Michael O'Connor was born on Thursday Island before moving to Darwin, where his home was destroyed in the air raids of February 1942. He served as an intelligence officer in the Royal Australian Navy following a period as a District Officer in Papua New Guinea. He is the author of *To Live in Peace* published in 1985 and, in his spare time, writes extensively on national defence issues.

Michael O'Connor is a widower and lives in North Queensland.

An Act of War is his first novel.

I0553422

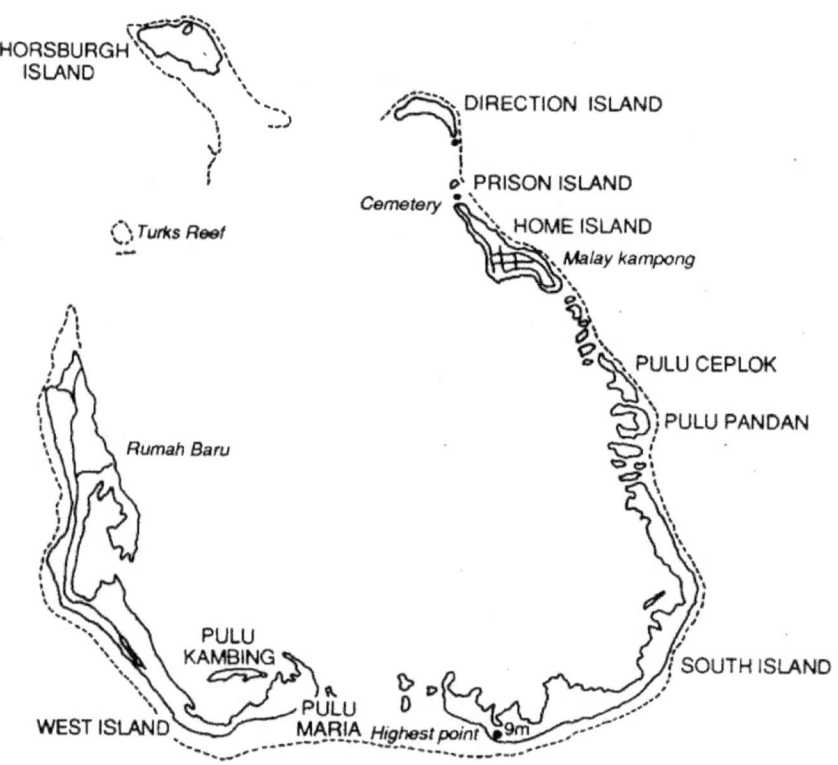

HORSBURGH
ISLAND

Turks Reef

DIRECTION ISLAND

PRISON ISLAND

Cemetery

HOME ISLAND

Malay kampong

PULU CEPLOK

PULU PANDAN

Rumah Baru

PULU
KAMBING

SOUTH ISLAND

WEST ISLAND

PULU
MARIA

Highest point

9m

COCOS (KEELING) ISLANDS

AN ACT OF
WAR

MICHAEL O'CONNOR

First published by Arrow Australia
1990

Second edition published 2016
Amazon Inc.

Copyright Kotali Consultants Pty Ltd

National Library of Australia
Cataloguing-in-Publication Data

O'Connor, Michael, 1938.
    An Act of war

    ISBN 0 900882 60 3.

    I. Title

A 823.3

For my family - who didn't laugh!

ACKNOWLEDGEMENTS

This is a work of fiction set in the not-too-distant future. All the characters are imaginary, as is the scenario itself. That is not to say that Australia could never find itself in a situation similar to that portrayed here. One can only hope we will never be put to the test. Listing the people who have helped with this book would take many pages. Many officers and other ranks of the Australian Defence Force have passed on knowledge and wisdom with an enthusiasm I found greatly heart-warming. I hope they will see the final result as a tribute to their high professionalism. If I have modified details and altered jargon and procedure, I hope they will not judge this fiction too harshly. Former residents of Cocos have described the islands while officials of private companies and public corporations have provided basic data with such warmth that I feel a great sense of obligation to produce something good. If I have failed, the fault is mine not theirs.

Note to this edition

Originally published last century, the book has been long out of print. To meet occasional requests for copies, it is offered here again. In the meantime, the world has changed significantly and the scenario here is even more imaginary.

To you the reader, enjoy!

GLOSSARY

AB	Able Seaman
ADC	Aide-de-camp (Senior officer's personal assistant)
AEW	Airborne Early Warning
AIM-9	Sidewinder heat seeking short-range air to air missile
ALA	Azanian Liberation Army (military wing of African National Congress)
ANC	African National Congress
APC	Armoured personnel carrier
ASW	Anti-submarine warfare
Baffles	Sonar blind spot blanked off by ship's hull
Bandit	Aircraft contact identified as hostile (cf. Bogey)
Barra	Australian-designed directional passive sonobuoy
BASSETT	Code term for Ikara missile
Bathy probe	Sensing device which collects water temperature at different depths
Bde	Brigade(Army)
BIG BULGE	Allied term for Soviet air-borne search radar
Blade count	Identification system for ships and submarines from passive sonar information
BMP	Soviet amphibious tracked infantry combat vehicle
Bogey	Unidentified aircraft contact (cf. Bandit)
BTR-60	Soviet-designed eight-wheeled amphibious armoured personnel carrier
CAP	Combat Air Patrol
CDF	Chief of the Defence Force
CINCPAC	Commander-in-Chief, US Forces Pacific
CLF	Cocos Liberation Front
CRU	Control and Reporting Unit (local area air defence radar and direction system)
CRV-7	non-guided airborne rockets
DDG	Guided missile destroyer

Difar	Passive sonobuoy
DIO	Defence Intelligence Organisation
Dogbox (time)	Defines a time until which a guided missile is in flight and active
E-2C	US early warning and control aircraft, often carrier-borne
ELINT	Electronic intelligence gathering
EMCON	Electronic emission control - all radar radios and other emitters shut down
ESM	Electronic surveillance measures
ETA	Expected time of arrival
EW	Electronic warfare
FFG	Guided missile frigate
FLIR	Forward-looking infra-red surveillance system
HALO	High altitude, low opening (parachute jump)
Harpoon	US-designed long-range anti-ship missile (can be launched from aircraft, surface ship or submarine
HARM	US-designed high speed anti-radar missile
HEAD NET	Allied term for Soviet ship-borne surface search radar
HUD	Head Up Display - instrument data displayed on a see-through screen immediately in front of the pilot
IFF	Identification Friend or Foe (coded signal which identifies friendly targets to a radar system)
Ikara	Australian-designed long-range guided anti-submarine missile
Il-38	Soviet-designed long-range anti-submarine patrol aircraft (NATO designation May)
IP	Initial Point - navigation target
IRDS	Infra-red detection system
Jezebel	Code term for airborne passive sonar search
Jindalee	Australian-designed very long-range over-the-horizon radar
Layer	Boundary between different water temperature zones
LCH	Landing Craft (Heavy)
LOFAR	Type of passive sonobuoy
MAD	Magnetic Anomaly Detector
MAG	Military Assistance Group
MICV	Mechanised Infantry Combat Vehicle

MiG-29	Soviet-designed fighter aircraft (NATO designation Fulcrum)
Milan ATGW	Brand of anti-tank guided weapon
Mulloka	Australian-designed medium range ship borne active sonar
NATO	North Atlantic Treaty Organisation
Navcom	Navigator-Communications officer in a P-3 crew
NGS	Naval Gunfire Support (for troops on shore)
Nixie	Decoy for homing torpedoes
Nocom	No communications procedure (does not apply to radar - for which see Emcon)
Nomad	Australian-designed light patrol aircraft
NSC	National Security Council
ODF	Operational Deployment Force
ONA	Office of National Assessments
PC-9	Swiss-designed training aircraft
PDMS	Point Defence Missile System
Phalanx	US-designed radar-controlled anti-missile gun system
"pickle"	Weapons release button - on joystick
POSSUB	Classification of possible submarine
PROBSUB	Classification of probable submarine
PT-76	Soviet-designed amphibious, air-portable light tank
PWO	Principal Warfare Officer
"racket"	Detected electronic transmission
"riser"	Surfacing submarine
Ro-ro ship	Roll-on, Roll-off merchant ship
SAM	Surface to air missile
SAS	Special Air Service Regiment
SCR	Sonar Control Room
Secure from	Stand down from battle stations action stations
SIGINT	Signals intelligence gathering (cf. ELINT)
SLOCs	Sea lanes of communication
SNOOP TRAY	Allied term for Soviet submarine-borne surface search radar
snort	Process by which a diesel-electric submarine breathes air to charge batteries without actually surfacing
sonar picket	Ship designated to conduct sonar surveillance for a force at sea

SOSUS	Fixed underwater sonar detection system
Sparrow	US-designed medium-range radar-controlled air-to-air missile
Sqn	Squadron (RAAF or Army)
SS-N-7	Soviet-designed submarine-launched anti-ship missile
TASS	Towed array sonar system
TDA	Torpedo danger area
U/S	Unserviceable
USAF	United States Air Force
VECTAC	Term for attack on a submarine by an aircraft directed by a ship in contact with the target
VR	Flying speed
XO	Executive Officer - second in command
ZSU-23-4	Soviet-designed four-barrelled radar- controlled 23 mm mobile antiaircraft gun system

PROLOGUE

Australian Defence Headquarters, Russell Hill, Canberra

The buildings that made up Defence Headquarters were laid out in neat array at the foot of Mount Pleasant. Like a totem pole in their midst rose the spare column of the Australian-American War Memorial. Its crown of a stone eagle with upswept wings, irreverently nicknamed "Bugs Bunny", looked down Kings Avenue towards Parliament House and the government triangle.

Deep underground in one of the anonymous grey concrete buildings was headquartered the Defence Intelligence Centre. Behind an array of electronically guarded doors, analysts pored over a stream of information constantly fed into their computerised databanks.

The northern end of the main passageway ended in a plain blue door with an electronic cypher lock. The legend on the door proclaimed HOSTILE INTENTIONS SECTION. No name plates were on the door but normally three officers, one each from the army, navy and air force, worked at speculating about possible military threats to their country.

The office was cold. White-painted, tile-floored and lit by harsh fluorescent strips, it looked more like a laboratory. It was underground and the air conditioning chilled the atmosphere. The furniture was basic government issue - a trio of plain desks, chairs on casters and a bank of grey filing cabinets.

The only occupant, a navy captain in summer whites, scowled at the word-processor screen in front of him. The green headline flickered at him: *The Collapse of South Africa - Implications for Australia.* Scrolling down the text, he came to the sub-heading: *The Military Dimensions*, and began to reread his draft.

What must clearly be understood is that the campaign against the defunct white regime in South Africa was only incidentally about demolishing apartheid and racism. Politically, South Africa was turned into a pariah state, isolated and friendless. External powers were forced to choose between competing black political forces and to accept the political and military programmes of those they supported.

Because the external dimensions of the struggle were pre-eminently about strategic influence, the Western powers were effectively bound to the group most likely to come out on top. Rightly or wrongly, this was judged to be the pro-Soviet African National Congress and its military wing, the Azanian Liberation Army.

Backing the ANC did not however give the West any leverage. That was earned by the Soviets who provided money, weapons and training. The Soviets persuaded the ANC to pursue an armed policy based initially upon terrorism, knowing full well that this would impose political limits to the amount of real support the West could give. Western influence on the outcome in South Africa was thereby minimised.

As is now apparent, the most important foreign figure in Pretoria is the KGB Resident at the Soviet Embassy. The Soviet Military Assistance Group is relatively unimportant, being concerned mainly with converting the ALA from a guerilla organisation into a conventional national army. The Soviet MAG co-ordinates the efforts of North Korean and East German military advisers.

The basing of a Soviet naval task group and naval air strike and reconnaissance aircraft at the old Simonstown installation gives the Soviet Armed Forces a wider global reach than they have ever enjoyed. Although the force consists of older ships and aircraft, they now have the capacity to interdict a large proportion of Western Europe's oil imports from the Middle East fields. The force is supplemented by the South African maritime force which was captured virtually intact. This is clearly the military pay-off the

Soviets wanted. At this date, American intelligence lists the group as comprising:

- 2 Victor-class nuclear attack submarines;
- 1 Kresta II-class guided missile cruiser;
- 2 Kildin-class destroyers;
- 2 Tu-20 Bear-D long-range ocean reconnaissance aircraft
- at least 6 Tu-16 Badger bombers, two of which may be tanker aircraft.
-

To this group can be added the captured South African maritime forces consisting of:
- 3 French Daphne-class diesel-electric submarines;
- 7 Israeli Reshef-class fast missile boats.

This force is relatively powerful provided it can be supported. It is clearly designed for anti-shipping operations and has an adequate self-defence capability against all but the most powerful enemy.

Elsewhere this paper comments that a large proportion of the world's output of such industrially vital commodities as platinum, diamonds, manganese and chromium are now available to western consumers only with Soviet permission. Soviet economic power is also reinforced by their access to and de facto control of South Africa's gold production.

Militarily, the fall of the South African regime represents a significant loss of strategic position for the West. From an Australian perspective, however, the immediate strategic damage is quite small. Relatively little of our own trade uses the Cape route so that any attempt to interdict shipping on that route will have only the most limited effect on this country.

Industrially, the ability of Australia to replace much of the lost production of diamonds, gold, manganese and platinum could be a bonus. I would argue that this is likely to be of only short to medium term benefit.

Abruptly, the text ended. This was the tricky part. Captain Tony Bellano was only a temporary intelligence officer. His posting to the Defence Intelligence Organisation was little more than an interlude in a career spent mostly at sea. And after almost three years in this underground vault, he wanted nothing more than to go back to sea again. But he had become convinced that Australia's almost unique ability to replace much of South Africa's strategic mineral production made it the next target for international pariah treatment. The bureaucrats upstairs would not like what he would now write. Nor, he thought cynically, would the politicians. If they ever saw it.

Focusing on the keyboard, he began, two-fingered, to peck out the words:

In geostrategic terms, Australia meets every condition that made South Africa a tempting target for the Soviet Union. In some ways, Australia is even more attractive.

Australia produces all the strategic minerals that the Soviets control in South Africa. Even if the quantities are currently smaller, we cannot be sure that an accelerated exploration programme will not disclose greater reserves. After all, most of Australia's mineral wealth has been discovered in the past forty years. Much exploration which could have been carried out was not pursued simply because many of the potential explorers controlled the South African mines. They had no interest in driving prices down by oversupply.

In addition to the high value minerals already listed, Australia provides a large proportion of the West's low cost basic minerals such as iron and aluminium.

Further, the development in Australia of cheap energy such as coal, uranium and natural gas make Australia a significantly more valuable target than South Africa.

Militarily, Australia's position at the junction of the Indian and Pacific Oceans offers the possibility of reducing the strategic options now available to the United States. Control of Australia coupled with that already achieved in South Africa would shut the

United States out of the Indian Ocean and make Western access to Middle East oil even more problematic.

Australian bases at Sydney, Fremantle and Darwin are of central importance to the existing global strategic balance.

It is outside our terms of reference to propose a political strategy for the isolation of Australia. We assume that such a strategy can and will be put into effect and that it will have some military dimensions. The difficulty for an aggressor would be to find a plausible casus belli.

Clearly, the military pressures upon Australia will be different from those used in South Africa. Australia does not have a significantly divided population. There is no opportunity for the land-based revolutionary guerilla warfare which led to the collapse of the Afrikaners.

At the same time, there is no serious chance that Australia could be invaded and occupied by a hostile power. Only the Soviet Union could achieve that and then only at the risk of expanding the conflict into general war with the United States. We see no possibility of that, especially given the Soviets' serious domestic economic and ethnic problems.

Nevertheless, Australia could suffer levels of harassment which would be expensive to counter and which, if coupled with political isolation, could lead to serious economic problems. The basic assumption is that a hostile political strategy would be directed towards the eventual installation of a puppet Australian government which would then implement the policies handed down by external "advisers".Such policies would include the abrogation of the ANZUS Treaty, closing down the joint US-Australian nuclear facilities, and the provision of facilities for Soviet naval and air forces.

For the purposes of this paper, we assume that any strategy of isolation will encompass three principal targets: sporting links, overseas trade and external territories. We further assume that attempts will be made during the campaign to have Australia expelled from the Commonwealth and from the United Nations, or at least from its specialised agencies. This last factor would help in breaking down the American alliance which underpins our limited defence capability.

Militarily, Australia is vulnerable to political and military assaults on overseas trade. Our economic dependence upon overseas trade for current living standards is total. A campaign of trade sanctions is almost certain to be implemented. If it were only partially successful, living standards could be expected to drop sharply with increased unemployment, high inflation and the political pressures that would result. These would be relatively more pressing than they were in South Africa because they would impact upon the whole body politic rather than a disenfranchised segment of the population.

Australia's vulnerability to such sanctions would be exacerbated by our dependence upon foreign shipping. Less than five per cent of all exports and imports are carried in Australian bottoms. A principal objective would be to dissuade foreign shipowners from servicing the Australian trade.

Militarily, selective attacks on Australian-flag ships would be expected to reinforce a sense of vulnerability among foreign shippers and increase pressures on them to withdraw from the Australian trade. Whether our importance to the world as a primary source of several strategic materials would overcome these pressures could only be tested by events. Certainly, to generate confidence, it will be necessary for Australia to demonstrate an ability to defend merchant shipping for occasionally considerable distances.

He paused as the phone rang. It was his director. "Tony, come round and see me, will you."

"Sir!". He saved his text, switched off and left the room.

In the director's office, Brigadier Abrams wanted to talk about the project.

"It's nearly finished, sir. We have to marry it up with the economics and political people so as to get an agreed version. That will mean a lot of hours in committee because I don't think they will like our hardline version. They will see it as unduly alarmist and overly cynical."

"All right, but don't let them pressure you into some bland lowest common denominator garbage. The strategic analysis of the South African collapse is the right one and I want to use it to generate some insomnia in high places." Abrams grinned, relishing the opportunity of assaulting bureaucratic complacency.

"Seriously, though", he went on, "our biggest problem, as always, will be to persuade people to act on speculation. We're not in the criminal court; we don't have to prove anything beyond reasonable doubt the way the bureaucrats want it. Intelligence is not about persuading a jury, it's about rational speculation. And we have to give the operations people a nudge or two in the right direction."

As Bellano nodded agreement, he went on, "Another topic, Tony. You're going back to sea in three months. The personnel director has picked you to go to the new ANZAC frigate, *Yarra*, in command. Congratulations!"

Bellano walked backed to his office on air. Command of his own ship - and the lead ship of a new class - was just about the best appointment he could have had. The next three months would drag even though there would be plenty to do.

Back at his desk, he recalled the draft paper and continued:

Trade sanctions will almost certainly be designed to cut this country off from its principal sources of military equipment, including ammunition. The obvious response, to divert resources now into the development of production facilities to replace imports will be expensive in both financial and political terms. Government would be faced with a choice of cutting politically sensitive programmes or raising taxation at a time when the need is not so obvious as it may become in future years.

It may also be necessary by some form of rationing or increased imports for non-essential use to ensure an adequate supply of oil for the Defence Force. With dwindling reserves, policy should ensure that the Defence Force can be guaranteed adequate fuel for operations without depending upon imports. This may mean cutting back production from Australian wells so as to hold reserves in the ground. Operations Branch should be able to provide the necessary consumption requirements.

Apart from trade sanctions, military action could involve attacks on both mainland and off-shore installations as well as our island territories.

Many installations, especially in the remote north-west, are difficult, if not impossible, to guard satisfactorily. This is particularly true of the off-shore oil and gas platforms which contribute heavily to energy exports. Together with the high-value extraction, primary processing, transport and loading facilities for on-shore mining developments, these are excessively vulnerable to low-cost sabotage attacks.

Australia's external territories have virtually no economic value. On the other hand, Cocos and Christmas Islands in the Indian Ocean have a substantial strategic value to the general Western interest though less so to Australia.

Christmas Island is virtually indefensible against an Indonesian attack but is less important than Cocos. At the same time, Indonesia is unlikely to tolerate any pressure on Christmas from a third country.

Cocos has considerable strategic value in global terms. Its airfield would allow an occupier to dominate the approaches to Sunda and Lombok Straits. If we are not prepared to defend Cocos, we should think in terms of offering the facilities there to either Indonesia or the United States.

Because of the lack of facilities, the Pacific Ocean territories of Norfolk and Lord Howe Islands do not have much strategic significance.

Nevertheless, it is worth considering that, in the context of a combined political-military campaign to isolate Australia, the loss of any of these island territories could be damaging to Australia's external prestige. Internally, such losses could seriously affect the credibility of the government and Defence Force, as well as community morale.

While Australian governments have been careful to integrate these territories and their indigenous populations into the Australian constitutional structure, it would not be difficult to develop a campaign based upon hostility to colonialism. After all, it is not necessary to be right, merely noisily persuasive.

Bellano paused. His watch told him it was time to go home and tell Anne about his new ship. He wondered how she would take it. They had been happily married almost fifteen years. Their early passion had mellowed to an almost placid contentment coupled with a fierce and shared pride in their four children.

For them, the posting meant yet another move, back to Sydney probably. The upheaval of moving, house-hunting, of changing schools for the children, and of adapting to a new social environment would bear more heavily on Anne than him. He would be at sea for most of the time, working up his new command. He would be doing what he wanted to do more than anything else.

Despite the sobering thoughts, he could not suppress his excitement. He wondered if his speculations about a future enemy might not come true. In that case, he could well be in the firing line.

Closing down the computer, he secured the office, collected his cap and headed for the door.

CHAPTER 1

Prime Minister's Department, Canberra

Four of the five men who gathered in the National Security Council boardroom were of a type. Middle-aged, their silver hair and elegant grey suits proclaimed a seniority in government service which could never quite be imitated by elected politicians or generals in mufti. As they waited for their chairman, their quiet, relaxed conversation told of years of intimacy spent moving up the public service ladder to the halls of power. Now, all heads of department, they formed one of Australia's most exclusive clubs. The easy familiarity which led to an almost total unanimity of outlook was further nurtured on the golf course and on Canberra's all-pervasive cocktail circuit.

The fifth man was clearly an outsider. His air force uniform only emphasised the distinction between Air Marshal Philip Noble, Vice Chief of the Defence Force, and his civilian superiors. Not only was Noble deputising today for his better-known chief but, as a recent arrival in Canberra, he enjoyed only a limited entree into this most powerful of élites.

All looked up as Sir Alan Scott, the Chairman of the National Security Council, came into the room. Scott, who was also Secretary to the Cabinet, was the most powerful public servant in Canberra. In his mid-fifties, he was tall, spare and quiet-spoken. Totally committed to the politico-administrative system he had served all his working life, he was also adept in the techniques of manipulating elected politicians. Scott rarely appeared in public except at the Prime Minister's elbow as his chief adviser. He would never be heard to publicly dispute government policy; indeed he would not even comment privately except to his closest colleagues. He abhorred the practice of leaking information to the media as no more than ill-mannered grandstanding. In his rare statements, usually to seminars on public administration, he would urge the superiority over all others of the Cabinet system of government with its professional and independent public service. Yet, by subtle combinations of flattery and pleas of administrative difficulty, he could frequently bend policy to what he and his colleagues deemed to be desirable in the national interest. It was the Canberra system, adapted from Westminster and defended against accusations of a lack of democracy by the plea that, however imperfectly, it worked.

Scott greeted his colleagues briefly and, as he took his place at the head of the table, they scattered to find their seats.

"Gentlemen", Scott opened. "I thank you for coming. We all know each other but I would like to welcome Air Marshal Noble representing the CDF who is interstate. I hope we will see more of you at these gatherings. We have for discussion today the Defence paper on the South African collapse. Gary, this is your department's offering. Perhaps you could lead off."

As Secretary of Defence, Gary Irwin was responsible for the Defence Intelligence Organisation and its inputs into the government's strategic analysis. He had studied the paper carefully and accepted most of its conclusions. But his organisational antennae told him that they were not popular in the club. How to deal with the paper was a problem he had worried over for some days. Loyalty to his own department dictated a vigorous defence of the paper and its conclusions. On the other hand, what Scott would call the 'bigger picture' called for moderation in any proposals for changes in policy.

"The paper presents a detailed analysis of the reasons for the sudden collapse of the white South African government and I do not know of any dispute with that part of the paper. In particular, the view that global strategic considerations determined the attitude of most foreign governments is one we have agreed here in the past. Equally, we were left with a situation where, with the best will, we could have only limited influence on the winners compared with the Soviet bloc. In that sense, there is no point in crying over spilt milk. We got what we expected and about what we could realistically achieve.

"On the question of the resultant trade opportunities for Australia, our view is essentially speculative. I would expect that Trade would have a better analysis. We put it in because of the impact any increased trade would have on attitudes to Australia. We would expect that Australia would become a more important country in the global strategic picture.

"DIO clearly expects that our growing importance will focus more attention upon us and that some moves against Australia could be expected. Again, this view is speculative, a sort of worst plausible case. Any such moves, however, could have a military dimension and raise questions of defence preparedness. This is essentially the issue that this Council needs to discuss."

Scott nodded to Paul McLeod, head of Foreign Affairs. "I am a bit worried about this rather excessive degree of speculation." Despite his position as Australia's most senior diplomat, McLeod liked issues to be cut and dried. "Is there any evidence at all for this supposed transfer of hostility to Australia? After all we have tried to emphasise our credentials as a non-racist, independent-minded country for more than 20 years.

"I might add", he went on, "that the paper suggests a strategic importance on the global scene that I find difficult to accept for a country with fewer than 20 million people. Are we not perhaps in danger of taking ourselves too seriously?"

Irwin hesitated. He did not like the speculation either and did not want to commit himself to defending a position he could not prove. He deflected the question, smoothly, appearing to defer to the military expert. "Perhaps Air Marshal Noble could expand on that", he suggested.

Momentarily, Noble stared at the papers in front of him, collecting his thoughts. "There is no evidence", he said bluntly, "at least not of any overwhelming kind. Of course, there won't be until it is too late to respond.

"What we are posing here is a possibility, a plausible one. There are indications of heightened Soviet interest in Australia. You all know about them - the increased pressure for Soviet pseudo-scientific research installations in Australia, more trade on unrealistically favourable terms for us. These are all on the public record. What has also been discussed is the escalation in Soviet intelligence activity both on and off shore. The fishing deal a few years ago has led to a large increase in Soviet hydrographic and oceanographic research in our vicinity..."

Scott interrupted. "But surely that is all outside Australian waters. They have been very correct, at least according to your own surveillance."

"Certainly they have kept out of territorial waters, sir", Noble responded, "but we do assess that they are working to develop safe submarine operating areas south and west of the continent. We must also assume", he warned, looking at each man in turn, "that they are collecting such intelligence as sound, radar and heat signatures on ships trading to and from Australian ports. Those developments are of concern at least for international trade which has been increasingly diverted south about Australia since the expulsion of the Americans from the Philippines and the steady decline of security in that country. I don't think we need to panic about these; to a great extent they are the basic nuts and bolts of intelligence but they do represent an increase in unwelcome Soviet interest in our part of the world." Getting a nod from Scott, he continued, "Our concern is that if things do go wrong, we ought to be better prepared than we are now. We would need to speed up procurement projects already in the pipeline, especially the frigates and submarines, lift our manpower base so as to bring more units up to combat-ready status and gear up industry to produce more ammunition, especially missiles, quickly."

"And what's that likely to cost?" As might have been expected, it was Dennis Arthurton, Secretary to the Treasury who asked the question.

Irwin answered that. "On our rough estimates, we think that defence outlays would need to rise about 12 per cent in real terms yearly and reach a ceiling in about three years, then hold at that level indefinitely."

Arthurton scribbled some quick calculations on a pad. "Good God, man, that's impossible! You're looking to around 3.5 per cent of GDP. You want to screw another $4 billion a year out of the taxpayer?" The question was rhetorical, brutal and clearly intended to intimidate.

"Or trim welfare programmes?", Scott asked quietly. "I don't think Cabinet would go for that."

Irwin was intimidated. "I know it's a lot", he offered tentatively. "The figures are preliminary and we need to work on them in more detail. I'm sure we could cut that back." Arthurton was not appeased. "I think it's quite ridiculous to come here with some old-fashioned 'Russians are coming' scaremongering just to try to get more money for your expensive toys", he snapped.

Noble flushed brick-red under his tan. "With all due respect, Mr. Chairman, these so-called expensive toys are supposed to dissuade people from attacking this country or its interests. We don't have too many of them and few have the sort of capability they should have because we have had to skimp not only on the extras but on some of the basics as well. We still have only one Jindalee radar, our Hornets don't have enough tankers and the new ANZAC frigates are being built without a surface-to-surface missile system. As for the Army, it's so starved of men and equipment that it can't get 1000 men into combat in less than a month. Do you want me to go on?"

In the silence that greeted his outburst, he ploughed on, ignoring the wave of hostility that filled the room. "I admit the assessment is speculative. Unfortunately, despite what some in the community seem to expect of us, we don't have a pipeline into the Kremlin, or anywhere else important for that matter. By the time we get the sort of evidence you want, we will be too busy digging trenches to worry about anything else.

"I've always understood that the best way to stop a shooting war is to look like a hard nut to crack. At the moment we look much too soft, except perhaps to the public relations machine."

"Ah yes, public relations". Scott was bland. "The problem is that public relations tends to be a bit too effective. We might have a problem persuading our masters that things are as bad as you say."

"Well, tell them the truth", Noble put in.

"What is the truth, old boy?" The question came from McLeod, his tone bland, almost cynical. "The truth can be what our masters want to hear. In our business, truth is a matter of perception rather than reality. The truth as I see it is that you have presented a case of special pleading based on pure speculation. As plausible as it might be, the extra resources you want may well be totally wasted, what Dennis here would call a serious opportunity cost.

"One thing you can be sure of is that our masters would not like us to propose a diversion of resources away from projects which might get them re-elected on the basis of some pure speculation — especially when we have been telling the public for years about what a great defence capability we have.

"In any case, can we be so sure the Soviets will be a problem. It seems to me that they have more than a few of their own these days." He settled down for a short lecture. "As we all know, Mr Chairman, the Soviets have been in serious trouble for a decade now. While they are still a formidable military power - I'll grant you that", he nodded to Noble, "they not only have serious economic problems but the union shows every sign of rapid disintegration from ethnic and religious unrest. Agriculture is still a mess, the technological gap between Soviet industry and the West is growing and they are perennially short of convertible currencies. My people just don't see them indulging in any adventurism, not even as a diversion from their domestic problems."

Irwin interposed a comment. "I don't think there is anything in the paper which contradicts what you say. The point remains though that, while they have lowered the temperature of confrontation with the United States and NATO, they have certainly not backed away from the low-cost limited operations on the periphery, especially when there was a prospect of success. The whole South African experience proved that and paid a handsome geo-strategic dividend into the bargain."

Scott decided to hose down the dispute. "Thank you, gentlemen. I doubt that this line of discussion is getting us anywhere. The real point is that the paper gives us no evidence upon which to base an acceptance of the highly speculative conclusions. Certainly, there seems to be no basis on which to go to our masters for an acceleration of the current defence programme."

"There may be one solution, gentlemen." The speaker was Max Coffey, Secretary of the Trade Department. "If the figures check out and we do pick up some of South Africa's mineral markets, there will be a significant growth of royalty payments to government, especially if we can swing an increase in prices on a seller's market. If that's the

15

case, Defence could make a case for more money as the increase starts to take effect in a year or two."

There was a sigh of relief around the table. A solution had been found. At least decisive action could be deferred without actually refusing the Defence proposals. In the meantime, something else might show up to provide a clearer picture.

Noble held his peace. Inexperienced as he was, he could read the mood of the meeting. It was pointless to argue that the money was needed now. Better to develop a campaign for more resources on a more solid base.

He reflected on the nature of the bureaucratic system he had worked in on and off for some years. The opposition to the paper had been cut and dried well before the meeting was convened. Probably, it had been refined on the Royal Canberra Golf Club's immaculate course, or perhaps over pre-dinner drinks at the Commonwealth Club.

The opposition was not direct. It was couched in terms of questions which implied a willingness to agree if only certain obstacles could be overcome. The outcome was just as inevitable. The answer was never a flat "no", merely a request for more information, usually the sort that could never be acquired.

The real problem, he thought savagely, was that these buggers had never been in the field. They had never commanded troops, had never experienced the sour taste of physical fear that went with driving man and machine to the limits of their endurance. They had never been - and never would be - shot at. They dealt in words and in pieces of paper. They intrigued and thought it was life. They manipulated people and communities, caring little for the effects which, in any case, they assessed from cold statistics. Not for the first time, he wondered why his own ambitions had brought him back to this soulless jungle.

Sharing a staff car back to their offices after the meeting, Irwin was sympathetic. "I know it's difficult, Phil. What you must realise is that these fellows, for all their seniority and expertise, are strangers to national defence problems. They all have their constituencies, whether it be their minister or the institutional outlook of their own departments. We've been at peace now for more than two decades, fifty years if you exclude the optional wars like Korea and Vietnam. To most of them, national defence is one of those motherhood things, something we have to have because it's traditional. A lot of them don't think we're necessary. Deterrence means nothing. It's all too theoretical for men who have never in their lives had to face any but bureaucratic conflict. They don't understand you chaps in uniform. Between you and me, I think some of them have read too many novels about military coups. They see you and your people as a bigger threat than the Soviets. It's not all peace or war, you know.

"What we need to do is generate some stories about how undermanned and equipped we are. I'll talk to the public relations people and tell them to play down the supermen image for a while. In the meantime, you ought to bypass the PR machine and arrange some deep background briefings for editors and selected journalists. Take some of them out on exercises but don't give them the usual snow job. Let them see just how shaky we are on the ground."

CHAPTER 2

The United Nations, New York

The chairman was from Mexico this month. As the delegates took their places around the conference table, he banged his gavel, American style, and announced: "This meeting of the Committee on Decolonisation will come to order." For more than an hour, the committee dawdled through a routine agenda. Most of those attending were junior members of their national delegations. For them, the meeting was a chore to be endured as part of their career development. The committee itself was almost an anachronism. The only colonies left in the world were those held in thrall by the dictators who blithely ignored the tentative appeals for them to grant independence in the occupied territories. At least two of the twenty or so delegates who bothered to attend dozed in their places. Eventually the chairman, looking at his watch, asked formally if there was any further business. His tone implied that none would be welcome. He had a luncheon date he expected to enjoy. Immediately, the Indian delegate raised his hand. "Yes, Mr Patel? Will this be quick?" "Mr Chairman, my government wishes to raise the question of the Cocos and Christmas Islands and the status of their inhabitants as an oppressed people." Patel ignored the chairman's obvious impatience. At the end of the table, the British delegate nudged his Australian counterpart. "Wake up, old boy", he whispered, "S.K.'s gunning for you." S.K. Gupta, the Indian Ambassador, was represented by his deputy, C.T. Patel, but no one doubted that he had masterminded this new development. The chairman temporised. "The matter of Cocos is not on my agenda and has not been referred to the committee." A tall Nigerian in flowing white robes muttered, *sotto voce*: "Where the hell are Cocos and Christmas Islands?" His neighbour chuckled. The Indian was unabashed. "My government has information that the peoples of these islands are being subjected to intolerable persecution by their colonial masters. We will be raising the matter in the General Assembly if this committee does not take up the question of its own volition. It would not look good if the Committee on Decolonisation declined for purely procedural reasons to consider a clear case of colonial oppression." The implied threat was unmistakable. The chairman looked around the table. "Who is the metropolitan power in this case?" Max Schofield, the Australian delegate, alert now, studied his fingernails and said nothing. The Indian smirked. "Perhaps our Australian colleague does not know his geography." "If you are referring to Cocos and Christmas Islands in the Indian Ocean, you have clearly forgotten your history." Schofield feigned boredom. "Mr Chairman, both the territories of Cocos and Christmas voted in a plebiscite a decade ago for incorporation into Australia. This was approved by the General Assembly and both islands are an integral part of Australia. There is no question of jurisdiction on the part of this committee." Patel was undismayed. "My government has been approached by a representative group from Cocos Islands seeking relief from an oppressive and illegal occupation of their territory. After investigation, my government is satisfied that the so-called plebiscite of 1984 was fraudulent and wishes this matter to be re-opened by the committee. We further wish the committee to hear a representative of the islanders at its next meeting." Schofield studied the Indian. This was clearly the beginning of a planned campaign. Patel would be in no hurry for a decision, wanting to squeeze the maximum political benefit from the issue. It ought to be killed at once. "Mr Chairman, I object to this matter being raised in this way. The matter of the status of Cocos is perfectly clear and was brought to finality by the United Nations over a decade ago. Under the UN Charter, any matters affecting Cocos are internal matters for the Australian government and people. I ask you to rule that the committee has no jurisdiction in this matter." The Mexican, more conscious than ever of his desire to close the meeting, briefly conferred with the UN official who acted as secretary to the committee. "I am advised that the Australian interpretation is correct and I believe we should now adjourn." Immediately, Patel was on his feet. "I am sorry, Mr.

Chairman, but I must dissent from your ruling and ask for a vote on my proposal." In the vote, the Indian proposal was carried by seven votes to three. Eleven delegates abstained. The Indians were supported by the Soviet Union and Hungary as well as a group from the Afro-Asian bloc. Only the British and Americans supported Australia.

HMAS *Yarra*

The sun flashed off myriad wavetops as *Yarra* passed through Sydney Heads. Directly ahead lay the low cliffs of Middle Head with their old gun galleries commanding the entrance to the harbour. Lounging in his chair on the starboard side of the bridge, Tony Bellano mused that any ship trying to force the harbour entrance in the old days would have faced a fearsome welcome with guns not only ahead but to port and starboard on South and North Head. "Port fifteen." The order was given quietly by the officer of the watch, standing at the pelorus. Acknowledging the order, the quartermaster, from his own seat, spun his tiny wheel, not much bigger than a saucer. "Midships, steer 210." As the vista of Sydney Harbour opened up, the bridge crew could see the famous landmark of the Harbour Bridge across Bradley's Head. On both sides, the hills were crammed with the homes of those suburbanites lucky enough to enjoy one of the most beautiful harbour views in the world. Multi-coloured roofs contrasted with the greens of many kinds of native and foreign trees. The sun flashed off the windows of cars on the roads which wound their way through the hills. The harbour was alive with craft of all kinds. Yachts and small motor boats abounded, suggesting that many workers were taking the day off, enjoying an unseasonably fine winter day. Large merchant ships were moored to buoys, waiting their turn at overcrowded wharves. Beetle-like ferries scurried from Cremorne and Mosman across to Circular Quay and back again while the more majestic Manly catamaran raced down harbour leaving a sheet of white foam in its wake. As *Yarra* rounded Bradley's Head and turned to starboard to head over to the Garden Island naval dockyard, Bellano could see a cluster of grey shapes huddled at the foot of the giant hammerhead crane overlooking the Captain Cook Dock still out of sight behind the island. Glancing over his shoulder, he noted the slim black shape of HMAS *Otway*. The submarine had provided the 'clockwork mouse' for Yarra's anti-submarine exercises over the past week. *Otway* was neatly in station in *Yarra*'s wake. "Yeoman", he called to the signal petty officer. "Detach *Otway* to *Platypus*. Tell him to go away and learn to make some noise." Despite her age, the old *Oberon*-class boat was very quiet and almost impossible to detect even with Yarra's modern sonar outfit. Bellano watched the submarine as the big signal projector clattered out its message. A brief acknowledgement flashed from the top of the submarine's sail and it slowly altered course to starboard, heading for the submarine base at Neutral Bay.

"Signal from the Island, sir. We're to berth outboard of Darwin at Cruiser Wharf."

"OK. Frank", he turned to the officer of the watch. "Let's see you bring her alongside."

Bellano would stand by as the young lieutenant manoeuvred the ship, watchful and ready to take over if anything went wrong. There should be no need. There was only a light southerly wind and, at slack water, mooring would be fairly simple. The past two weeks had been spent in work-up exercises to drill the new crew and train the command team in simulated combat operations. The crew had shaken down well in the post-commissioning cruise. F/A-18 Hornets from Williamtown RAAF Base near Newcastle had carried out mock attacks while F-111s from Amberley had simulated sea-skimmer missiles, attacking the ship at ultra-low level to exercise the Phalanx radar-controlled gun. Off Jervis Bay, the ship had conducted radar calibration and tracking exercises against target drones. At the end of that period, an elderly drone had been sacrificed to the ship's Point Defence Missile System. Bellano grinned to himself. It was always good for morale to actually destroy a target. Every spare officer and sailor had been on the upper deck to watch THAT. Their exercises had been shadowed by the ever-present Soviet spy trawler. This vessel, designated AGI but more commonly known as 'Snoopy', had appeared on the fringes of the Jervis Bay exercise area about three years ago. Every three months, it was relieved by a replacement out of Vladivostok. Bristling with aerials, it cruised slowly around the exercise area listening to communications and recording all electronic transmissions for later analysis. Coping with the intruder had become a ritual. Specific frequencies were reserved for exercises to ensure the Soviets never gained access to secret operational frequencies. In some ways, it was good training fo crews, sharpening up their security consciousness.

Bellano felt a bit sorry for the Russians. Wallowing around in all weathers, barely keeping way on, and doing nothing but listen for three months was a hell of a way to earn a living. For all his sympathy, though, they were a bloody nuisance. Occasionally his people became irritated by the constant spying and rude messages were flashed to the Russians. There was never any reply.

Later, they had worked against the submarine. Using their own helicopter, and twice with the help of a P-3C Orion from Edinburgh near Adelaide, they had tried to detect the elusive submarine outside the range of its Harpoon missiles and Mk. 48 torpedos. Detection had been easier with the P-3 present. Their own towed array sonar with the greater weapons capacity and speed of the P-3 provided improved flexibility.

Bellano shuddered to think how vulnerable his ship would be if its sole helicopter should be immobilised through damage or breakdown. The P-3 took too long to get to the operating area from its base so the helicopter was his only means of keeping the submarine out of range. Even so, it could carry only one anti-submarine torpedo. If that missed, or failed, the ship was almost defenceless.

The FFGs had two helicopters so that the chances of being totally without support were greatly reduced. Even the old DDGs had Ikara anti-submarine missiles although their range was now less than the Harpoon missiles of the submarines.

Twice, the submarine had penetrated the screen and simulated attacks, once with a two torpedo salvo and once with a Harpoon missile. The Harpoon was notionally destroyed by the Phalanx but they were plain lucky with the torpedos. One had been seduced by the Nixie decoy but the other failed to acquire its target.

On that occasion, there had been a minor confrontation with 'Snoopy' who had tried to recover the spent exercise torpedo but, after some gentle pushing and shoving, the Russians had backed off.

On balance, Bellano was pleased with the work-up. The weather had been kind, too kind perhaps. Exercising in light seas with clear sunny skies was almost a pleasure, especially in winter. It would be different in heavy weather and poor visibility with the troops sick and battered. Individual performance dropped off sharply, as did sonar performance against the dangerously quiet Oberon submarines.

The crew's morale was good. They had performed well and their ship had few of the defects that plagued new designs. It was a small ship's company and he had a solid core of good chiefs and petty officers. They called him 'The Wop', taking a perverse pride in explaining to other ships' companies that their captain was actually a fifth generation Australian, despite his name.

Now it was time for some leave, a few minor repairs and touching up the paintwork. In three weeks, the ship would sail for Darwin and a six month deployment in northern waters. It would be a time for hard work. Most of the men would not mind that. Like him, they would be leaving their families behind in Sydney and the work would be a necessary anodyne. They could look forward to some foreign port visits, the dream of every young sailor, in Singapore, Manila and perhaps Surabaya to break the monotony.

He climbed out of his chair as the ship turned to port between the dockyard and Fort Denison, lining up her mooring.

The United Nations - New York

Nobody had been bored at this meeting of the Committee on Decolonisation. As she left with her two political advisers, Barbara McKinnon, the Australian Ambassador to the United Nations, was fuming. She stormed down the corridor to the lifts to return to her office.

McKinnon was one of the few women ambassadors to the United Nations but she was no feminist symbol. A career diplomat for 20 years, she had made a name for sheer professionalism in several trouble spots. Earlier in her career, a remarkably insensitive - or possibly vicious - superior had sent her as Australian ambassador to a strict Muslim country. It nearly caused a rupture of diplomatic relations because the Emir had initialy refused to accept her credentials. But, within a month, she had so charmed her hosts that she had become a close confidant of the old ruler.

An hour later, she scanned the draft of her cable to the Foreign Affairs department in Canberra.

At the meeting of the Committee on Decolonisation this morning, S.K. Gupta, the Indian Ambassador, introduced one Haji Mohammed bin Rahmani who claims to be the chairman of an organisation called the Cocos Liberation Front apparently based in Madras. Gupta tabled a document (appended) which purports to be a statement of claim by the CLF against the Australian government. This demands:

> - complete political independence for the Cocos Islands;
> - recognition of the CLF as the sole representative of the indigenous people of Cocos, and of Haji Mohammed bin Rahmani as interim head of government;
> - admission by Australia that the plebiscite of 1984 was fraudulent; and
> - payment of an indemnity of A$1 billion over a ten year period to the Cocos Islands government.

Gupta made it clear that his government supported the claim and was actively seeking to have the matter inscribed on the agenda of the Committee and ultimately of the General Assembly.

It was clear that the matter had been discussed with the Soviet ambassador who supported Gupta. Most delegates abstained from discussion clearly because they lacked instructions from their governments. However, I am concerned that the fact that this matter has not been laughed out of court reflects a lack of support for our sovereignty over Cocos.

On the committee, we can count on the British and the Americans. The best we can hope for from the French will be abstention. I believe the whole Afro-Asian bloc may well be against us. Request instructions.

24

As she authorised the draft for transmission, the intercom buzzed. "I have Mr Gupta on the 'phone, Ambassador", her secretary announced.

"What are you up to, S.K.?", she asked as he came on the line. "My dear Barbara", Gupta was suave. "Could I come around for a chat about this Cocos business? And I would like to bring Mikhail with me if you have no objection. I'm sure we can clear it up without any real problem. And I know your office brews the best coffee in the UN."

As Gupta was announced, McKinnon flicked on her tape recorder. There were several microphones but the one set in the coffee table in the corner would pick up everything that was said in the room.

He was accompanied by Mikhail Arbutov, the Soviet ambassador. They were a good pair, top-notch professional diplomats, experienced, sophisticated and, she admitted to herself, quite charming. Gupta was in his fifties, dark, stocky, silver-haired and impeccably dressed. A military background was betrayed by a regimental tie and his British education by spoken English, quite free of the customary chi-chi Indian accent.

Arbutov was as elegant. His tailored suit lapel displayed a discreet Order of Lenin, the only clue to his nationality since his English was as correct as Gupta's, distinguished only by an American accent.

They fenced gently as coffee was served.

Gupta opened the batting. "Barbara, I think I should make it plain that my government has accepted the credentials of the CLF. In our view, the Cocos islanders will never achieve any prosperity or independence as an appendage of Australia. Without wishing to give offence, you Australians are simply too contemptuous of coloured people."

McKinnon sipped her coffee, cogitating briefly. "You are pretty forthright, S.K. Let me be equally blunt. What's in it for India?"

"We gain no benefit. But you must understand that India regards the people of Cocos as entitled to our protection. We believe that historically we have a responsibility for the security and welfare of the peoples of the Indian Ocean and we are in a position to support them.

"On the other hand", he continued, "what have you done? The people work as little more than slaves on low wages. They have no prospects and, whatever you say, they are ruled by imported white bureaucrats from the mainland. Your only justification for being there is to use the airfield to support American surveillance operations in the Indian Ocean. As you must know, we have never been happy about that ever since they tried to pressure us with their navy during our war with Pakistan in 1971." "Where did you dig up Rahmani, S.K.?", McKinnon asked curiously.

"Haji Rahmani is a refugee from Cocos. He sought asylum in India after he objected to your fraudulent plebiscite. We believe he has the support of the majority of the islanders, those you so often refer to when it suits you as the 'silent majority' if I am not mistaken."

"It seems they are your silent majority, S.K. They certainly have not said anything to us. Mikhail", she turned to the Russian, "what is your interest in this?"

Arbutov put his cup down. "I think, Barbara, you will find that my government will also support Rahmani and our Indian friends. As you know, we have always supported the aspirations of indigenous peoples against their colonial overlords. We also are not happy with the use of Cocos as a base for the Americans.

"I might also point out", he added, "that since Rahmani is a Muslim, he can expect the support of his brethren in all the Muslim countries. I do think you should advise your government to concede on this matter. After all, what have you to lose? A few specks of land 2000 kilometres from your mainland, some 400 people you ignore anyway and nothing of value."

"And what do we get for this small sacrifice?" McKinnon was sarcastic.

"I think you will earn some good will in the Third World." It was Gupta who replied. "I rather suspect that you may need it in the years to come.

"Look", he added, "if it makes it any easier, I am sure I can get Rahmani to drop the demand for an indemnity. I believe we could handle his financial needs as a mark of our good will both to him and to Australia."

"Thank you, gentlemen." The ambassador was dismissive. "I will of course report your démarche to my government. No doubt you will hear the decision one way or another in due course."

Later that day, she cabled a report of the discussion, adding:

I have also spoken to Ambassador Sudjono of Indonesia. He was emphatic that you should take up the issue with his government. He believes it will be difficult for Indonesia to support us publicly but they would want us to retain control of Cocos. He indicated that Indonesia would be seriously concerned if India acquired the use of the airfield on Cocos.

Canberra - Russell Hill Defence Headquarters

It was later the following day when Gary Irwin strolled into Air Marshal Noble's office. Once again, Noble's superior was away on an inspection trip.

"Philip, I'm sure you will remember our discussion about increasing support for defence readiness some months ago. This cable from New York should be helpful if you dropped the word to a few people."

"I saw that", Noble replied. "But I'm not too sure that we'll be able to do much with it. I doubt if we could defend Cocos anyway, even supposing there were any public support for our doing so. It's not big enough to hold much less deploy a useful number of troops."

"You may be right. But look at it this way. If we abandon Cocos without a murmur, there is unlikely to be any comeback. It might even be sold as a good idea politically. Strategically, I am not so sure. This could become a tussle between India and Indonesia over what is legally our territory. My guess is that if our Indonesian friends believe we won't defend Cocos, they will move in to pre-empt any possible Indian occupation. That would hurt our relations with them even though they would in fact be doing us a good turn.

"The point is that if the choice were offered to the community, I am sure there would be a lot of Australians who would look askance at our tamely giving up our territory.

27

"Then again, there is the fact that we do find that airfield useful for our P-3 patrols out into the Indian Ocean. It's a pity we don't have a small RAAF detachment on the airfield. That might make it a bit harder for the Indians to press their case. Unfortunately, it's too late now to put people in there.

"If I were you, I'd have Andy Firebrace around for a good dinner and a whisper in his ear. You know him, editor of the Advocate. I think you'd find him sympathetic."

CHAPTER 3

Coastguard Headquarters, Brisbane

The bell on the teleprinter by the wall rang as the machine came to life and chattered briefly. The duty signaller strolled over and tore off the sheet. Her languid demeanour on this quiet pre-Christmas day vanished as she scanned the message. She almost ran as she took the signal to the duty watch keeping officer.

"Sir, we have a ship missing." She handed over the slip of paper. Lieutenant Denyer scanned it briefly. It was short and to the point.

```
DTG 231400Z DEC 95
IMMEDIATE
UNCLAS
FROM:    DARWIN RADIO
TO:      COASTGUARD BRISBANE
INFO:    COASTGUARD DARWIN
         COASTGUARD HEDLAND
         MARITIME HQ SYDNEY
GOVE ARGOSY HAS FAILED TO REPORT PASSING 15 DEG
SOUTH STOP REPORT DUE 231200Z STOP SHIP HAS NOT
RESPONDED TO THIS STATION STOP DEPARTED DAMPIER
FOR PUSAN VIA LOMBOK 220600Z COURSE 352 DEG ETA
LOMBOK 241800Z
```

Denyer glanced at the clock. It was almost 1.30 am. on Christmas Eve. He reached for the operations manual and reference publications stacked on his desk. After a quick scan, he picked up the 'phone and called the Vice-Commandant's home number. "Sorry to disturb you, sir." He could hear a party in the background. "We have a ship failed to report. *Gove Argosy* is one of BHP's bulk carriers out of Dampier for Korea. She's two hours overdue with a routine report about 400 nautical miles south of Lombok Strait. The book makes her 140,000 tonnes with a crew of 27. Weather is fine but it's two hours after sunset local time.

"I recommend we get the Hedland Nomad airborne immediately and ask Maritime Commander to send us a P-3.It will take them a good seven hours from now to get to Learmonth, then say another two to fuel and get to the search area. They should be on task by 0530 local time so they'll have plenty of daylight for a visual backup to radar. The Nomad can't stay out that long but her radar may give us a head start."

There was a brief silence as Captain Czulak cogitated. "All right", he agreed. "You'd better ask Maritime Commander if Jindalee can pick out that ship among the rest of the traffic up there. I'll join you in about an hour."

Denyer put down the 'phone and walked over to the signaller's computer terminal to draft his messages. Once they were on their way, he would scrounge a cup of coffee. It would be a long wait on this one.

RAAF Base, Learmonth, Western Australia

Learmonth was always a dump, Vidulic thought, as he climbed down the ladder from his P-3C Orion aircraft.Beyond the floodlit apron, it was deep night, that darkest hour before the dawn, with only a few lights showing around the so-called 'bare base'.

Squadron Leader Marko Vidulic was not happy. He and his crew had been called just as they had been about to turn in after a long day. As the duty crew, they were packed and ready to go but there had been no time to freshen up. Now, as the ground crew hooked up fuel hoses to his aircraft, he and his crew headed for the mess. A quick shower and shave followed by a bolted breakfast would prepare them for a long over-water search.

The big P-3 lifted off the runway an hour later. Although based on the civil Lockheed Electra of the1950s, the only resemblance to that famous airliner was in the airframe and the four big Allison turbo-prop engines. Even then, the magnetic anomaly detector (known naturally as MAD) boom projecting backwards from the tail told of something more lethal than a passenger aircraft.

On closer inspection, the P-3 revealed a number of hard points under the wings as well as bomb bay doors and sonobuoy chutes in the fuselage. Small antennae projected from many points. This P-3C model was the most advanced submarine hunter in the Western world. The fuselage was packed with electronic gear which could interrogate and process information from sonobuoys, the MAD, an infra-red detector known as IRDS, an ESM system which listened for and classified radio and radar transmissions from ships, submarines or other aircraft and, of course, long-range search radars which sought out targets all around the aircraft.

The Orion's tactical officer, known naturally as Tacco, manned a console which constantly updated a tactical plot from all the sensors. On an operation, he directed the pilot who was otherwise the aircraft's captain.

When configured for combat, the Orion carried the airborne version of the American Mark 46 torpedo and Harpoon missiles that could be used against hostile surface ships. The airborne version of the Harpoon sea skimmer missile had an effective range of more than 65 miles. Flying at some ten feet above the surface, even a radar-equipped ship would have less than a minute's warning from the time the missile popped up over the radar horizon.

Inside the pressurised cabin, the crew switched on radios and radar. The radar operator's screen glowed showing the shoreline of Exmouth Gulf fading away behind the aircraft.

"Pilot—Navcom", the navigator called Vidulic. "Distance to search datum about 470 nautical miles, say 80 minutes at this speed. I suggest we go up to 5,000 feet for optimum radar coverage."

"Shepherd 52, this is Coastguard Hedland."

The call came over the tactical frequency.

"Go ahead, Coastguard."

"Shepherd 52, our Nomad was on task for three hours doing a radar sweep on track from Dampier to 13° South. We had numerous radar traces but all small craft. Nothing like a bulk carrier more than 50 miles from Dampier. Neither Darwin Radio nor Dampier Harbour Control have any contact. Oh, and Jindalee was no help; they have had sunspot problems and have no reliable data at this time.

"Our aircraft will be back on task at 1000 local time; until then, it's all yours."

"Roger, Coastguard. We'll keep you informed."

Vidulic called the navigator. "Give me a plan for a creeping line ahead search using 15○ South and 116○ 20' East as search datum and backtracking to Dampier. When we reach datum, I'll cut back to three engines but we'll stay high for optimum radar cover. Search speed will be 240 knots."

For hour after tedious hour, the P-3 droned on. Inside the fuselage, the muted roar of the engines dulled the brain as tired eyes tried to focus on the radar display. Crewmen squinted through high-power binoculars backing up the electronic waves with the sardonically named Mark I Eyeball.

From a cloudless sky, the sun slowly moved across the heavens as the aircraft gradually extended its search coverage. From the datum, it searched back along the ship's estimated track, zig-zagging for 50 miles on either side of the missing ship's presumed course. The radar waves reached out 100 miles ahead and 80 miles on either side of the aircraft's track.

Targets there were and in plenty. Small fishing vessels, oil rig supply ships and coastal traders were detected and identified visually. Three big bulk carriers were spotted and identified as foreign ships heading for Dampier to load iron ore. Contacted by radio, they denied having sighted the *Gove Argosy* either visually or on radar.

Coffee was passed around hourly. Lunch was eaten but there was no sign of the missing ship.

"Sir", the co-pilot was green, "how come a ship that size can disappear out there? We've covered more than60,000 square miles with perfect radar and visual conditions."

"Yeah", the voice came from aft. "I've seen each wave at least ten times."

"We keep it going, fellas. That's a big ocean out there."

Vidulic called Hedland. "Coastguard, this is Shepherd52. We will be going off task in another two hours - back to Learmonth. We've seen nothing suggesting the target. I think we may have to revert to low level search for wreckage or survivors."

"Roger, Shepherd 52. We'll get the Nomad in the air for the rest of daylight commencing at the search datum. Can we expect you up bright and early tomorrow?"

"Yeah, roger that, Coastguard. We'll call you."

Coastguard Headquarters, Brisbane

In his operations room, Captain Czulak looked over the log of the search for *Gove Argosy*. Now the day after Christmas, the Hedland Nomad had now already flown five sorties in three days and the crew was approaching exhaustion. Soon the aircraft would have to be grounded for urgent maintenance. Shepherd 52 had flown two 12 hour sorties and was now on a third. Shepherd 55 sent up from Edinburgh was completing a second. No trace of the *Gove Argosy* had been found. Nor, he thought grimly, had they seen any sign of wreckage or survivors. It was time to reassess. He strode down the passage to the Commandant's office, pushing aside the weariness that clogged his brain. He knocked at the open door and walked in.

"Jack, you look buggered." Rear Admiral Wilson looked concerned. "When did you last get home?"

"Dunno, sir. Lost track of time. But I think it's time we called off this search. I think that ship has gone. We've scoured the relatively limited area it could be in and there's no trace. No sign of wreckage or survivors."

"Could we have missed anything?"

Czulak pondered. "I don't think so. Weather conditions in the search area could hardly have been better. We've had three good aircraft on the job as well as ships keeping lookout. The thing is - if she's sunk, well, those ore carriers would go down like a stone and it's over 5000 metres deep at the search datum. There would not be much trace and, if it was at night, most of the crew would have their heads down. She'd be sunk before they woke up."

"What about navigation hazards?"

"I can't see it, sir. Hedland did a detailed search along the track from Dampier. Once clear of Dampier Archipelago, you're into deep water pretty quickly. In any case, if she hits a rock, there's usually time to get out a Mayday and the wreck has something to sit on."

The Commandant agreed. "All right, call them off and tell them well done. I'll get on to BHP's Marine Superintendent. He's been giving me a hard time. You'd better start the ball rolling on the formal enquiry too."

He reached for the 'phone as Czulak left.

"Sandy!" Captain 'Sandy' McDermott was at his Melbourne home. " 'Tug' Wilson. I'm sorry but I'm calling off the search for *Gove Argosy*. We must assume the ship's been lost with all hands. I can't justify any more search time in the circumstances."

McDermott agreed sadly; the master of the missing ship was an old friend. His love of the sea did not blind him to the reality of its dangers, the sudden emergencies that came from nowhere to sink ships and kill men. People on land were backed up by all sorts of emergency services; for the seaman, there was only himself, his experience and his ship against the awesome power of the sea.

"Any idea what might have happened?", he asked.

"I thought you might be able to help", Wilson replied."It could be accident - an internal explosion in a fuel tank, something like that. There's nothing to go on. I assume at this stage that the ship was in good shape in which case we may have to think about some kind of sabotage or terrorist attack. Have there been any threats made, d'you know?"

McDermott shrugged. "None that I know of. And the ship was OK. You know we don't skimp on them and she was only ten years old. It should have been a milk run. I guess there'll be an inquiry but I'm damned if I know where we start to find an answer to this one."

CHAPTER 4

12°13' South, 110°14' East

The Orion droned steadily through the night heading almost due east on a course from Cocos to Darwin. The aircraft was on automatic pilot with the co-pilot relaxed in his seat staring out into the moonlit night.

Aft, the crew was mostly dozing. Marko Vidulic was leaning over the main radar display sipping a cup of coffee and watching with his radar operator as the strobe of light slowly circled the screen. A little earlier, they had passed by Christmas Island to their north but it had been out of radar range.

The crew were looking forward to arrival in Darwin, the end of a patrol which had taken them from that city to Butterworth in Malaysia, far out into the Bay of Bengal for a look at the Indian bases in the Andamans and Nicobars, then south to Cocos for fuel. After Darwin, they would head south for home at Edinburgh with the tapes of their surveillance mission.

Suddenly, the operator's head jerked up. "Sir, you're wanted up front. Flare spotted to starboard".

"OK, on my way. Anything on the radar?"

"Not a thing", was the puzzled reply.

Vidulic climbed into his seat. He could see the flare well off the starboard wing. It was red and fading now as he flicked off the autopilot and banked the large aircraft to head for the spot.

"Anything on radar or IRDS yet?", he asked through the intercom.

"I've now got an infra-red trace ten degrees to starboard, distance 3000 yards. Course to target is 165. Computer is plotting".

"Roger. That's the flare. It's almost out now but I've got a good fix. Wake them up back there and let go a smoke marker as we pass overhead", Vidulic ordered. "I'll circle and come down to 1000 feet after we drop. Then I want every spare body on visual lookout.

"Tacco, once the marker's gone, I'll feather No. 3 and cut speed to 160 knots. Co-pilot, give me 18 degrees manoeuvring flaps.

"Pilot—Tacco, smoke away."

Vidulic banked to starboard, cutting his No. 3 inboard engine throttle and losing height. The smoke marker ignited on the water. Smoke billowed and drifted downwind while the burning marker provided a point of reference both visually and on the infra-red detector.

"Pilot". The call came from aft. "Dinghy in the water about 50 yards upwind from the marker. It's an open dinghy and looks like there could be three men in it."

"Got him, sir". The co-pilot pointed out his side window. "At about 4 o'clock."

Vidulic hauled the big aircraft around to port, heading away from the marker to give manoeuvring room while losing height. "Tacco, I'll turn 180 degrees to port and come back over the top at 400 feet. Standard rescue procedure. Two smoke markers together, then three more at five second intervals. Keep me on course with IRDS and you drop the markers"

"Pilot—Tacco, roger. Course to target is 037 degrees."

"Navcom—pilot, call it in to Coastguard when we've dropped the rafts."

The big aircraft roared towards the dinghy, crabbing slightly with the wind on its starboard beam.

"Smoke, smoke away!"

Three more markers were dropped at five second intervals, then Vidulic banked away to starboard to bring the aircraft around in a circle and head back to the dinghy. Height was eased to 300 feet and he lined up approximately 50 yards downwind of the markers.

Vidulic checked the markers and the dinghy. Good, he thought, they seem to be drifting at the same speed. He reached down to his weapons panel, opened the bomb bay doors and selected the switch which would drop the rescue pack.

As it drew abeam of the double smoke marker, Vidulic flicked the switch and the package dropped away.

"Raft away!"

As they circled again, Vidulic saw that the pack had dropped perfectly. The two ten-seat rafts had inflated and were linked together by two rations and survival packs. The survivors' dinghy slowly drifted down on to the rafts and they could see men scrambling into one of them.

The navigator switched to the Coastguard frequency. "Coastguard Hedland, this is Shepherd 52. I have a raft with survivors in the water at approximate position 12° 14' South, 110° 14' East. I can remain on station for up to seven hours. Can you get me some surface support to pick them up."

"Roger, Shepherd 52. We have HMAS *Yarra* in the area. I'll give you an ETA as soon as we have it. Well done."

HMAS *Yarra* was cruising at 14 knots on a sou-south westerly course heading for Fremantle and a maintenance period after a visit to the Indonesian naval base at Surabaya. The night was dark and the ship was rolling gently in the slight swell from the north west. After clearing Lombok Strait the previous day, Yarra had diverged from the usual shipping lanes and her radar was now clear. The crew was at normal cruising stations with most of them in their bunks. The bridge team gossiped easily about the visit to Surabaya and their impending stay in Fremantle as they waited for their middle watch to end.

The 'phone by the head of his bunk buzzed insistently. Bellano, with the practice of years, was awake immediately.

"Captain", he answered.

"Officer-of-the-watch, sir. Signal from Maritime Command to proceed to 12° 14' South, 110° 14' East to pick up survivors in a raft. There's a P-3 on the scene. Course to the pickup point is 318 degrees, six hours at 25 knots." The officer of the watch had done his sums before calling his captain.

"All right. Alter course to 318 and set speed to 25 knots. I'll be up immediately." Bellano hung up the 'phone, walked out of his cabin and climbed the ladder one deck to the bridge.

Three hours later, dressed and eaten breakfast, Bellano was sitting in his bridge chair waiting, as was so common at sea, for something to happen. Subconsciously, his daydreaming began to focus on his wife. Just before they had sailed, Anne told him she thought she was pregnant again. That had been a surprise. Not that they had consciously tried to avoid more children. She claimed he only wanted another toy as well as his new ship but the smile had softened the accusation. He relaxed for a time, indulging his dreams. Then the Ops Room 'phone buzzed, breaking into his reverie. He snatched up the handset.

"Captain—Ops. We have the P-3 on radar at 80 miles dead ahead."

Bellano picked up a microphone. "Yeoman", he called to the signals petty officer, "patch me through to the aircraft, please.

"Shepherd 52, this is *Yarra*. Good morning. We have you on radar at 80 miles. ETA three hours."

"Roger *Yarra*. We are orbiting the raft. Three men on board all apparently alive. We'll bring you in and then go home. We're getting dizzy flying round in circles here."

The quartermaster grunted. "He should try going the other way." The comment brought a chuckle from the bridge team at the hoary old joke.

Bellano conferred with his Executive Officer. "Frank, I think I'll put the helo up. It can go on ahead and drop a swimmer to the raft. If these guys have been in the water for a while, they won't want to climb the ship's side. The helo can hoist them in and bring them back to the ship. See to it, will you please. I'll tell Shepherd what we're doing."

An hour later, the three men were in the ship's tiny sick bay with a horror-struck sick berth petty officer trying to treat their terrible burns. Days, if not weeks, of exposure to tropical sun and salt water had flayed and blistered almost every part of their emaciated bodies. Two of the men had lost consciousness and were in shock, as though rescue had exhausted their last reserves of willpower. The third mumbled deliriously as the XO tried to extract his story.

Later, with the ship heading south east at full speed, the XO reported to Bellano.

"They're off the *Gove Argosy*, sir. She went missing a month ago about 400 miles south east of where we picked them up. There was thought to be no survivors until now. One of these is the second officer who had the watch and the other two were on the bridge with him.

"Funny thing is, he says there was an explosion outboard just aft of the bridge. Everybody else, apart from the engine room crew, had their heads down and the ship went down so quickly, none of them had a chance to get out. The three of them got into a life raft that floated away and they've been drifting ever since. They had one flare left when they heard the Orion last night."

Bellano thought for a moment. "I don't understand this bit about an explosion outboard. An engine room or fuel tank would blow from inside the ship."

"He's pretty incoherent, sir", the XO responded. "He's on the verge of going into shock."

"All right", Bellano replied, "we'll let others worry about it when he's fit again. Send a signal to Coastguard at Hedland with what you have. And tell them we'll make best speed for Onslow, I think, and helo them into the hospital there."

Coastguard Headquarters - Brisbane

Czulak studied the report on the survivors picked up by *Yarra*. Nothing much to go on, he thought. Two of the survivors had died in hospital while the other was still in a serious condition but was expected to live. Under further interrogation by a Coastguard team from Port Hedland, he had insisted that, when his ship had been sunk, there had been an external explosion with a column of water shooting up on the port side aft of the bridge.

It didn't make sense. If the second officer was right, the only explanation was a torpedo. But that only made sense if the country was at war. Of course, if there had been an internal explosion with a secondary explosion from a fuel tank, that could possibly account for the column of water but only one explosion had been reported. The only safe assumption was that the survivor's recollections were too vague to be reliable after his appalling experience adrift for more than a month under a tropical sun.

The real problem, he decided, was the failure to find the survivors. Canberra would want to know why the search had been called off and why they had not been found more quickly. They might even want a scapegoat and he was a logical candidate; after all, he had recommended calling off the search.

It was easy for those chairborne buggers, he thought. As far as they were concerned, the survivors had been there in the water; they should have been found. It didn't matter to them that the dinghy had no radar reflector and that the sun's glare off the water made visual searching for a small object a matter of chance.

He mused that if the search had continued, the same individuals would have been complaining about the cost. He'd decided long ago that you couldn't win.

Sighing, he picked up his pen and began to draft his own report.

United Nations Headquarters, New York

The Australian Broadcasting Corporation maintained an office in New York and had access to a small studio in the UN Secretariat Building on 1st Avenue. Brett Lumsden rose to greet the two men who entered.

"Mr Patel, Haj Rahmani. Please come in."

After settling his visitors before their microphones, Lumsden began the introduction to his interview for a nationwide radio current affairs programme.

"Early today, the United Nations General Assembly voted 47 to 9 to condemn what it called Australia's illegal occupation of the Cocos Islands in the Indian Ocean. The decision follows six months of lobbying by the Cocos Liberation Front and its Indian sponsors.

"Cocos has been an Australian territory since 1955 and, in 1984, under an act of self-determination approved by the United Nations, the islanders voted overwhelmingly for incorporation into Australia.

"In its decision today, the General Assembly has instructed the Security Council to institute wide-ranging sanctions against Australian exports, especially mineral exports.

"In making its decision, the UN has been influenced by the Cocos Liberation Front and the outright support given to it by India, the world's second most populous nation. In the studio, I have Haji Mohammed bin Rahmani, the chairman of the CLF and Mr. C.T. Patel, deputy Indian ambassador to the United Nations.

"Haji Rahmani, if I can ask you first. What is the basis of your claim that the 1984 plebiscite decision should be set aside in favour of your organisation?"

"Well, Mr Lumsden, it is our contention that the so-called plebiscite in 1984 was fraudulent. Not all islanders were given the opportunity to vote while those that were suffered a large degree of coercion.

"We believe that Australia has not given our people the freedom they are entitled to. There is outright apartheid practised by Australia on our islands which are also used for military purposes without our approval."

"Mr Patel", Lumsden was smooth. "What is India's interest in this issue?"

"India has given sanctuary to Haji Rahmani and his colleagues of the CLF. We have also undertaken to support all oppressed peoples in the Indian Ocean region as we believe that to be consistent with our national principles. In our view, Australia should withdraw from Cocos and hand over authority to the CLF pending a further plebiscite to be conducted this time by the UN itself."

"It has been suggested, Mr Patel, that India's real interest is in enforcing trade sanctions against Australia and taking over some of our more important markets?"

"Mr Lumsden, there would be no need for these sanctions if Australia handed over Cocos to its legitimate rulers. It seems extraordinary to me that your country would wish to risk such a rich trade so as to maintain your rule over a small community of less than 400 people such a long way from your own country. Do you not have enough land of your own?"

Lumsden decided to cut the interview short. "Haji Rahmani, what is the future of the people of Cocos under your rule? How can you assure them of a good standard of living?" Rahmani paused before answering. "As a westerner, you probably cannot conceive that my people are not seeking inordinate wealth. We have enough to get by with. We expect Australia to pay a $1 billion indemnity over ten years to compensate us for years of occupation and our security is guaranteed by our Indian friends. Frankly, Mr Lumsden, we don't want anything else."

Lumsden wound up quickly. "The CLF and India have sold their programme to the UN General Assembly. Despite the low vote in favour of a new plebiscite, the fact that only eight other countries, all white and all Western, supported Australia indicates the degree to which we have been isolated in this forum of the world. Now the focus will switch to Canberra where the Australian government must decide whether to stand firm on Cocos and risk not only political isolation around the world but a threat to Australia's vital markets.

"This is Brett Lumsden at the United Nations for AM."

Prime Minister's Department - Canberra

Sir Alan Scott was in the chair again for this meeting of the National Security Council.

"Well, gentlemen, the Prime Minister has asked for an urgent assessment of this United Nations decision on Cocos and this liberation front. He also wants our advice on the line to be taken in public. Now, I presume you have all seen the report from the Office of National Assessments. Who wants to start the ball rolling?"

McLeod from Foreign Affairs looked up. "Of course, we all know this nonsense started some six months ago. We tried to kill it at that time but I think we misjudged the determination of the Indians.

"I think ONA have it right; this liberation front is just that, a front for the Indian government itself. They are calling the shots. This Rahmani is just a puppet. It's a classic operation."

"Then why don't we just let them have the place? Apart from the airfield, it has no value for us - or does it?" The questioner was Treasury's Dennis Arthurton.

Philip Noble responded immediately. "Realistically, Cocos is not of direct importance to us. We use the airfield a lot for deployment of our long range maritime patrols but the information we collect is of broad background value for the Americans as well as ourselves. It's not vitally important.

"It appears to me that the Indians want that airfield. They already dominate the approaches to the Malacca Strait. With the airfield on Cocos, they will be able to dominate the approaches to Sunda and

Lombok as well. That means they would be able to control all traffic through the Indonesian archipelago. Whether or not they exercise that control does not matter; their position would confer some substantial coercive potential."

In the ensuing discussion, McLeod pointed out that the Indonesian government had made plain their desire and expectation that Australia would not give in to the CLF.

"That's all very well", Scott commented. "It would have been more helpful if they had not abstained in New York. "Max, how serious is this trade threat? Can the Indians replace our mineral exports in our usual markets?"

Coffey from Trade thought not. "I agree with Philip. In general, India could not take our place and I would expect our usual customers to continue to deal with us. We might lose a little if they decided to reduce their dependency on us which some have done for quite different reasons. By and large though, trade sanctions don't work."

McLeod thought that the high abstention rate on the UN vote indicated a lack of support for sanctions. "Frankly, I think we should play this whole thing down, certainly in public. After all, there is no evidence whatever that Rahmani has any following on Cocos itself. There is no suggestion that I am aware of that the Indians plan any military action against us over Cocos. It has to be a bluff and I think we should call it."

Noble raised his hand. "I hesitate to raise the matter with the Council in the light of past discussions but it would be helpful to the situation if we could at least do something to build up ammunition stocks and boost our readiness somewhat. If, at the same time, we could make some public announcement of that, it may have some deterrent effect."

Arthurton grinned. "I take your point. I think we could go along with a modest increase along those lines. If we had a formal proposal, I believe the funds could be found. What about Cocos itself? Do you want to put some of your own people on the ground there?"

Noble laughed. "I don't know if you've had a look at the map but there's not a whole lot of room on the islands and we would have some difficulty with keeping them supplied. I'm not too keen on the token force concept that we followed up north in 1942. Those poor devils were just hostages to fortune, militarily useless political sacrifices."

"Very well, gentlemen", Scott wound up the meeting. "I shall suggest to the Prime Minister that he have a suitably anonymous spokesman make a statement rejecting the credentials of the CLF and suggesting that the UN vote received insufficient support for us to regard it as binding." He turned to Noble. "The defence spending statement should be separate, I think, and would best come from your own minister."

CHAPTER 5

Port of Dampier, Western Australia

Dampier Harbour's youngest pilot was Charlie Evans. A product of Britain's merchant service, Charlie had submitted to his wife's pleas to settle down and had left the sea, except for the chore of taking the huge iron ore carriers into and out of this remote port. It kept his hand in and left plenty of time for fishing, a pastime he intended to pursue with single-minded devotion during a spell of leave due next day.

Short, red-headed and with his neat white tropical uniform a stark and dazzling contrast to his fiery sunburn, Charlie climbed the last ladder to the bridge of the 148,000 tonne *Weipa Argosy*. Airconditioning reduced the temperature inside the wheelhouse to a cool 20 degrees. Outside, it was already over 30 in what little shade could be found, and it would climb higher.

" 'Morning, Captain", he greeted the ship's master. "Ready to proceed?" The BHP captain was less formal. "Take her out, Charlie, but don't bend her. She's carrying 45,000 tonnes of dirt and drawing 16 metres. There's only two metres under the keel, old boy."

"No worries, Captain. We can handle bigger ships than this without hitting the putty." Evans was confident, almost cocky.

He called Dampier Control on his portable radio and was given clearance to proceed. The ship edged away from the East Intercourse Island ore loader. Pointing in the direction of the first channel buoy, the pilot ordered, "Quartermaster, just scrape the buoy to port and follow the channel. Once past the middle ground buoy, your course is 007 degrees. Captain, can we have revs for 5 knots please."

The huge vessel, longer by a third than a city block, slowly made her way down channel with the pilot occasionally giving quiet helm orders. Five decks below and 220 metres away in the eyes of the ship, crewmen stowed mooring lines which would not be required until the ship berthed at Kaohsiung in Taiwan to unload. In the distance, Charlie could see the pilot boat which would take him to another carrier waiting to enter the port. There was always a queue for the two huge loaders which, as long as ships kept coming, would dump 16,500 tonnes of iron ore into the gaping holds every hour.

Time passed slowly as the buoys slipped by to port and starboard. After half an hour, the bulk of East Lewis Island had dropped astern and the bridge crew could see the fairway beacon marking the end of the narrow dredged channel about a mile ahead.

The explosion, when it came, threw everyone to the deck. Later from his hospital bed at Karratha, the quartermaster claimed to have seen a flash in the water but no one cared very much by then. The noise came first, a loud crack like a rifle shot followed by a roar. A huge column of water rose almost slowly into the air on both sides of the ship about 80 metres forward of the wheelhouse. Hundreds of tonnes of water reached higher than the mast before thundering back into the sea and across the decks. Simultaneously, and almost drowned by the thunder of the explosion and falling water, a rending, tearing screech told of the main deck tearing across like paper at No. 6 hatchway as the ship's keel, hammered upwards by the blast, bent the massive hull like a banana.

With bow and stern almost anchored by the weight of ore in the holds, the leviathan's back broke. The rent across the deck spread down both sides and the ship split in two. The bow section sank almost immediately, settling nearly upright on the bottom with the deck just awash on the rising tide.

The stern, made more buoyant by fuel tanks and accommodation spaces, took longer to sink. As it did, it rolled to port. Water pouring into open scuttles and doorways crashed along passageways and down ladders, sweeping loose fittings and furniture with it. Men moving about were picked up and smashed against steel, mercifully losing consciousness before they drowned. As the fury of the explosion spent itself, the upper works settled on the bottom lying across the channel. The starboard side lay exposed like a stranded whale, the huge screw propellor still idling slowly, uselessly, part in, mostly out of the water.

A few bobbing heads showed where men on deck had been thrown into the sea.

According to later estimates, the ship broke up and sank in less than 30 seconds. The bridge crew were catapulted to the port side of the wheelhouse. Water poured in through the smashed-in door as stunned and bleeding men fought their way past jagged steel fittings torn from their mountings by the blast. As he struggled to the surface, Evans found that the starboard side wheelhouse door was now some ten metres above him. Looking around, he counted heads. As far as he could see, all the bridge crew were floating although one or two, including the master, were clearly unconscious.

Helped by the others, he tore life jackets from the stowage in the deckhead, now vertical instead of horizontal, and put them on the unconscious survivors. Holding on to a pedestal, he kicked out the remains of one of the bridge windows and sent the men out, passing the stunned survivors through to the others.

Looking around he saw the pilot boat tearing towards the scene, her bow wave reaching higher than the upper deck. Other small craft were putting out from the petroleum wharf. From Dampier township behind East Intercourse Island, he could hear a siren begin its mournful wail. Supporting one of the survivors, he looked at the quartermaster, treading water close by. Spitting water, he offered a comment. "Shit, that's one way to start a holiday".

Canberra, the Prime Minister's office

In Canberra, the Prime Minister's office was an oasis of calm. His office was large, elegant and comfortable. Pale timber panelling was complemented by pastel green carpets and drapes. One wall was solid bookshelves, packed, as were all ministerial offices, with bound copies of parliamentary debates going back to 1901. They made a photogenic backdrop for the television cameras but were rarely read. Expensive paintings glowed from two walls while a national flag on its stand made a splash of stark colour in one corner.

The Prime Minister's desk was set, large, solid and reassuring in front of the bookshelves. Two telephones, sat on the desk. The red one for classified conversations was connected to a sophisticated voice scrambler before being switched to the normal network. The other was an extension from his office switchboard.

In one corner, a group of easy chairs set around a small table provided for small meetings. Usually informal, nevertheless much of the government's business was done in that corner

Chapman kept his desk clear and the tone of his office quiet. He resented the political hype of the ambitious young men who thought they ran the country. "I like ladies and gentlemen around me", he once said at a party meeting. "If anybody is going to shout in my office, it will be me." He was wading through a too-long and unutterably tedious Cabinet submission when the 'phone rang. With a sense of relief, he reached for the receiver. His secretary announced Sir Stephen Carter.

"Stephen, my dear fellow, what can I do for you?", he greeted his old political ally.

"Arthur, what the bloody hell is going on? One of my ships has been mined and sunk in Dampier Harbour." The voice was that of an angry, even frightened, man rather than a friend. "First reports say that ten men have been killed and the damned port will be closed indefinitely. Are we at war?"

Chapman thought briefly. Carter was no alarmist but Defence Minister Grayling had merely told him there had been an accident, playing it down. "I'll get right on it, Stephen. According to my information, it has been an accident, an internal explosion maybe." His voice was soothing, a party meeting voice.

Carter was contemptuous. "Bullshit", he shot back. "My ships don't blow up and sink in 30 seconds. That was a mine." He paused. "Now look", he was dictating now, Chairman of Australia's biggest corporation, "you get your people off their backsides and get that channel cleared. Have you any idea how much of your spending money comes from exports out of Dampier. That port is closed now until the wreck is cleared and your bloody bleating Treasurer will have to start worrying about his deficit."

Chapman felt trapped, defensive. "But Stephen, it's only one port..."

Carter interrupted, impatient. "Don't you understand. Dampier sends out 50 million tonnes of iron ore a year. It will be months before it's cleared. Other ports are already overloaded and can't handle the ships. It will cut exports and slow down our own steelmaking. And even if we can divert some shipping, how many foreign ships will come here if they think they will be mined. Don't be a fool, man! Someone has done this to us for a reason. You're the Prime Minister. Bloody well do something about it." The 'phone crashed down in Chapman's ear.

He thought for a moment. Carter's right, of course. We have got a problem even if we don't know why. He buzzed for his Principal Private Secretary. "John, organise a meeting of the Cabinet Security Committee in here in half an hour, please. Get General McCarthy over too. Oh, and cancel everything else."

The meeting was not going well. The five members of the Cabinet Security Committee sat round the table with the Chief of the Defence Force at its foot. The Prime Minister struggled to convey a sense of urgency and threat that he only imperfectly felt himself.

"Lord", Chapman thought at one stage, "what on earth possessed me to give Defence to this fool, Grayling."

Major (he insisted on the title as recognition of 20 years undistinguished part-time military service) Eric Grayling had got the Defence portfolio because he wanted it. He liked being saluted by generals and being received by honour guards. Also, he was an important figure in his State's party machine. Chapman groaned under his breath as he recalled Menzies' dictum: never give a portfolio to anyone with experience in the job. He would always think he knew better than his expert advisers. The trouble with Defence was that no-one wanted it; Defence was no road to political preferment, at least not in peacetime.

Grayling was holding the floor now. "This sinking is clearly accidental. There's not the slightest evidence of a mine explosion. Carter just won't admit to incompetence in his own company. It's obviously the same problem as with the *Gove Argosy* back in December. Sure, it's a problem. But it's a problem of clearing the port. That's the Transport Minister's job."

The Prime Minister looked around the room. "Any other views", he asked? "General?"

Sir Gerald McCarthy was a big man, smooth-cheeked and clean shaven, bulky in his khaki dress uniform. His leather and badges gleamed while three rows of medal ribbons proclaimed not only 40 years service but a decoration for bravery awarded as an infantry company commander in Vietnam. The knighthood went with the job of the nation's top military commander. McCarthy was no genius but he was loyal and dependable. Plainspoken, he was a soldier's soldier who would do his political masters' bidding without seriously questioning their demands. Nevertheless, he was not afraid to differ with his own minister especially on technical matters; their mutual antipathy was a common topic of conversation on Canberra's cocktail circuit.

"Well, sir, I think it is too early to be positive that it was not a mine. Sir Stephen's view has to be respected." He paused, considering. "I think we must establish a number of things. First, whether it was a mine or an accident. If it was a mine, we need to know where it came from and how it got there. Obviously, we must work out why it was laid although the culprit is likely to tell us before long. He must want something.

"Also, we need to find out whether he has laid any others. And that means looking at all the other key ports, a huge job with our limited resources", he added gloomily.

The Foreign Minister interrupted. "But surely you can't seriously see this as a military attack on us. There is no reason. We have no real quarrel with any other country at this time. I must be one of the least busy members of Cabinet."

Everyone laughed at that. Unlike most politicians, Foreign Minister, Brian McDonald, was not noted for being a workaholic. In the House, he was noted for doing as little as possible while a competent electorate staff guarded his political back. Suave, elegant and lazy, he nevertheless counted a wide range of world leaders as personal friends. Newspaper files and television archives were packed with pictures of McDonald, tete-a-tete with kings, presidents and prime ministers the world over. Nonetheless, he was effective, and they all knew it. At the laughter, he grinned back, totally unabashed.

"Well, Minister," the CDF replied, "I hear what you say. But the fact remains a ship has been sunk and the locals are persuaded it was a mine. It could be a terrorist enterprise. It could even be aimed at someone else, Japan for example. "Prime Minister, I think we should look at this very closely. Obviously there will be a marine board of inquiry set up by Transport but I think some of my naval people should go up there and look for evidence around the wreck."

He went on. "We must now consider that the loss of the *Gove Argosy* last year may not have been an accident. I think you should let me move some forces to the north west in case this thing escalates. That may help deter any escalation and I think we should make it very public to ram the point home. Also, we had better get what limited mine clearance forces we have up to Hedland and elsewhere to make sure we don't have any other nasty surprises."

And so, after some discussion, it was agreed.

Defence Operations Centre, Canberra

The Defence Operations Centre was established in the basement of the Russell Hill Defence complex. The new electronic plotting table which was the centrepiece of the operations room could display any map required. A small team of plotters with electronic pointers stood ready to move units as ordered. Office cubicles around three walls housed the operations and intelligence staffs who collected and displayed information on Australian, allied and possibly hostile forces. Along one wall, flanked by entrance doors, was a raised platform with a long desk for the commanders. A battery of telephones and speakers faced each place while clocks on the opposite wall showed the time in ten zones from New Delhi to Washington.

The duty operations officer, a navy captain, stood to attention as the Chief of Defence Force and his Assistant Chief for Operations entered.

"Good afternoon, Ops", McCarthy wasted no time. "Put the north-west coast from Geraldton north and west to Sunda Strait on the table, please. Have we got a navy spook on duty?"

"Here, sir." The intelligence officer was a grey bearded lieutenant commander.

"Good, I want you in on this."

As the map took shape in its different colours and outlines, he asked for communications. "I want Maritime Commander in Sydney and Air Commander at Glenbrook patched in on the secure line. If they aren't there, I want the deputy commander and ops officer. Put them on the speaker. Set us up for data transmission too. While we wait for them, I want your views.

"Briefly, he described the mining of the *Weipa Argosy* and his discussions with the Cabinet Security Committee.

"This is going to be primarily a naval and air operation so you fellers will have to guide me. Let's assume that a mine was responsible for the sinking. How did it get there? Spy?"

"It would have to be a surface vessel, sir." The intelligence officer was emphatic, insistent, determined to forestall argument. "A submarine would be too dicey, trying to lay in the channel, while an airborne drop could not guarantee the accuracy without giving itself away.

"The ship could be a freighter or a fishing vessel; something quite small would do. Trouble is, it could have been laid weeks or months ago and programmed to activate at this time, or even to take out the *Argosy*. We need to look for any unusual ships using the port, maybe since the last time the *Argosy* called there."

"Why do you say that?" asked McCarthy.

"Well, sir, the smarter mines can be programmed to pick out a particular ship. I am assuming, for no particular reason, that whoever he is wanted to sink an Australian ship rather than a foreign one. There aren't too many of ours. If they had a magnetic or acoustic signature on the *Argosy*, they could have made sure by programming the mine accordingly. It's guesswork but something to go on until we have some hard evidence on the mine itself."

"OK, I'll accept that. How do we get the evidence?"

"Dampier Port Authority should be able to give us the details on shipping movements, sir, but we'll need some divers up there to look for bits from the mine." He paused. "They may have to move a lot of ore to find anything useful. It could be a slow job", he warned.

"All right. Get on to Dampier about the movements. Ops", he turned to the operations officer, "you'd better get a diving team moving. We need that identification as quickly as possible. Get on it straight away, please."

As the captain picked up the 'phone, a signaller interrupted. "I have Maritime Commander and Air Commander on the speakers, sir."

McCarthy greeted his two top field commanders and quickly outlined the situation.

"We must work on the assumption that this mining will be followed up by some political or further military moves against us. We must also consider the possibility that the loss of the *Gove Argosy* last year was no accident, in which case we have a submarine operation on our hands as well. The PM agrees with me that we should put on a show of strength up north. Any ideas? You first, Peter."

Air Vice Marshal Peter Forbes had been Assistant Chief of Defence Force (Operations) for just a week following a tour as Head of the Australian Defence Staff in Washington. Originally a fighter pilot, he was widely regarded as an intellectual airman, a likely contender for the CDF's job in four or five years. One of the new breed, he had abandoned the traditional RAAF belief that air power should be exercised independently of surface operations. Tall, lean and with a reputation as a bon vivant, he was well-liked by his colleagues of all three Services.

"Yes, sir. First, I think we need all the mine countermeasures forces we have available to do a check of Port Hedland first, then the other mineral ports going clockwise around the coast." He thought for a moment. "Perhaps we should have another diving team look at the oil and gas wells up there too."

As the commanders agreed, the plotters recorded the proposals on the map display, the markers glowing in the half light. Other plotters set up estimated departure and arrival times.

"Next priority would appear to be surveillance, sir. We have been caught on this one. We've got one Jindalee station operational and that will give us a readout of ships and aircraft in the area. But we will need a lot more follow-up to identify any targets. I think we should get some more P-3s operating. Could we have 11 Sqn deployed north and split between Learmonth and Darwin to really saturate the area?"

From Glenbrook, the Air Commander, Air Vice Marshal Alan Johnson, demurred. "That will leave us pretty thin on the ground on the Pacific side", he argued. "As well, we have the commitment to the Americans up in the Bay of Bengal with the Butterworth detachment. We are still short of crews and a maximum effort by 11 Sqn is not something we can keep up for long."

"I'll talk to the Americans", McCarthy replied. "I think we have a real problem here. I'll get the orders to you today. 11 Sqn is assigned to Maritime Command for surveillance ops in the north east Indian Ocean. If you have to cut patrol times elsewhere to conserve assets, so be it. Carry on, Peter."

"Yes, sir. Next up, we should get some destroyers up to Darwin. We only have *Yarra* up there at present and she's a bit light on muscle. Perhaps Admiral Cartwright could advise on that."

From Sydney, Rear Admiral Ian Cartwright, the Maritime Commander replied. "I can let you have *Canberra*, *Sydney* and *Perth*. Everything else is in refit. I'll have to send *Success* in support. Poor old *Perth* is a bit tired but her Ikara could be useful if there is a submarine problem. I can have the whole group off in three days and in Darwin in ten. *Yarra* is at 48 hours notice in Darwin. I'll bring her to immediate notice if you need her. Meantime, my air people can get to work on a programme for 11 Sqn."

Before McCarthy had digested this, Cartwright came back. "Just a thought, sir. Perhaps I should send a couple of our submarines on a long-range snoop. *Otama* and *Waller* are available now in the west and I could push them out south and south-west of Christmas. With their long-range passive sonar, they could pick up any submarine activity supplementing the SOSUS detectors as well as being available for anything more active."

Getting a nod from his staff, McCarthy approved this. Quickly, they agreed also to detach sections of F/A-18 Hornets from 3 Sqn at Tindal to Learmonth and Derby. As well, the Air Commander offered to put 6 Sqn's F-111s at Amberley near Brisbane on stand-by. McCarthy closed the conference. "Thank you gentlemen. Your orders will be confirmed within the next hour or so. In the meantime, please look to the future. If this thing escalates, and I think it must, we will need to conserve men and materiel." On that sombre note, he departed.

CHAPTER 6

9° South, 96° East, Indian Ocean

Colonel Kapil Sharma woke with a start as his orderly nudged him. "Sun is coming up, sir. Thirty minutes to ETA."

Sharma went forward rubbing sleep out of his eyes as he climbed up to flight deck of the big Russian-built Ilyushin Il-76 transport. Nicknamed Candid by the NATO powers, the Indian Air Force called them *Gajraj*. Peering out of the cockpit side window, he could see the ocean far below bathed in the new dawn. He glanced at his watch; it was almost three hours since the eight aircraft had lifted off from the air base at Car Nicobar. Mentally, he went over the briefing he had given his airborne regiment, the lead battalion of which was in this group of aircraft.

It was a little over 1300 nautical miles from Car Nicobar to Cocos, about three and a quarter hours cruising for the big planes. Two thirds of his 300-man unit were packed into the leading pair of aircraft while the other six carried vehicles and their crews. He would have a couple of PT-76 light tanks and a similar number of BMP infantry combat vehicles, BTR-60 APCs and, most important, ZSU-23-4 radar-controlled 23mm quad anti-aircraft guns in case the Australians reacted aggressively with air strikes.

He didn't think it likely. They would land before the locals were up and about on this quiet Sunday morning. There was no Australian military presence and the civilians would be looking forward to a lazy day of sun, surf and picnicking. Without radar, they would not know what was happening until the aircraft were on the ground. Even then, they would be curious rather than alarmed, especially since his men had painted American markings on the aircraft.

The returning 'planes would take all the whites back with them, leaving the islanders untouched. There would be fewer than 250 to go back, many of them women and children. He had given the strictest orders that they were to be treated with care and courtesy. There would be no urgency and the evacuees would be allowed to take all their personal possessions with them.

He looked up as the two pilots sprang into life. The automatic pilot was switched out and the throttles cut back. The nose slowly sank below the horizon as the plane began to lose height. The co-pilot passed him a headset already plugged in to an outlet on the bulkhead. The aircraft's captain pointed to the main radar display.

"We have Cocos on radar, colonel. Looks like about six-tenths thin cloud cover with bases at about 3000 feet and wind from the south-east. We'll be able to go straight in, as planned. Landing in about 15 minutes if you want to wake your boys up."

Sharma nodded. "All right. Don't forget, if they call us from the ground, don't answer. And get this monster of yours off the runway and into the parking bay as quickly as possible to let the others in." He unplugged the headset and went aft.

Back in the cargo compartment, he picked up the microphone of the public address system. "All right, pay attention. We will be landing in 15 minutes. There will be a delay in disembarking because we will have to taxi back along the strip to the parking area. The crew will open the tail doors as we taxi. Landrovers will be out first on my signal with full crews and move to the parking bay perimeter.

"6 Section will be aircraft guard. 7 and 8 Sections to secure any vehicles in the vicinity. 9 Section to unload the aircraft. The rest of you form up out of the way and be ready to help unload the other aircraft as they come in.

"Now, ensure your weapons are loaded and magazines charged. I want no shooting under any circumstances without my direct order."

Cocos Airport Flight Services

Ross Bingham stood on the edge of the parking apron outside his office in the Flight Services building and glared at the airstrip. He saw little point in running a 24 hour flight information service from Cocos. They had few callers. The fortnightly charter flight from Perth, an air force

Orion twice a week and the occasional American navy plane were hardly reason for him to turn out of bed at five o'clock on a Sunday morning. Must be due for leave, he thought. This place is starting to annoy me.

As he looked into the distance, he started as he saw an aircraft to the north. Ducking inside, he picked up his binoculars and tried to make it out. Big, he thought, but can't see what it is yet. It's coming in too, on long finals already. Returning to his desk, he flicked on his microphone.

"Aircraft in the circuit, this is Cocos Flight Services. Identify please."

There was no answer as the huge machine came ever closer, its 20-tyre undercarriage dangling from the fuselage, ready to absorb the shock of almost 70 tonnes of aircraft and payload hitting the ground at 125 knots.

Through his binoculars, Bingham could now make out the stars and the US Air Force legend. Must be a Starlifter, he thought. Wonder what they want here.

There was a double burst of smoke as the wheels touched down gently right on the "keys", the parallel white bars marking the threshhold. As the nose wheels settled, there was a roar as the pilot deployed thrust reversers to slow the landing run. Bingham grunted his appreciation of a pretty landing.

As he watched, the roar of a second aircraft overhead made him look up. "I'll be buggered", he breathed. "What's going on?" He scanned the sky and picked up two more of the giant planes. He picked up the 'phone and dialled a number.

It was quickly answered. The whole island was waking up, he reckoned. "Sir, it's Ross Bingham at the strip. We've got a US Air Force Starlifter on the ground and another in the circuit. I have two more, no, make that three, in sight. There's been no notification and no response to my calls."

The Administrator did not hesitate. "All right, I'll come straight down. You'd better go and meet them while I get dressed."

Bingham watched the big aircraft turn onto the parking apron. As it did, the rear cargo doors swung open and three Landrovers packed with troops in battle order rolled down the ramp. Hitting the tarmac, they roared away from the aircraft, one heading for the administration block where the crew dismounted quickly and burst in to secure the building.

One vehicle headed for Bingham and screeched to a stop where he stood by the fence. A dark-skinned soldier in a green uniform jumped down, pointed a rifle at him and ordered him to put his hands on his head.

Stunned, Bingham hesitated. Sharply the soldier repeated the order, reinforcing the message by prodding him in the chest with the muzzle of his rifle. Slowly, the young Australian complied.

The Indian backed off and muttered something to his colleagues in a language Bingham could not understand. The soldiers relaxed, broad grins splitting their brown faces. The driver switched off his engine and they all got down, looking around curiously.

The big *Gajraj* taxied onto the apron, coming to a stop in front of the old terminal building. Troops poured out of the aircraft as the pilots cut the engines. Bingham noted that a few deployed around the aircraft, weapons at the ready, while the others formed up on the apron. NCOs barked orders that suddenly sounded loud as the engines ran down to silence.

Intent on the first plane's arrival, Bingham had not noticed the second plane until it swung into the parking area. As it did so, a third *Gajraj* landed, sweeping down the airstrip before slowing sufficiently to turn and taxi back after its predecessors.

As the second aircraft pulled up behind the first, three more Landrovers rolled down its ramp to be followed by two tracked vehicles looking like light tanks. Both had a small gun mounted in a cupola. As he watched, a crewman appeared from the cupola and loaded a small missile on to a launching rail above the gun.

At an order, eight soldiers climbed into the troop compartments of the two vehicles, Soviet-built BMP infantry combat vehicles, and they clattered away to opposite ends of the apron. Other soldiers clambered into two of the Landrovers which followed.
Sharma and his headquarters team stepped into a Landrover which drove to the terminal building. A signals team followed and began to set up their radio sets. A messenger was sent to collect Bingham.

As he was escorted into the building, Bingham saw a tallish, slightly-built dark soldier dressed in green combat fatigues. He was hatless with short, dark brown hair. A neatly trimmed moustache added to the impression of a military professional. Bingham knew nothing of badges of rank but gathered from small red patches of flannel on his collar that he was faced with a senior officer. As he watched, the officer unbuckled his web equipment and dropped it on a chair.

Sharma looked at the young civilian. Suddenly, he smiled, a gentle, somewhat mischievous grin. "Good morning", he greeted. "Please put your hands down and have a seat. I apologise for not letting you know we were coming but we thought it best to make it a surprise." The tone was gentle, the English impeccable and unaccented.

A soldier put his head around the door and spoke to the colonel. At an order, he ushered in another Australian. Bingham recognised Charles Savage, the Administrator. Not surprisingly, having been called out of bed, Savage was unshaven and untidy.

"Ross, what the hell's going on here? Who are these people?"

Sharma interrupted. "Who are you, please?"

"I'm Charles Savage, the Administrator of Cocos. Who are you?", he snapped.

Sharma smiled engagingly. "I am Colonel Kapil Sharma, commanding 2nd Airborne Commando Regiment, Indian Army. I am now in command here as military governor until President Rahmani of the Republic of Cocos arrives to install his government... "

"What sort of bloody nonsense is this?" Savage interrupted, confused and increasingly angry. "You've no right to be here. This is an act of war."

Sharma was polite. "I understand that you must be upset. However, I must point out that our rights here are based upon my men and their weapons. If you have a close look outside, you will see that I have more than 300 men with tanks, armoured personnel carriers and anti-aircraft guns. I think you will find it difficult to argue against that.

"As for a war, we are here as liberators under the terms of an agreement between my government and that of President Rahmani. There is no basis for any war but my task is to defend the security of the Republic of Cocos against any threat whatsoever.

"Now, Mr. Savage, may I introduce my second-in-command, Major Murthy, who will work with you to evacuate you and your colleagues with their families by the aircraft which brought us here. I have no wish to rush you but the aircraft must leave by sunset today. There will be plenty of room for everybody and their belongings."

Sharma ignored Savage's expostulations and left the building with a signaller, sprinting across to the Flight Services building. As he ran, he noticed that troops were moving out into the settlement, led by English-speaking officers with loud hailers, warning residents to begin packing. In the radio room, the signaller switched the transmitter to a frequency which he checked against his notepad and plugged in a morse key. At a nod from Sharma, he keyed in the codeword which told New Delhi that the landing had been successful and the airfield was secure.

Sharma turned as the air force commander came in. Wing Commander Mehra's flying suit was rumpled and his eyes showed his weariness from the long over-water flight.

"What now, sir?" he asked.

"You've got ten hours to refuel if you need it, have a rest and some food, and get the evacuees aboard. I want you off not later than 1730. You'd better paint out those American markings, too. They've served their purpose.

"Also, when you go, keep low and fly east for 30 minutes or so. I don't want any of them to see the landing ships bringing the other battalion and our heavy equipment. They should arrive from the west during the night and land in the morning. The MiG-29s will fly in tomorrow with a *May* from the navy's long-range maritime patrol squadron.

"In the meantime, we have to find and shut down the Australians' Jindalee radar beacon here. It gives them a reference point and, if they lose it, it throws a lot of their solutions into question."

"Won't they be alarmed?"

"I doubt it." Sharma was unconcerned. "They will think it's just a breakdown and try to find out. If we don't respond, they're just as likely to conclude that everyone here has gone off fishing. After all, would you work too hard in a paradise like this on a holiday?

"Anyway, so long as we get the ships and additional aircraft in unscathed, I don't care what they think, and it's too late now for them to react quickly. Their system is slower than ours - or so intelligence tells us."

The airman chuckled. "They must be bad! Incidentally, what about our honoured president?"

Sharma laughed. "Don't be irreverent. I have to be nice to the old boy as well as tell his subjects they have a new boss. He's coming in on the ships. Doesn't like to fly, he says."

The airman grinned. "Well, sooner you than me. We'll get out of your hair as soon as possible. What will you do if the Australians react?"

"I doubt if they will." Sharma became serious. "Intelligence thinks the Australians will let the place go without doing anything more than protesting politically..."

"Which of course, we'll ignore."Mehra was contemptuous.

"As you say, we'll ignore them. But even if they do react militarily, we believe they will find it difficult to do anything beyond some harassing air raids. And with our ZSUs already here and some SA-7s and 8s coming in on the ships, we'll give them a warm welcome.

"We could have a problem if they use their submarines against our supply ships but the navy claims to be able to handle that. If they can't, you may get some more flying down this way."

"OK", the airman was dismissive. "We'll look after you, sir. Now, I'd better go and sort out my boys and make sure we're ready to go. I'll see you before we leave."

Sharma nodded. "Thanks, old boy. And very well done, too. It all went like clockwork."

Later that afternoon, Sharma stood with Savage and watched as the evacuees filed aboard the aircraft. Most had recovered from the shock of their brusque expulsion but there were some tears as residents took a last look at their recent home. Soldiers helped them aboard the big planes. Sharma smiled to see one of his men leading two chattering youngsters to their aircraft. Excited by the novelty, they earnestly quizzed their escort about his rifle and other equipment.

Finally, he turned to the Administrator. "I think it's time for you to go", he said gently.

As the two men walked over to the aircraft, Savage controlled his emotions with an effort. "I would like to thank you for your courtesy, colonel. You and your men have made things a lot easier than they might have been. I hope you won't have too many losses when we take the place back."

Sharma was philosophical. "That's the risk we take", he remarked. "We do what we're told and hope the politicians sort things out before the shooting starts. Have a safe trip home."

The two men shook hands. The Indian stepped back and saluted as Savage walked up the ramp into the aircraft and the huge doors closed with a thump.

Next day, Sharma watched from the jetty as the first of the *Polnocny*-class landing ships nosed into the gently shelving beach. As it slowly ground to a stop on the coral sand, the double bow doors opened and a ramp dropped down. Soon, men and vehicles began to stream ashore to be directed to their bivouacs by the beachmaster.

As he watched, a boat pulled away from the accommodation ladder close to the ship's stern and headed for the jetty. Sharma went to meet it and was on the landing as it drew alongside.

A short, slight elderly man in a sarong and round black cap stepped ashore.

Sharma saluted. "Good morning, Your Excellency. Welcome home. I am Colonel Sharma in command here and at your orders."

President Rahmani beamed as he looked around. "Thank you, colonel. It is very good of you to take this trouble for my people."

"Thank you, sir. It is my pleasure as well as my duty.

"If I may make a suggestion, most of my forces will remain here on West Island. The Australians have all been flown to India and will be sent home from there. All of your people are on the other side of the lagoon on Home Island. There is a modern launch here which the Australian administrator used. I can make that available to you to go over to Home Island and establish your government. If you will permit, I will send a platoon of my soldiers over with you to act as a garrison."

Rahmani bowed. Despite Sharma's deference, he knew only too well who was in command on Cocos. He would be allowed some political freedom among the Cocos Islanders provided he did not interfere in any way with the Indian military. His jurisdiction would certainly not extend to West Island where the airport was.

"Thank you, colonel. Those arrangements would be most acceptable."

As they spoke, four MiG-29 fighters screeched overhead in tight formation before breaking off to join the circuit and come in to land in line astern. After they had rolled into the parking area, a big four-engined, Russian-built anti-submarine *May* aircraft followed more sedately.

Later, having disposed of Rahmani, Sharma called his staff together.

"All right. Pay attention, please. These will be the deployments. 1st battalion will be at the northern end of the island. You'll have all the 105s and I want them to cover the entrance to the lagoon. You'll be responsible for the security of the fuel tanks and the loading facilities, as well as the boats. Boundary with 2nd battalion will be the east-west road from Rumah Baru. You will also provide the guard platoon for Home Island. Understood?"

Major Dewan, the battalion commander, nodded as he furiously scribbled notes.

"2nd battalion will be responsible for the rest of the islands but especially the airfield. You will have all the armoured vehicles and these can be used for patrols of the other islands.

"Now, I expect that, if the Australians react, they will send F-111s against us and will concentrate initially on the airfield and our aircraft. So, the ZSU-23-4s will be deployed at each end of the runway. I want SA-7 detachments on the points on the other side of North and South Lagoons, and the SA-8s at the Quarantine Station. If you have any farmers among your troops, put them on to looking after the animals there."

Amid chuckles, he went on. "You fly-boys had better get some sandbag revetments for your birds. Ask Major Pandya here for some soldiers to form a working party. Put the MiGs at the northern end of the parking area in case you need to get off quickly. You sailors won't

64

be able to do much to protect your bird. I suggest you put it at the southern end and we'll see if we can get some camouflage on it.

"Regimental headquarters will be at the administration building. You can use the former club as an officers' mess but don't drink it dry too quickly.

"Set up your perimeters and fields of fire as quickly as possible. You won't be able to dig in too deep because of the water table. Use coconut logs to build sangars and pack them up with sandbags. Any questions?"

"Sir, can we use the empty houses to billet the men?" The questioner was Major Pandya.

"Good idea. Yes, but don't let them get too comfortable and make it clear there will be punishments for any looting or other damage. And no settling in until the work is finished. That goes for officers as well. All clear? In that case, thank you, gentlemen. You may carry on."

Parliament House, Canberra

Grayling surveyed his desk gloomily. The paperwork tide never receded and most of it was either incomprehensible or unnecessary. Most of the mechanical work could be handled by a public servant or, at least, a junior minister but the constitution would not permit that. There was so much to do that there was little time left for the political work in Cabinet and in his electorate. Sighing, he reached for the pile of letters to be signed. At least, he could get those out of the way with the extraordinary scrawl that passed for his signature these days.

It was almost a relief when his intercom buzzed. "It's General McCarthy to see you, Minister", his secretary announced. "He 'phoned ahead and said it was urgent."

"Good morning, Minister." McCarthy was terse, bypassing the usual small talk. "We are receiving information from a variety of sources indicating that Cocos has been invaded. The analysis is not yet complete but there are indications of military aircraft and a large number of troops on the islands."

Grayling's shock was palpable. His face paled and he felt his pulse begin to race as the adrenalin flowed. He had risen to greet McCarthy but sat down now, gripping the edge of his desk to still hands that had begun to shake.

Controlling his voice with an effort, he demanded "What's the evidence?"

"Civil Aviation tell us that Cocos went off the air yesterday. They failed to send normal weather reports and did not answer any calls. Also, according to Alice Springs Jindalee, the Cocos beacon has failed.

"Then, later yesterday, one of the weather people rang through to Cocos on the normal radiophone. The 'phone at the other end was picked up but nobody answered before it was put down again."

"Not much to go on". Grayling was dismissive, beginning to regain his composure.

"Agreed, sir. But when this happened yesterday, our duty intelligence people asked the Americans to have a look. As you know, they have a photo satellite which can look at Cocos although it is normally tasked for Soviet targets.

"They agreed to photograph Cocos on a routine pass which was actually during the night. They have reported that initial analysis of the infra-reds shows troops and armoured vehicles as well as aircraft. They are sending us the photos for full analysis and we should have them later today.

"Also, an E-2C on an exercise from the USS *Coral Sea* in the Indian Ocean has reported a lot of UHF and VHF plain language transmissions in Hindi from Cocos. That was yesterday but the word has just come through from CINCPAC. They also spotted a number of ships in formation, apparently approaching Cocos.

"I have asked the Americans in the meantime to let us have anything they can spare in the way of surveillance of Cocos. CINCPAC has agreed and so has Pine Gap. Jindalee has been told to concentrate on ships and aircraft in the Cocos area but the loss of the beacon there will make any sort of precision tracking difficult.

"In any case", McCarthy explained, "I'm told Jindalee will not be able to detect troops and aircraft on the ground or ships which are moored at or near the islands."

"What about Geraldton?" Grayling was referring to the Australian communications intercept station near that West Australian city.

"They report nothing out of the ordinary with Indian HF traffic but that means nothing. They would be expected to maintain normal traffic levels in case we were alerted by any changes.

"Geraldton had not been tasked for VHF or UHF in the Cocos area so they did not copy what the *Coral Sea*'s aircraft picked up. I have changed that tasking this morning."

Grayling, calmer now, thought briefly. "This is obviously a matter for Cabinet. The question is: do we wait for a better analysis or go with what you have? It's still a bit uncertain, isn't it?"

McCarthy cursed inwardly at the response. Grayling's words were carefully chosen, he thought. If this thing turns out to be a mare's nest, I'll get the blame for hitting the panic button and he'll get the credit for his caution. Bugger you, he thought, I don't mind sticking my neck out even if you do. His reply was formal.

"I strongly recommend, Minister, that this matter go to Cabinet now, as a matter of urgency. If it is confirmed, I will need a directive as to our response as soon as possible. If it turns out to be a furphy, the worst that will have happened is that some ministers will waste some time." Not for the first time, he thought to himself.

"All right, then." Grayling bowed to pressure. "Let's walk round and see the Prime Minister now."

CHAPTER 7

Parliament House, Canberra, Monday morning

In the Prime Minister's office, McCarthy completed his briefing to a stunned Cabinet Security Committee. Chapman was the first to comment.

"It looks as though the Indians were more determined than we thought. I assume we are talking about Indians?"

Grayling pre-empted McCarthy's reply. "That conclusion is still tentative, Prime Minister. All we have is some local radio transmissions said by the Americans to be in Hindi. In my view, our first priority must be to find out what is actually happening on Cocos."

All eyes turned to McCarthy who shrugged. "Certainly, the reports must be confirmed. I would hope we could have more detail from the photos by tonight, and Geraldton should begin to generate some intelligence within a few hours. At best, I could have confirmation by midnight.

"What I will need to know, though, is how the government intends to respond if this is an Indian invasion. If there is to be a military response, then we will need to step up our level of readiness, and that will inevitably lead to publicity."

Chapman looked around the table. "The advice we had before is that we should let Cocos go. I must say I am inclined to accept that. After all, what do we have to lose", he asked rhetorically, "an airfield that Defence say they can manage without and a quarantine station. It's hardly the stuff wars are made of."

Brian McDonald, the Foreign Minister, was appalled, especially when he heard the mutter of agreement from the rest of the group. It was too easy to rationalise away the loss of the islands but he knew that many of Australia's friends would expect a vigorous response. The Indonesians certainly did not want Indian forces on Cocos where they could dominate the approaches to Sunda and Lombok Straits. The Americans found the Cocos airfield and the Australian patrols which used it of no little value in supporting their Indian Ocean squadron.

Apart from anything else, the Indian invasion was an act of international lawlessness. If they got away with it, a nasty precedent would have been established, whatever the United Nations vote had been. The problem was, he mused, we just don't know how to behave internationally. We prance around full of platitudes but run away from the tough ones.

Nevertheless, he decided to temporise, knowing that his colleagues would welcome an opportunity to delay any decision.

"I think we should wait for confirmation from Defence. CDF says he can give us a better story later tonight. And let me call in the Indian High Commissioner and see what he has to say. I'll get our people in New Delhi to check around urgently but discreetly, and perhaps, CDF, you might get your attach, over there to do the same. I think we should also talk to our departments before we jump to any conclusions."

The discussion continued briefly but the essential decision to postpone action had been agreed. McCarthy had to be content with the delay, realising that little of substance could be done in the meantime. Reading the mood, he decided to limit himself to having the planners look at a few theoretical contingencies.

"What about Bill Newman?", McDonald wanted to know. "Are you going to let the Opposition in at this stage?"

Chapman pondered that for a few moments. Whatever the government did, their opponents would use the decision against them, he thought. Sooner or later, he would have to tell Newman - and certainly before any announcement. He expected the Labour Party would oppose any use of force to recover Cocos. Certainly, their Left wing would make it hard for Newman to support a military response. If Cabinet decided to let Cocos go, they would most likely be publicly critical but privately supportive. The government could live with that, even with their narrow four-seat majority in the Reps. In fact, Labour's basic support would ensure he would be able to control any back-bench dissidence in the Coalition. Inevitably, there would be some from the militaristic element.

69

On the other hand, if Newman were told now, he might want a say in the decision. While that might defuse any political fallout, he did not want Newman to feel he had a right to any input into the government's decision. Better to decide first and tell the Opposition later, he concluded.

There was no dissent from his explanation and the meeting prepared to break up.

"I don't think there's much point in coming back tonight, gentlemen. We'll reconvene at 9.00am tomorrow morning. CDF", he turned to McCarthy, "perhaps you will attend and have a more detailed brief for us then. In the meantime, of course, no-one goes public on this."

Monday afternoon

Later, in his own office, McDonald welcomed Vijay Natarajan, the Indian High Commissioner. Paul McLeod was present. The three men sat in easy chairs around a low table, making small talk until coffee was served and McDonald's secretary left the room.

The Foreign Minister opened the discussion. He came straight to the point. "Vijay, I have asked you to see me because of some disturbing information we have that Indian military units have landed on the Cocos Islands. As you know, they are Australian territory and we would be very concerned if India had landed forces there without our permission."

Natarajan was a professional diplomat. Short, stocky, almost plump, and clean shaven with dark brown hair slicked down over a broad scalp, his manner was bland. The blunt accusation from McDonald made no obvious impression.

"I'm so sorry, Minister, he responded. "I have no knowledge of this.

"Of course", he volunteered, "in the light of the UN General Assembly decision last January, we do not accept that Australia has any sovereignty over the Cocos Islands.

"Er..", he paused, "are you sure of your facts?"

McDonald was equally urbane. "We are waiting on confirmation but I have no reason to question the information we now have available.

"I would be grateful if you would communicate our concern to New Delhi and let my government have an explanation. We are not only concerned about any violation of Australian sovereignty but also for the safety of Australian citizens. I have to brief Cabinet on this tomorrow morning at 9.00am. It would be helpful if I could pass on your government's answer at that time." Behind the mask, there was steel in McDonald's demand.

After the Indian took his leave, McDonald looked at his top adviser. "The bastard knows. That bland front instead of a hot denial is confirmation enough. I wonder what they'll say." McLeod was pessimistic. "I think they will admit it, using the UN resolution as justification and thumb their noses at us. After all, they're in possession now after what looks like a very efficient little *coup de main*." He raised an eyebrow, quizzically. "What will we do, kick them off or ...?" He left the question unfinished.

"Cabinet—or the security committee, anyway—is inclined to let them have the islands. And that's even without asking the soldiers whether they can get them back." McDonald made it clear he was not happy with Cabinet's attitude.

The two men discussed the options. McLeod argued for resistance, making the point that Australia's prestige would suffer if the islands were passively surrendered. He emphasised the bad effect surrender would have on relations with Indonesia and, to a lesser extent, Malaysia and Singapore.

McDonald worried more about domestic opinion. Despite a climate of pacifism which had been long and carefully nurtured by the intelligentsia, he thought that the public would be angry about an invasion of Australian territory, however remote and insignificant. The media, he accepted, would climb on to any bandwagon. They had peddled the peace line for decades but could just as easily become more jingoistic than Margaret Thatcher. There would be demands for the government to act forcefully.

It was not too early to take some soundings, he thought. Seeing McLeod out of the office, he decided to spend the rest of the afternoon and evening making a few phone calls.

Defence Headquarters, Russell Hill, Tuesday morning

McCarthy rubbed his eyes tiredly as he looked over the photos. The wall clock showed 0330hrs as the briefing officer picked up his pointer and stood in front of a display of photo blowups on the wall. These looked fuzzy, a mixture of light and shadow making no sense to the untrained eye. At a nod from McCarthy, he began to describe the features to the assemblage of senior officers.

"Sir, the photos were taken just after dark on Sunday evening, that is the day before yesterday. They show a force of troops not less than 200 and probably not more than 400 all on West Island where the airfield is. Some of these are in formed bodies while others appear to be working on vehicles. Oddly, there seem to be very few individuals, especially in the residential areas. This would suggest that the civilians are either confined to their residences or they have been removed. There are indications of troops bivouacking under cover of the trees.

"We can identify a number, approximately 15, of distinctly military vehicles. These are marked on your copies and shown on the blowups. There are at least six armoured vehicles including two ZSU-23-4s. These are tracked, radar-controlled quad anti-aircraft guns of 23mm calibre. We can also make out one PT-76 light tank and a BMP infantry combat vehicle. The others appear to be light trucks like Landrovers and they seem to have some sort of weapons, probably machine guns, mounted.

"Sir, all these armoured vehicles are of Soviet origin but they are in use by the Indian Army. Landrovers would suggest Indians also but we cannot be positive about the identification from the photos."

"All right", McCarthy growled, "anything else from the photos?"

"Not at this stage, sir. We may get additional data from a more thorough analysis. What we do have from more recent pictures the Americans took this, sorry, yesterday morning is a *Polnocny*-class landing ship beached just south of the jetty on West Island and discharging vehicles. There are two more *Polnocny*'s standing by off the beach. At least one of these is carrying artillery. Although these are also Soviet-built ships, there is a *Godavari*-class frigate standing offshore. This is definitely Indian.

"We will get more out of these photos with more detailed analysis but we've only had time for a quick look so far."

"What about SIGINT?" The question came from Philip Noble.

"VHF and UFH intercepts from Geraldton are coming in now. They confirm the use of Hindi so they are certainly Indian forces there. They have been using plain language fairly loosely so either they think we can't hear or they don't care if we can. Most of the chatter is domestic, things like bivouac areas, billeting, ration issues and so forth. They are using encrypted call signs so we'll need more time to put together a detailed force structure. There are certainly some troops detached to Home Island where the Malay population lives.

"One thing, though. The photos don't show it but SIGINT says that there are aircraft on the ground. Presumably they arrived after the satellite pass.

"I should add, sir, that all attempts to communicate through normal civil channels with Cocos have been unsuccessful. They simply aren't answering."

McCarthy thanked the intelligence officer who collected his papers and left. After a short discussion, the meeting broke up with officers aiming to get as much rest as possible in what was left of the night.

Parliament House, Canberra, Tuesday mid-morning

It was a full Cabinet which gathered to hear McCarthy's briefing. As well as the 14 senior ministers who made up the Cabinet, all five members of the National Security Council sat behind their respective ministers to advise. The CDF distributed copies of the photographs he had seen during the night.

The briefing was precise, almost brutal in its uncompromising simplicity. There was no room for argument. Cocos had been invaded and occupied in a well-planned but essentially simple operation, and without a shot being fired. McDonald described Natarajan's response at their meeting the day before. The Indian had not reported back and there was nothing of use from the post in New Delhi. The meeting would decide how Australia would react.

Discussion was confused. The oldest minister present, now looking after Health, muttered that he had always opposed the granting of citizenship to the islanders. "We were never able to defend them. I said so back in 1982 and I say it again." As usual no-one took any notice of him.

When Primary Industry asked about the fate of the animals in the quarantine station, McDonald exploded. "What's this", he demanded, "some sort of Orwellian 'two legs good, four legs better' nonsense? This is not Animal Farm, you know. There are some 400 Australian citizens on those islands. More than 200 are mainlanders with their families. Don't we owe them anything?" Offended, Primary Industry subsided.

Grayling claimed the floor. "On the basis of what CDF has told us, an operation to recover Cocos would take some months and cost not less than $500 million." At that, a number of ministers visibly flinched. McCarthy looked at Irwin who shrugged; Grayling had not asked him for a figure.

Asked for an estimate of casualties, McCarthy hedged. "I have no estimate at this time, and, in the absence of any detailed planning, I could only hazard a guess - probably 500 overall of which 60 would be killed. But that could be too optimistic."

"Could we do it?", Chapman asked.

"Frankly, Prime Minister, without more detail at this time, I don't know. The Indians are good and, if they are properly supported, it will take us a lot of time, men and money. If we don't get American help, I would have to say we could not do it.

"I don't want to sound negative but the discussion is too vague for me to advise you. I need time to work out some options."

Attorney-General wanted to know what the media should be told. There was general agreement they should be told as little as possible.

McDonald demurred. "I don't think we can sit on this for long. We could have a real problem if we try to hush it up. Remember the uproar over cover-ups in Vietnam, never mind the perennial dredging up of the attempts to deny the Darwin bombing fiasco in 1942 or the Brisbane

Line nonsense. The more we cover it up, the more outrageous the speculation becomes and the sillier we look eventually.

"I think we should go on a diplomatic offensive on this one, cast the blame on the Indians for an act of aggression."

"That's all very well", Grayling replied, "but then we'll be expected to go and take it back and that's a job we may not be able to do."

Treasury waxed sarcastic. "D'you mean to tell me I've been giving you $9 billion a year for you to tell me you can't do anything when we need to. There could be a nice old Royal Commission in that." Offended, Grayling retired from the debate.

Eventually Chapman called a halt. There was general agreement to a proposal that a low-key statement be issued announcing a loss of communications with Cocos and that attempts were being made to regain contact. Only McDonald dissented but he agreed that the Opposition Leader should be briefed on developments.

Back in his office, he called in his press secretary. "Frank, you know Andy Firebrace, don't you?" The question was superfluous; McDonald had fed leaks to the editor of the Canberra Advocate for years.

"Why don't you go and have a chat with him. Give him the Cocos story on a strictly non-attributable basis. He can do what he likes with it but what I'm really interested in is his own personal reaction. You can tell him if you like that Cabinet is divided on the question.

"Oh, and on your way out, ask Jenny to get that bastard Natarajan over here, on the double ... " he grinned, "politely and through proper channels, of course."

Tuesday, late afternoon

McDonald was working through his in-tray when the intercom buzzed.

"Frank here, boss. Andy says to make sure you watch Channel 6 news tonight. He wouldn't tell me any more."

Later, he flicked on the television. The lead story was about Cocos. The anchorman led with a bald assertion that Indian forces had invaded and occupied Cocos before introducing Reg Baker, the network's chief political correspondent. Like many in the Parliament House press corps, Baker was no friend of the government and his tone was a mixture of hostility and triumph.

Standing in front of the ministerial entrance to Parliament House, he spoke into a hand-held microphone.

"Confusion reigns in the government tonight over rumours that the Australian Cocos Islands in the Indian Ocean have been invaded and occupied by an unknown military force.

"According to a very brief statement issued from the Prime Minister's office earlier today, there has been a breakdown in communications with the islands which lie more than 2000km from the Australian mainland.

"However, unconfirmed reports from Parliament House sources say that the government has evidence of military forces landing on the island and there is speculation that these could be Indian, or even Indonesian.

"I contacted both the Indian High Commission and the Indonesian Embassy but they denied any knowledge of any invasion.

"A spokesman for the Prime Minister's office said he had no knowledge of any invasion and other government sources have declined to comment."

The camera switched to the studio set as the anchorman interrupted. "Reg, what is the Opposition saying?"

"I spoke to Bill Newman, Leader of the Opposition, just a short while ago as he was leaving to catch a 'plane home to his electorate. He says he has spoken to the Prime Minister about the rumours and has demanded a full statement which will either confirm them or prove that they are false.

"Apart from that, we do know that there was a full Cabinet meeting today and that General Sir Gerald McCarthy, the commander of the defence forces, attended.

"If there are any further developments, we'll let you know immediately. This is Reg Baker at Parliament House for the Six Network."

McDonald flicked off the set as the anchorman began an interview with an academic who clearly had been given neither the time nor the information to discuss the Cocos issue coherently. He told his secretary to call the Prime Minister's office and tell him he was coming around.

Chapman was defensive as McDonald urged him to make a full statement. The Foreign Minister argued that any attempt to fudge the issue now that the media were on the scent would rebound later.

"Damn it all, Arthur. We know they are there. You can't do a Mr Micawber, hoping something will turn up. The Indians won't leave unless they are forced out, so we have basically three options. Either we let them have the bloody islands, we try political pressure internationally to have them withdraw or we use the military to boot them off.

"If nothing else, if we come clean now, we retain some control over the story. The feedback from both the media and the public will indicate what sort of support we are likely to get on the three options."

Chapman hesitated. McDonald's arguments made sense but he did not like to be pushed. He thought the most sensible solution was to let the Indians have the islands, to wash his hands of the place and negotiate the return of the mainlanders.

Newman, though, had shocked him. He had briefed the Opposition leader fully, expecting support for the abandonment option. To his surprise, Newman had argued strongly for a military response. He had agreed to maintain confidentiality for the time being but insisted on being kept informed.

As they talked, the PM's principal private secretary came in.

"Excuse me, sir, but the switchboard has just lit up with demands for interviews. It's about this bulletin that's just come from Reuters on the AAP link." He handed a copy to each man. They scanned it quickly. The message was unmistakable. It read:

NEW DELHI TUESDAY 0730GMT BEGINS INDIAN FOREIGN MINISTRY HAS ISSUED THE FOLLOWING STATEMENT QUOTE INDIAN VOLUNTEER FORCES HAVE TAKEN CONTROL OF THE AUSTRALIAN-OCCUPIED COCOS ISLANDS AND INSTALLED THE LEADER OF THE COCOS LIBERATION FRONT, HAJI ABDUL BIN RAHMANI AS PRESIDENT OF REPUBLIC OF COCOS STOP INDIAN

GOVERNMENT IS PROUD TO BE FIRST COUNTRY TO RECOGNISE THE REPUBLIC STOP INDIAN VOLUNTEER FORCES WILL REMAIN IN COCOS TO ENSURE SECURITY OF THE NEW REPUBLIC THE ESTABLISHMENT OF WHICH IS CONSISTENT WITH THE UNITED NATIONS GENERAL ASSEMBLY RESOLUTION OF LAST JANUARY STOP AUSTRALIAN CITIZENS FORMERLY RESIDENT IN COCOS HAVE BEEN EVACUATED AND WILL BE RETURNED TO AUSTRALIA VIA SINGAPORE THIS WEEK UNQUOTE FOREIGN MINISTRY SPOKESMAN CLAIMS THERE WERE NO CASUALTIES AND ALL AUSTRALIAN RESIDENTS ARE UNHARMED AND IN GOOD HEALTH STOP QUESTIONED HE SAID QUOTE INDIAN TROOPS ARE ALL VOLUNTEERS AND HAVE BEEN GRANTED LEAVE FROM REGULAR INDIAN UNITS UNQUOTE HE WOULD NOT ELABORATE AND DISPUTED THAT VOLUNTEERS WERE ACTING UNDER INDIAN GOVERNMENT DIRECTION ENDS

The three men looked at each other, almost with relief. The decision had been made for them. Chapman broke the silence.

"John, Security Committee of Cabinet to meet here in 15 minutes please - and get General McCarthy over as soon as he can get here. I'll give the media something to go on while we decide where we go from here. You can let them in for a short press conference in five minutes."

Ten minutes later and facing a forest of microphones in the glare of television lights, the Prime Minister read out a hastily drafted statement that said:

The Australian government unequivocally condemns the unjustified and unprovoked act of aggression by India in its invasion of the Cocos Islands.

The islands are, by free decision of their inhabitants in 1984, Australian sovereign territory. The United Nations General Assembly is not entitled to overturn that decision unilaterally, a fact which was clearly recognised by the majority of its members who abstained from voting last January.

The Indian government has admitted that its forces were involved in the aggression. It must accept responsibility and take the consequences for its lawless act.

There was an immediate clamour of questions.

"Prime Minister, Richard Norton, AAP. What will the government do?"

Chapman kept the answers short. "Cabinet will meet in a few minutes to consider the options"

"Sir, Mary Petrelli, ABC. Can you indicate what those options are? Do they include an invasion of Cocos by Australian forces?"

"That is one option, certainly"

"Prime Minister, Reg Baker, Six Network. Why was the government not aware of the invasion? What's wrong with our intelligence people?"

Chapman smiled at the sally, remarkable only for its predictability. The thought passed through his mind that some of the journalists, Baker among them, were as programmed as robots on a factory floor. He riposted gently. "The government did have reports of the invasion. We were in the process of confirming these. I presume that you never report anything without confirmation, Reg." There was laughter at that, easing tension. "Now, if you'll excuse me, ladies and gentlemen, I have a Cabinet meeting."

CHAPTER 8

Cabinet Room, Parliament House

The Cabinet was not only unhappy; it was frightened. Probably not one member had ever seriously expected to find himself facing up to a military invasion of Australian territory. For most of them, their only experience of war had been in their political youth, fighting the battles over conscription and the Vietnam war, mostly at the level of student politics where it was all a bit of a game, strident but harmless. With the exception of Grayling who had been a reservist, none had actually served in the military.

Most of the ministers had little experience of or interest in the outside world. Some would happily debate international politics but only with a sense of detachment, believing that the issues involved were far removed from those that concerned them and their constituents.

Almost all had matured in an intellectual climate which regarded peace as the normal condition of rational people. Nothing was worth actually fighting and dying for. Modern civilised states did not seriously consider using force as an instrument of national policy. That concept, they believed, belonged to a world now happily consigned to history. It was detached view, one they had never seriously been forced to confront. Now they were confronted and their discomfort was palpable.

What was worse was the fact of the Opposition's hostility to their own preference for appeasement. According to Chapman, the Opposition Leader had made plain his belief that Australia should fight to recover Cocos, preferably by diplomacy but by force if diplomacy failed. Newman had also made plain that he was not seeking mere electoral advantage; he and his colleagues were prepared to fight and, he believed, the people would be with them.

McDonald was no help. He claimed the Indian announcement and the invasion itself ruled out any chance of any diplomatic solution other than surrender. His was a lone voice for the military option. In his more savage moments, McDonald thought his colleagues were poltroons. More realistically, he recognised their confusion and understood. In his world of international diplomacy, the parochialism of the Australian politician was taken for granted.

McCarthy listened to their discussions, making no comment. He was not optimistic that he could successfully invade Cocos and he doubted if the Indians would withdraw voluntarily. Not now when they were well established. Answering a question, he explained.

"The Indians are there in some force. They have an air defence system apparently based on fighter aircraft, guns and missiles although we don't yet have full details.

"Theoretically, they are very exposed—over 1300km from their nearest base. But, and this is the catch, Cocos is just as far from our nearest air base at Learmonth. If they sit there and can be supplied, we must mount a major operation to get rid of them.

"Our biggest advantage is that Cocos is simply too small for them to put large numbers on the ground. So, if we do invade, we won't need a very big force. And, I suspect, it would not be a very big or long battle so logistics should not be an insurmountable problem.

"What we don't have is the shipping to get troops there, nor do we have air cover to protect them all the time.

"What we can do is lay on some air strikes to harrass them, knock out installations, aircraft and men. With our submarines, we could attack their resupply ships but, if they resupply by air, I doubt if we could stop them."

"Can't you knock out the airfield?", the Treasurer wanted to know.

"I'm not sure how successful we would be or whether we could maintain enough pressure to keep it permanently out of commission. We just don't have enough aircraft or bombs. If they dig their heels in, I doubt if we can keep up enough pressure to persuade them to pull out."

"Why not hit them elsewhere, sink some of their ships with our submarines?" This time, it was Transport who asked the question.

McDonald interposed. "I believe we would have a problem with other countries if we did that. The fencesitters would jump down on India's side and our friends might take their place on that fence. To retain support, we must focus our efforts on Cocos itself."

McCarthy killed the speculation. "I doubt if it would have any more than nuisance effect but it would escalate the conflict. And we would risk our whole submarine force. The Indians are pretty good at ASW, you know."

"Are you saying, then, General that we should let them stay there?" There was no doubting what answer the Prime Minister wanted to that question.

McCarthy passed the buck back. "No, sir. That is up to the government. There are military options. They are not easyand they would be expensive. I want you to understand that. But we will give it a go if that is your decision."

Discussion went on well into the night. To the extent that there was a consensus, it was for making the best of the situation and letting the islands go. But no minister wanted to put it into so many words. Only McDonald clearly favoured retaking Cocos for a range of political and other considerations. He took the floor to summarise his arguments.

"First, and at the most practical level, Cocos is valuable to us. We have the animal quarantine station there. I think most of us understand how important that is to the economically important pastoral sector, and the problems we would have if we had to put it elsewhere.

"Defence also use the airfield—and they need it. Not too many of us understand just how much extra reach it gives us for surveillance. Perhaps most of you don't care about that but I do.

"The fact remains, too, that the people of Cocos are Australians. There has never been any evidence of unrest that this Cocos Liberation Front might use as a justification. And when we offered them—and they accepted—the right of Australian citizenship, we implicitly undertook to defend them, not cut and run as soon as trouble loomed. Surely we aren't as gutless as that?"

The question was rhetorical but stirred a few present to angry mutters.

"Then", he continued, "we get down to the more philosophical questions. What happens next if we tamely give up Cocos? Does anybody here seriously think that running away from this issue means we'll have bought immunity for the future?

"And there's the responsibility we have to other countries to resist. We cannot afford to appear to endorse the principle that military aggression is ever legitimate."

He pounded the table—passionately. "Even if we lose, we must make the effort for our own sake and that of every other potential victim in the future."

He sat down, his hands trembling. Looking around the room, he saw that he had made little impact. It's not that they don't understand, he thought, as he listened to the arguments; they just don't want to face up to the decision.

The debate continued, increasingly focusing on the military options but in a detached sort of way. It was getting nowhere.

Chapman listened for the most part, feeling his own inadequacy. He had no clear idea of the best course. Like many of his predecessors, he knew he could have his way if he knew what he wanted. He could dominate the Cabinet through sheer force of personality if he wished. Without his intervention, though, there was no leader. McDonald came closest to it but his hard line was clearly not popular.

Not for the first time, Chapman cursed the system that gave him such an unwieldy Cabinet. Achieving consensus among eight or ten people was always easier than having to persuade fifteen. The larger number was not more democratic; a small group would still have to answer to the party, the Parliament and, ultimately, the electorate. Packing up a Cabinet with so many people really was a case of jobs for the boys.

Grayling was a case in point, he thought. The man's a bloody incompetent. To placate the party, I had to give him a job so I gave him Defence partly because he wanted it and no one else did, but also to keep him out of a politically sensitive job. So what happens; we have a war on our hands and he is the responsible minister.

Eventually, and after midnight, McDonald asked, "What exactly do they have on the ground there?"

McCarthy was vague. "We're not absolutely sure at this time. The satellite photos we have are helpful but we need more information. I would have to get an RF-111 over the islands and maybe even put some people in on the ground before we can be certain."

At that, Chapman saw his opportunity and decided to postpone the discussion. He closed the meeting, smoothly. "Shall we agree, gentlemen, that we defer any decision until General McCarthy can give us more detail. I will tell the media we are pursuing a military option but operational secrecy will not allow any disclosure at this time. That should shut them up for a while."

There was no dissent and the meeting broke up.

RAAF Base, Learmonth, two weeks later

Learmonth was no longer a sleepy bush airfield. The RAAF base on the western side of the runway was alive with men and vehicles. Long rows of tents were set back from the taxiways and parking aprons. At the northern end, F/A-18 Hornets and F-111s stood in sandbagged revetments while at the southern end, a single Orion was running through pre-takeoff checks prior to departure to relieve another P-3 on anti-submarine patrol to the north-west.

The weather was hot and sunny, the sky a startling blue when contrasted with the red-brown earth and pale green-grey saltbush scrub. The pilot and navigator of the RF-111 got out of the small, olive-drab van and waved to the driver as he accelerated away. They walked over to the aircraft which seemed to crouch on its landing gear, its multi-coloured camouflage a stark contrast against the white concrete apron.

The two men were dressed alike in green flight suits with gaudy unit badges. Each carried a white flight helmet. The navigator climbed the ladder and settled himself in his right-hand seat to programme the inertial navigation system. Meanwhile, the pilot walked around the aircraft for a last minute visual check.Finally satisfied, the pilot boarded and began working through his pre-takeoff checklist.

With the wing-like canopies shut and locked, the aircraft taxied out to the runway. Apart from a single 330 gallon drop-tank under each wing, it was clean. Its real weapons were the six cameras in the bomb bay space. Today, they would be searching for details of the Indian force on Cocos.

Two days before, another RF-111 had set out for a high level photo reconnaissance. Briefed to fly at 28,000 feet and 450 knots, its radar had been programmed to 'squawk' as a civilian airliner. Five hours after takeoff and at least an hour after it should have returned, it had been sadly marked down as missing. No radio transmissions had been heard. The Alice Springs Jindalee installation had reported tracking the aircraft as far as Cocos but had then lost it. Other aircraft had been operating in the vicinity. Presumably Indian fighters had intercepted and shot it down. This time, Jindalee had been used to study the Indian combat air patrol and the sortie had been planned to arrive over Cocos with the CAP approaching the end of its endurance.

The slim shape, misnamed the Pig, thundered down the runway, lifting off smoothly. As the landing gear came up, the pilot turned on to his course of 302 degrees and climbed slowly to his transit height of 26,000 feet.

They were briefed for a low level photo run this time. At 120 miles from Cocos, they would let down to low level, about 500 feet. At an estimated 20 miles out, the navigator would flick on the APR-113 radar for a quick check of his inertial navigation system. He hoped there would not be too much drift. There were no reference points to fly to over water and they had to hit Cocos on the button. At low level, looking for a low lying island group hardly more than six miles across left little room for error.

The Indian CAP would be a pair of MiG-29s. Their look-down radar could pick up the Pig a long way out. Coming in at low level, the fighters would most likely report them in for the ground defence to deal with. If they got through that, the MiGs would try an intercept as they departed for home. And they had to get home; photos, unlike bombs, were of no use unless they were delivered back to base. With luck, the MiGs would not have the fuel to chase them too far. They would rely on a burst of speed on afterburner to outrun them.

From 500 feet, the water had lost the hard, smooth, blue colour seen from high level. At this level, it was a deep ultramarine. The waves which were easily seen had white caps which provided a stark contrast as they flashed past under the long nose.

At 95 minutes after leaving Learmonth, the navigator triggered the radar. Peering into the shroud of the radar scope, he saw the outline of islands away to starboard and adjusted the inertial system. The aircraft swung gently to the right reaching out for a fly-to point some two miles north of the outlying Horsburgh Island.

Both men heard the beep of the radar warning receiver in their headsets. If there was a CAP above, they had no way of knowing. It could have been a MiG or the CRU radar believed to be on Cocos.

As they approached the fly-to point, the navigator picked up the low-lying islands. Horsburgh was the last in the chain, separated from the main group by a two-mile wide channel. As the island came abeam, he called to the pilot.

"I have the IP visual. Come left to 220 degrees."

"Roger, have the IP. Coming left."

The island flashed by to port. Again, the navigator looking out spotted his target, the cluster of fuel tanks at the northern tip of West Island. Height was reduced to 250 feet.

"Target visual, come left five degrees."

"Roger, target visual."

"Cameras on." The navigator checked his film counters on the panel below the radar. The numbers were winding back smoothly. "Pulling film."

"Course from target is 172." The pilot knew that from his briefing but the navigator would remind him and check.

The tip of the island disappeared under the nose and the aircraft headed down a midline along the northern part of the long strip of coconut groves and secondary jungle.

More beeps sounded from the threat receiver. They ignored them; that was only the search radars reaching out for a fix.

The navigator checked his clock and theisland landmarks disappearing under the nose. After 15 seconds he spoke again.

"Come left 22 degrees; course 150."

The aircraft eased around to port to fly the length of the airfield runway. Here they were in the open. More beeps from the warning receiver. The navigator toggled a switch. Chaff bomblets spewed from the tubes aft and bloomed into clouds of tiny foil strips to jam the fire control radars. Small flares dropped away to confuse the hand-held SA-7 heat-seeking missiles.

Tracer appeared under the nose from behind but missed below the aircraft. That was the ZSU-23-4 blazing away by eye as its radar tried vainly to penetrate the chaff. It took 16 seconds for the shoreline to disappear under the wing as he looked back out of the aircraft.

"Cameras off. Let's get to buggery out of here."

The pilot cut in his afterburner and swept his wings back to 45 degrees. The aircraft leapt ahead, the speed rapidly rising. He kept low for another hundred miles, climbing and reducing speed only when he judged he was out of range of the MiGs. They did not follow.

Cocos Islands, Indian Ocean

The C-130 Hercules transport from 36 Sqn droned on through the night. On a course to pass within a few miles of Cocos, its transponder would identify it to the Indian radar on the islands as an American military aircraft. The pilot hoped it would look like a USAF aircraft en route from Central Australia to the American base at Diego Garcia. His briefing officer had told him the Indians would be unlikely to fire on an American aircraft. He hadn't said what the Americans would say if they found out. That was not his problem anyway.

Flying at 15,000 feet, the flight crew looked down on scattered cloud, silver in the light of the quarter moon that was rising behind them. The cloud base was supposed to be at around 5000 feet, giving the paratroopers in the back plenty of time to orient themselves to the drop zone.

In the cargo compartment, the loadmaster chatted to the paratroopers. There were six of them, all from the Special Air Service Regiment. An ugly lot, the loadmaster decided. Not that they were the hulking type. They were pretty unremarkable physically but there was an air of ruthless efficiency about them. Their conversation was relaxed, polite but reserved. They were giving nothing away. None showed any sign of tension, no nervous checking of weapons and equipment, no chatter about what lay ahead. These blokes knew what they were going to do and were mentally as well as physically ready. I won't have to kick any of these jokers out the door, he thought.

All were dressed in dark green coveralls over their uniforms. They were travelling light with only small combat equipment packs and the standard Steyr AUG-1 rifles although with their T-10 parachutes, weapons and equipment packs, each man would be carrying something over 50 kg. None of the team was wearing badges of rank although their commander was a captain.

Captain Peter Jeffreys walked forward to the flight deck. The pilot looked up as Jeffreys leaned over between him and the co-pilot.

"Come to look at the scenery?", he asked.

"Nah. The boys are getting tired of the noise. Want to know when you're going to let us out." The noise levels in the C-130 were a standing joke among soldiers.

"About fifteen minutes", the pilot replied. "We'll have Cocos on radar shortly and we'll open up the tail gate with five minutes to go. You should have plenty of light to pick up your landing zone but the wind factor will make it a bit hairy."

Jeffreys knew that. The prevailing wind was from the south-east so they would have to drop along that axis. That meant landing on West Island where all the Indians were, or the eastern chain from Pulu Atas to Home Island where, according to the photos, the Indians weren't.

He hoped the pilot was right about the light. A HALO jump from high altitude and skydiving down to about 500 feet before opening the 'chute was enjoyable in daylight, much less so at night and downright difficult when trying to hit a narrow strip of beach bordered by surf on one side and coconut trees on the other. The moon looked bright enough, he thought, and there was not too much cloud about.

Their job was to infiltrate the Indian positions and collect intelligence on their strength, dispositions and operating procedures before being picked up off the northern tip of Pulu Atas by submarine in a week's time. They would hole up for a day before making their way across the reef at the night low tide to West Island.

The pilot interrupted Jeffrey's cogitations. "Better get organised. I'll be opening up in a couple of minutes."

Back in the cargo compartment, the other five troopers were collecting their gear and moving to the rear door. Jeffreys joined them as the loadmaster checked that their equipment pack suspension lines were attached to harnesses, helmet straps were secure and rifles correctly slung.

There was a rumble of hydraulics as the huge tailgate swung down to provide an extension to the floor. The six men moved to the edge and watched the loadmaster who held one hand over his headset, frowning in concentration as he waited for the signal.

"Stand-by!" Then—"Go!"

One soldier gave the two-fingered salute with a sardonic grin but the rest simply stepped out together, ignoring their former host.

The night air was cool as the six men flew themselves towards the sea. The rush of wind soon drowned out the drone of the Hercules as it flew on into the night. The aircraft would continue on past Cocos until it was out of radar range, then make a long sweep to the north and east so as to land at Christmas Island for fuel.

Below, all was silent. In the distance, Jeffreys could see lights on Home Island and away to the west along the long strip which was the airfield on West Island. The moon glittered on the sea, showing up the land as deep shadow. He quickly made out the long dark line of Pulu Atas stretching away to the north west. Recalling his map, he looked at the eastern shore for the big sand dunes at each end. He soon picked them up, glowing white in the moonlight and offering a perfect reference point.

For a moment, he allowed himself to luxuriate in the extraordinarysensation of actually flying himself towards his destination before checking the luminous dial of his wrist altimeter.

At 500 feet, he tore at the ripcord handle. He heard the parachute deploy and then it wrenched at his harness as it caught the air and slowed his fall. Looking down, he picked a point on the beach just short of the big nine metre dune and began to steer himself towards it. To his right, the line of surf showed up white while the moon carved a silver path across the sea towards him.

And then he was on the ground, his boots crunching into the soft sand. He was brought up short by his suspension line which anchored him to his equipment pack now embedded in the beach. The wind pulled at his 'chute which he quickly collapsed as it threatened to drag him along the beach.

Slipping out of his harness, he looked around to check as his men floated down out of the sky within a few metres. They exchanged quick waves before bundling up their 'chutes and moving up the beach into the shelter of the trees. Loaded magazines were snapped into place in their rifles which were then cocked ready for immediate action.

Still silently, the six men slipped out of their overalls which they buried in the soft sandy soil together with their helmets and parachutes. Dry sand was scattered over the holes which were then covered with some of the many dried palm fronds that lay around.

The men were dark shadows in the gloom. Jeffreys recalled the argument with a staff officer who wanted to know why they wanted jungle green uniforms instead of the standard disruptive pattern camouflage outfits. The 'cams' would be useless in this terrain, Jeffreys thought, with their pale greens and browns so typical of the Australian outback. In daylight in this terrain, they would stand out like the proverbial country dunny. With the greens and dark face paint, he and his men could melt into the background.

Using only hand signals, Jeffreys motioned his men to spread out among the trees and they trudged south past the end of the vehicle track which ran down most of the length of the island, looking for a safe harbour for the coming day.

Parliament House, Canberra

The press conference was being held in one of the Parliament House committee rooms; there was not enough space in Grayling's office for the horde of journalists who were now crowding around the committee table. Television lights overpowered the normally bright fluorescent lighting as technicians struggledwith cables, cameras and sound gear.

At the head of the table Grayling faced a forest of microphones and tape recorders. He was flanked by McCarthy in full uniform and, on the other side, by his departmental head, Gary Irwin. Grayling had called the conference without telling the Prime Minister who was back in his home state on this day. Neither McCarthy nor Irwin were very happy about the decision and had advised against it. Neither wanted to be there but their minister had insisted - on both counts. The media have a right to know what we are doing about Cocos, he had argued.

The conference opened quietly enough. Grayling read a prepared statement which his staff distributed to the journalists. Not that it said much. Like most government statements, its significance lay in what it did not say. Grayling admitted the Indian invasion of Cocos, condemned it as an act of flagrant aggression and revealed that the government had ordered reconnaissance flights over the islands. These, he concluded, had given the government a good idea of the Indian strength on Cocos. Then the questioning started.

"Minister", it was Baker who got in first, "what is the Indian strength?"

Immediately, Grayling began to hedge. "We know they have fighter aircraft there and anti-aircraft defences. There are also a number of tanks and other armoured vehicles."

Baker pressed. "How many aircraft? What sort of missiles and how many troops?" Irwin whispered in his minister's ear. Grayling nodded as he replied. "I don't think it would be desirable on security grounds to give that sort of detail, Reg."

"Why not? Presumably the Indians themselves know."

Grayling was rescued by another questioner - but only temporarily.

"Minister, Michael Rogan, Reuters. Is the Australian government going to mount an operation to recover the islands?"

McCarthy muttered, sotto voce. "Told you so!"

Grayling, however, was unfazed. "We have the planners looking at that right now."

"But surely, Minister, it's for the government to decide its policy rather than have the planners decide for it? If the planners come up with a satisfactory plan, will the government put it into effect?"

"The government will look at all the options when those options are available for consideration." Grayling was smug.

"In other words, the government does not have a policy of kicking the Indians off Cocos." It was a conclusion, not a question.

"General McCarthy, Mary Petrelli, ABC. I have heard that we have already lost an F-111 shot down over Cocos. Would you confirm that?"

McCarthy did not dissemble. "Yes. An RF-111 sent on a photo mission did fail to return. The crew of two is presumed lost. A later sortie was successful and provided good intelligence."

Attention turned to McCarthy who appeared to be more forthcoming than his minister.

"Can you then tell us how many troops the Indians have on the islands?" No, I'm sorry I can't. We have some ideas but we cannot confirm them. As you are aware"—he knew they weren't but it didn't matter—"Cocos is covered by heavy vegetation which provides good camouflage. The photos therefore did not give us a good idea of troop strengths although we are confident of our figures on air defences and armour. We are getting information from other sources which should give us a better idea."

"What sources are those?"

"I'm sorry but I cannot discuss those without disclosing intelligence methods and capabilities. I'm sure you will understand."

"Can you recover Cocos, General?" It was Baker again.

"The Defence Force will do what it is told to do by the government."

"General, let me put it more plainly. Have you advised the government whether you can recover Cocos or not?"

"Sorry, Reg." McCarthy smiled. "The advice I give the government is privileged."

"OK. In that case, Minister, has the CDF advised the government that it can—or cannot—recover Cocos if it gets the go-ahead?"

Grayling tried to dodge. "Well, of course, the government has every confidence in the ability of the Defence Force to carry out its role. As you know, this government has significantly increased the resources devoted to defence compared with our predecessors."

AAP's Richard Norton interrupted. "Are we then to assume that the Defence Force can do the job but the government will not let it do so until it has a plan? Why does the government believe it is more competent than its professional advisers to decide whether the plan is suitable?"

Grayling reddened, then decided to bluster. "In case you hadn't noticed, this is still a democracy. The government will decide whether the cost in money and casualties is too high a price to pay. We will judge what the value of Cocos is and what we as a nation are prepared to pay to get it back. That is our duty as the elected government."

"In other words", Baker sneered, "you can't make up your minds. Thank you, Minister."

The conference quickly broke up. McCarthy and Irwin departed in silence.

Canberra - the Prime Minister's office

Chapman was back in Canberra and in his office, alerted by his staff about Grayling's disastrous conference. It had been the lead item on the early TV news and would lead every other news broadcast. He had spoken to Scott who had not been much help. Now he was waiting to see Grayling whom he had summoned.

As the Defence Minister entered, his direct line buzzed. It was Barney Gills, the government Whip.

"Arthur, I'll keep this short because I assume you've got that drongo in there with you." Chapman grunted, whether in confirmation or agreement Gills was not sure. "The troops aren't happy. I've been getting non-stop 'phone calls ever since the six o'clock news started. They're even passing messages through my staff that just aren't fit for their tender ears. Either shut him up or make up your minds what to do, or we'll have trouble with the backbench."

Chapman hung up and looked in silence at his Defence Minister. As if I don't have enough problems without you, you dumb bastard.

CHAPTER 9

Cocos Islands

Jeffreys crouched in the undergrowth looking across the airstrip. From his vantage point, he could see the whole expanse of the parking apron and the administrative buildings beyond. Deep in the shadow of the coconut groves, he used his binoculars to watch the scene, confident that with the sun behind him there would be no revealing flash. He was relaxed but alert, determined not to miss any significant activity but maintaining a reserve of nervous energy.

Behind him, his partner guarded his rear while two other pairs of SAS troopers examined the northern half of the island. After nightfall, they would filter back to him so that they could compare notes. At 0200 next morning, they would squirt a brief coded report by line of sight transmission to a communications satellite high in the night sky in geostationary orbit over the Australian mainland.

From where he crouched, Jeffreys could see two MiG-29s in sandbagged revetments at the northern end of the apron. Two hours earlier, another pair of MiGs had thundered down the runway, climbing steeply to port before disappearing into the heavens. Occasionally, he heard their faint rumble but could not pick them up through the tree cover and scattered cloud. Presumably that was their Combat Air Patrol. Yesterday, they had flown three hour patrols with two hours between. Today, he would check for a repeat of the pattern.

An Il-38 had flown in early in the morning and was now parked at the southern end of the apron. It had been fuelled immediately from a hydrant and now he could see men working on it. The air shimmered off the bare concrete of the apron but here, under the trees, it was cool, the edge taken off the heat by the shade and the prevailing south-easterly breeze.

A single ZSU-23-4 was parked on the grass at each end of the apron with its crew sitting beside or on top of the tracked vehicle. Occasionally, a Landrover drove along the length of the runway. Each vehicle had a driver with a gunner manning what looked like a .50 calibre machine gun.

Small parties of troops moved around. They looked like soldiers the world over, carrying out the minor chores of any camp. He kept count of the groups and numbers, trying to isolate each one by identifying the NCO in charge. But it was all guesswork.

Clearly, the old Flight Services building was the Indian headquarters. Not only was an Indian flag flying from the pole outside but he caught glimpses of at least one red-tabbed officer coming and going. Later that night, the six men compared notes. They could not get an accurate figure on the Indian manpower, reckoning it at more than 500 but less than 600. They had an accurate count on vehicles and had placed the CRU radar and the SA-8 vehicle. The latter, like the ZSUs, appeared to be in a generally static location.

Jeffreys' sergeant had formed a good opinion of the troops. "They're pretty relaxed, boss, but they seem to be on the ball. Plenty of patrols around, mostly in vehicles, and they've got their eyes open. They're not bored yet."

Of course, the F-111 flights would have woken them up, Jeffreys thought.

After calling in their report, he decided to pull back to Pulu Atas. They had collected as much intelligence as was available without revealing themselves. That island was not patrolled as intensely as West Island and they would be able to observe the harbour from there.

The six men silently made their way through the trees towards the narrow neck of land at the end of the airstrip. Here the trees had been cut back to clear the approaches to the airfield. The area was a mass of jumbled coral, broken only by the road which ran down the length of the island. Dead palm fronds scattered thickly on the ground made deep shadows on the white coral.

Suddenly, the trooper scouting ahead froze. Silently, the six men sank to the earth. Above the tumble of the surf away to their right, they heard voices. Jeffreys moved his head fractionally to make a skyline for himself. Then he saw it, a few metres away. The cut-down Landrover was stationary, the driver standing with his back to them at the side of the road, urinating. The gunner was squatting in the back of the vehicle, one hand resting on his machine gun as the two men chatted easily.

The SAS men were no more than shadows in the bright moonlight. Jeffreys looked around. His sergeant, close by, swept his finger across his throat. Jeffreys shook his head. Their orders were not to fight unless a fight was forced on them.

As they watched, the driver finished and walked back to the truck. The two men laughed at some private joke as the driver climbed in and started the engine. Suddenly the gunner called out something, sharply. The engine died and there was a clatter as he cocked his gun, swinging it towards the place where the SAS men lay. The driver slid out of his seat, reaching for his rifle as he took cover behind the vehicle.

Jeffreys lay still. Despite the sudden surge of adrenalin making his heart pound, training took over. As long as they lay still, they would not be seen unless the Indians actually fell over them. He slid the safety catch off his rifle, already cocked and pushed forward in front of him. He moved his head minutely to bring his eye to the telescopic sight.

The gunner spoke again, the voice peremptory, challenging but the language foreign. There was no answer. The gun appeared to be pointing away to Jeffreys' right, at one of his men.

The gunfire shattered the night, tracers flaring briefly. The heavy machine gun hammered bullets into the sand as it traversed across the ground. A few ricocheted off coral blocks, whining away into the night. Sand and coral chips flew into the air. Then Jeffreys heard the thud as at least one bullet, maybe more, tore into flesh and bone. He aimed his own weapon, the sight centred on the gunner's chest black against the moonlit sky, and fired—a three round burst.

The man was hammered backwards, dead before his body collapsed half in, half out of the vehicle. His finger contracted on the trigger, sending a long burst of gunfire into the night sky before he fell away.

His mate lay prone, firing underneath the truck. But his field of fire there was too limited and he had no target. One of the commandos slithered away to a flank and shot the man as he peered into the night.

"Wally's dead, boss." The sergeant had checked the men. One would never get up. Hit by two heavy bullets in the head and neck, he lay in a blood-soaked patch of sand, his rifle still pushed forward, finger on the trigger, facing the enemy who had killed him and who had been killed.

"Let's get moving. Leave the bodies. This place will be swarming with Indians in no time." Jeffreys knew the odds were against them now. The submarine was not due for another two nights and, by daylight, the islands would be swarming with men looking for them.

The scout moved off and the rest fell in behind, making quick time now to put as much distance as possible between themselves and the garrison. Passing across the open ground, their shadows melted into the black mass of the treeline.

The White House - Washington

The regular weekly meeting of the National Security Council was ready to break up. The main item on the agenda had been the growing tension in the Middle East with Syria and Iraq at each others throats again. Sporadic clashes had already broken out on the border while their various allies in what was left of Lebanon were indulging in even more intense artillery duels than usual. The Israeli Cabinet was meeting and the CIA reported the possibility of Israeli air strikes on air bases in both countries.

But the Middle East was not the only problem. The break up of the Soviet empire was continuing with large scale riots, this time in Kiev, capital of the Ukraine. Moscow's reaction was confused. Unrest seemed to be boiling up all round the empire's borders and the Chinese were threatening to take advantage of the troubles to recover territory lost more than a century ago.

President Forrest could see no immediate danger for the United States. But there was no doubt that the Soviet Union's neighbours were feeling nervous and looking for outside help. The whole shooting match would come to a head within a couple of years at the most, the NSC thought. It was time to do some work on contingency plans.

As the meeting approached its end, Forrest asked if there was anything else on the agenda. Secretary of State Soulsby raised his head from the pile of papers in front of him. "The Australians want to know what help we can give with their problem with India." He quickly outlined the events leading up to and including the invasion of Cocos.

"So, what are they going to do about it, Fred - or do they want us to do it for them?", Forrest asked.

"I don't think they know yet. I guess they want us to lean on the Indians to get out but, if that fails, they'll decide what to do when they know what we'll do. To be fair, they are facing up to a much bigger country and military capability."

"What do you say, Bill?" Admiral Bill Rauchberger was Chairman of the Joint Chiefs of Staff, a former naval aviator of long service and extensive combat experience.

"Well, Mr President, the Aussies have always been there when we wanted them. I guess we owe them. On the other hand, taking on the Indians at that distance would be no small undertaking if it got out of hand."

Dr Peter Danowski, the National Security Adviser, objected. "This is not our fight, Mr President. Our treaty with Australia commits us to nothing, especially in the Indian Ocean. The Indians have presented the issue as an anti-colonial thing and it's a real landmine for us.

"We're gonna have big trouble with the Indians in that part of the world before too much longer. In my opinion, we can't afford to be seen initiating any quarrel with them. If we have a fight with them, it should be on our terms. They're so damned touchy and aggressive, it's likely to happen sooner than we think. We can't afford to be dragged into it by an ally, no matter how loyal."

"What's the feeling over at State, Fred?" Forrest wanted to know. "My people think the Australians don't know what they want to do. They maybe want a push from us, one way or the other. If we try to push them into taking the islands back, they'll expect some help, maybe naval.

"On the other hand, if we back off, my guess is they'll decide to let the Indians stay.

"Also, I've had the Indian ambassador on my neck pressing us to stay out. He keeps reminding me how our move into the Bay of Bengal way back in '71 soured relations. It's a load of crap but they like to have a stick to beat on us."

"Does it matter to us if the Indians do hold Cocos?" John Sutherland, the CIA director wanted to know.

Rauchberger looked at the wall map before answering. "It's not a good deal for us, the Indians having that airfield. It gives them a good position on the SLOCs through the Indonesian archipelago. And it puts them between our base at Diego Garcia and the Australian mainland. The Indonesians won't want the Indians there, I guess but I can't see them doing anything about it."

There were mutters of agreement before he went on. "If we wash our hands of this, we'll have alienated the Australians, Indonesia, probably Singapore and Malaysia and, of course, South Africa's gone. Our hold on Diego Garcia would be pretty tenuous then."

"So, are you saying," Forrest demanded," the Australians are the guys in the white hats? We want them back on Cocos but we can't afford to help them? That won't make us look real good if we just dump an ally."

Danowski answered for them. "That's about it, Mr President. It's almost a no-win situation for us. It's also true, though, that Diego Garcia is not as important now as it once was given the turmoil in Russia. And the fact remains that, politically, you can't afford a fight with India at this time. Congress would go ape, especially now in election year. On the other hand, if we privately pat the Australians on the head and tell them to go to it, the ball's back in their court.

"Of course, we don't have to pull the rug from under them. We keep giving them all the intelligence and logistics they need, without any fanfare and within reason, but no forces and no joint operations.

"I suggest Fred tell their ambassador that formally but perhaps you could call Prime Minister Chapman and lay it out in detail."

Forrest looked around the table. There was no dissent. "OK, gentlemen. We'll leave it at that. Just let Pete know if we get requests for anything not previously approved and hold it for my decision. Meeting's adjourned."

Defence Operations Centre, Canberra

Peter Forbes looked up from his desk as the duty intelligence officer came in with a pink signal slip.

"Just got this in from Pearl Harbour, sir. It's pretty old. They apologise. The original report came from a sub on patrol and was not picked up until she came in. Then it seems to have disappeared in their system before someone realised it could be important to us."

Forbes read the message. It was brief.

DTG 172043Z MAY
PRIORITY
CONFIDENTIAL
FROM: CINCPACFLTOPS
TO: DEFENCE CANBERRA
SUBSURFACE UNIT IN TRANSIT DETECTED UNIDENTIFIED SSN VICINITY 16 DEG SOUTH 113 DEG EAST 20DEC95 STOP SIGNATURE CONSISTENT WITH SOVIET CHARLIE CLASS BUT ASSESSED AS NON-SOVIET STOP CLASSIFIED POSSUB HIGH ONE SPECULATE INDIAN STOP CONTACT NOT PROSECUTED FOR OPERATIONAL REASONS STOP REGRET INFORMATION NOT PASSED EARLIER

"So, what's the point, Spy?" Forbes was puzzled.

"Well, sir, it was just three days later in the same area that the BHP bulk carrier *Gove Argosy* went missing. That was before you joined. The inquiry called it an accident but there was conflicting evidence which raised the possibility of a torpedo attack. That was considered pretty way out then but it could be they were right. We looked at it again after the Dampier affair but there was still no evidence.

"Now we have some evidence that the Indians could have been responsible for one sinking. We should speculate that the mining was an Indian operation as well given the escalation of hostility with the invasion of Cocos. I suggest, sir, we should be looking at a possible campaign against shipping in the north-west."

"OK. I'll buy that. Thanks. Ask the duty ops officer to see me, will you."

In discussion, Forbes and his staff decided to implement a limited naval control of shipping to and from the north-west ports at least as far as Lombok or Wetar Straits. Maritime Commander would be told to hasten the refits on his surface ships and hold them ready for a northern deployment. The Personnel branch would have to mobilise some naval reservists to run the control of shipping operation. Circumstances were beginning to force a stepped-up response to the Indian aggression.

After an intense half-hour, Forbes stood up. "All right. Start drafting the orders. I'll go upstairs and tell the boss what we're doing. He'll have to square it with the politicians."

Jindalee Control Centre, near Alice Springs

The sergeant radar plotter looked at the screen again and checked his calculations. The contact was clearly an aircraft. The bearing was changing through a range from 325o to 341o but the range was remaining constant at about 800 miles. The Jindalee system was not more precise than that but it was right within about three per cent either way.

He had been watching the contact for a couple of hours. Its speed worked out at about 500 knots and it was flying courses of about 60o and its reciprocal after having come in from the north. At that speed and with its flight path, it had to be a military aircraft. He had reported it as a bogey and had been told by the duty officer to keep tracking.

He picked up the 'phone to report his latest calculations.

RAAF Base, Tindal

The briefing room was practically empty. Flight Lieutenant "Wokka" Norris scribbled notes as the 3 Sqn Operations Officer made his points. His wingman worked on his part of the plan.

"We don't know who this joker is", the briefer pointed out. "Your job is to find him. We'll give you the best vector we can from Jindalee but he's out of range of 2CRU at Darwin and staying that way. The navy's either tucked up in harbour or operating out to the west so they won't be able to give you an intercept either.

"Keep your weapons load to two Sidewinders and your gun. Carry two extra tanks. You shouldn't need them unless you have trouble finding him. He's operating at about 300 miles from Tindal. Go up to 40,000 feet and use your own radar to hunt him.

"When you find him, we want an identification first and then report back to 2CRU for further instructions. You are on NOCOM until you actually make contact, then you can talk as much as necessary. Your call-sign is Dragon."

Thirty minutes later, Norris climbed the ladder into his cockpit and strapped in. The ground crew stood by with fire extinguishers as the engines were started. He locked his canopy shut, armed the ejection seat and taxied out to the runway. Flaps were lowered for take-off as he worked through his checklist.

The two aircraft waited together, Norris' wingman just behind him to starboard. Left hand wrapped around the dual throttle and right hand lightly grasping the stick, he waited for clearance from the tower, the engines idling easily.

As his headset crackled with the clearance, he lifted the throttle stops and pushed smoothly forward. The engine note rose to a roar, reverberating off the buildings that surrounded the airfield. Then the aircraft moved forward slowly at first, then gathering speed fast, the acceleration punching him back hard against the backrest. Nose wheel steering was flicked off as the twin rudders began to bite into the air.

The speed built up rapidly. VR and he eased the stick back. The aircraft lifted off smoothly, the ground disappearing from his forward view as the nose lifted to the sky.

Gear up, then flaps and the speed and angle of climb increased. He banked the aircraft around to his course of 295ø, stealing a glance over his right shoulder to check that his wingman had tucked himself in behind and to starboard. The two aircraft continued to climb, pushing up to cruise altitude. Speed was stabilised at 450 knots.

His headset crackled again. It was the controller from 2CRU. "Dragon One, vector 310." He was being given an interception course based on the best position Jindalee could give.

Half an hour passed. He had no new course to steer so assumed he was still close to intercept. He checked his watch and flicked on his APG-65 radar for a wide-angle search.

No contact. He altered course slightly and flicked the radar into vertical search mode. The invisible beams reached out in a narrow wedge hunting above and below the aircraft.

Ten minutes passed. No sign of the bogey despite frequent course alterations and radar mode changes.

Something there, on the screen. Focus the beam. Got him. He read off the details. "Contact bearing 219, range 22 miles."

The radar gave him an interception course as he eased the throttles forward, tipping into a shallow dive and accelerating to close the target several thousand feet below him.

He peered ahead through the Head Up Display. Two minutes. "Tallyho. Bogey 12 o'clock. Estimate angels three zero."

Converging on the target from behind, he recognised the type as he drew closer. It was a Soviet-built Bear. Diving and pulling up under the huge aircraft, he checked the details. Big ventral radome and chin radar. That made it a Bear-D. Red stars under the wings and —he looked up, yes—on the vertical fin. Aircraft numbers behind the glasshouse cockpit and at the top of the fin— 07. It would be Soviet air force or naval air arm.

He called in the details to 2CRU and asked for instructions, dropping astern of the big bomber. He looked it over as he waited. All over silver with black exhaust streaks behind the four Kuznetsov turboprops. She was big. Wingspan was at least four times his and it was almost three times as long. Two propellers on each engine rotating in opposite directions. Guns too. He could see the rear gunner crouched in his turret with its twin 23mm guns. Top and ventral turrets had been removed, he noted. The gunner was training his turret, following him. He slipped away to port coming up alongside the cockpit. His wingman stayed astern. He could see faces turned towards him from the Soviet plane, otherwise they ignored him.

As he followed, the big aircraft swung away in a wide turn to starboard, towards the distant coast and away from him, eventually settling down on a reciprocal course.

Must be doing an ELINT run, Norris thought. Just stooging up and down in international airspace, listening to our radars and recording frequencies, pulse widths and the like. Listening to our tactical communications for later analysis as well. Not much to be done about it, he thought. He's not breaking any laws.

"Dragon One, this is Echo Niner. See if you can persuade your friend to go home. No rough stuff, though. Standard rules of engagement. Over."

"Echo Niner, roger. Stand by. Dragon Two, cover me."

Norris moved up again alongside the Bear's cockpit and flashed his wings to gain attention. He saw the faces turn towards him and lifted his hand, pointing to the north. He banked gently to starboard, commencing a long turn across the Bear's nose, trying to push him around to the north.

The Bear ignored him, ploughing straight ahead. Norris pulled up to avoid a collision. He saw the angry gestures from the Russians. He throttled back and let his aircraft fall behind the Bear. The tail gunner shifted target to him, the gun muzzles following until he slipped out of the arc of fire.

He repeated the manoeuvre. Again, the Russian ignored him.

"Echo Niner, this is Dragon One. Ivan doesn't want to play. Over." A pause. The controller was checking with Operations.

"Dragon One, roger. Abort the mission. Course is 148."

Norris flicked his aircraft around to port, waving to the Russians as he departed. His wingman tucked himself in and followed.

HMAS *Yarra*, Indian Ocean

Further to the west, HMAS *Yarra* was conducting surveillance operations in slight seas. Alternately sprinting and drifting, she ran at 24 knots then slowed to six to listen on the towed array sonar streamed astern. The ship was on a southerly course running into the low swell that rolled in from the broad expanses of the Indian Ocean. As the swell passed under the ship, the bow heaved upwards and then dipped with a slow roll first to port and then starboard. Some 150 miles to the north-west was a group of three bulk ore carriers en route to load cargoes at Port Hedland. Two months after the sinking of the *Weipa Argosy*, Dampier was still closed to large ships. The ship's company was in Defence watches with the operations room and weapons systems operating with minimum crews.

Yarra was covering the merchant ships on their track from Lombok Strait to Port Hedland but was observing full EMCON procedures with radar and active sonar shut down. Trailing astern was the passive towed array sonar listening for underwater sound.

Bellano was in his quarters working on an accumulation of paper work when the 'phone buzzed.

"Captain!"

"Ops, sir. EW is reporting BIG BULGE transmissions bearing zero-two-four degrees from us and distant, almost certainly from a Bear. Given the likely detection range, that should put the merchant group within the Bear's radar coverage."

Thirty seconds later, Bellano was looking at the plot in the Ops Room with his Principal Warfare Officer. The PWO sketched out the tactical picture.

"Sir, on this course, we are heading away from the merchant group which, on dead reckoning, bears 050○ at 155 miles. Their course is 165○ at about 13 knots. The aircraft now bears 026○ and is less than 150 miles and probably more than 60 miles away. I would estimate that the Bear has the merchant group on radar and his current course is easterly rather than westerly so he is closing the group.

"I recommend we alter course and increase speed to close the merchant group. This should open the bearing and give us a somewhat better idea of the aircraft's intentions. I suggest we recover the tail and go to an interception course of 073○ at 25 knots."

Bellano cogitated briefly. "Yes, I agree. Let's flash up our air search radar for 30 seconds only, just to let the Bear know we're around." He picked up the bridge 'phone as the PWO gave the order to switch on the radar.

"Sir!" It was the radar plotter. "I have no target on the scope so he has to be more than 100 miles away."

As the two men studied the plot, the EW operator reported constant bearing changes on the continuing BIG BULGE transmissions. The pattern suggested that the aircraft was flying an elliptical course out of visual range of the merchant group and some 120 miles north of *Yarra*'s track.

Maritime Headquarters, Sydney

It was early afternoon when *Yarra*'s signal arrived. The operations officer quickly scanned it.

DTG 260512Z MAY
IMMEDIATE
SECRET
FROM: YARRA
TO: MHQ SYDNEY
INFO: DEFENCE CANBERRA
        PERTH
BOGEY REPORT BIG BULGE TRANSMISSIONS BEARING 21 TO 26 DEG ESTIMATED 120 MLS MY POSITION 14 DEG 51 MIN SOUTH 115 DEG 14 MIN EAST MY COURSE 73 DEG SPEED 25

Intelligence quickly confirmed that the Alice Springs Jindalee radar had an unidentified air contact at the approximate position indicated by *Yarra*. Although Jindalee could not give a more precise position, it did confirm that the aircraft was orbiting within range of the merchant group. A check was being made with the Americans to locate the Soviet Bears based at Cam Ranh in Vietnam.

HMAS Yarra, Indian Ocean

Bellano, still in the Ops Room, skimmed the signal slip. It was brief.

DTG 260538Z MAY
IMMEDIATE
SECRET
FROM: MHQ SYDNEY

TO: YARRA
               PERTH
INFO: DEFENCE CANBERRA
YOUR 260512Z JINDALEE CONFIRMS YOUR BOGEY
CONTINUE TO CLOSE MERSHIP GROUP AND IDENTIFY
BOGEY PERTH TO JOIN YARRA WITH ALL DESPATCH

He wondered if the Bear was still around. EW had reported that its radar transmissions had shut down abruptly in the past ten minutes. The aircraft could still be there. A Soviet Bear operating from Cam Ranh at that range could stay on station for at least ten hours even allowing for diversions around Indonesian air space. Alternatively, an Indian Bear from Car Nicobar could remain in contact for some seven hours. That the transmissions had simply quit rather than faded out suggested it was still in the area. Jindalee confirmed that although its information could be too old by this time.

Time passed as the ship hurried eastwards. Just over two hours from the change of course, *Yarra*'s radar picked up the merchant ships, showing as a single trace at the edge of the plot. Slowly, they crept closer to the centre.

Suddenly, the radar plotter's head jerked up. "Contact, sir, aircraft bearing 012, range 91 miles. Tracking."

Simultaneously, the symbol for a hostile aircraft appeared on the plotting screen.

"Interrogate", the PWO snapped. The ship's radar sent out an IFF signal in an effort to identify the strange aircraft.

"Aircraft squawks Soviet military, sir." The Bear's radar transponder was indicating its identity and peaceful mission. "Aircraft is closing—course 160, speed 300."

Maritime Headquarters, Sydney

The operations officer was puzzled. He read Yarra's signal again.

```
DTG 260805Z MAY
FLASH
SECRET
FROM:      YARRA
TO:        MHQ SYDNEY
           PERTH
INFO:      DEFENCE CANBERRA
BANDIT BEARING 012 DEG RANGE 90 MY POSITION 14
DEG 29 MIN SOUTH 115 DEG 48 MIN EAST COURSE 73
SPEED 25 BIG BULGE AND IFF INDICATE SOVIET RPT
SOVIET BEAR
```

According to intelligence, all Soviet Bears in the region were on the ground at Cam Ranh. The information was less than three hours old. He walked across to the Command Intelligence Officer.

"What do you make of this?", he asked, dropping the signal slip on the desk.

'Spy' looked thoughtful. "My guess is it's Indians with a spoof identification. The info on the Soviets is pretty solid and given our relations with the Indians at present, we'd be pretty safe in the assumption. Their Bears are the Tu-142F. They are primarily ASW aircraft but they have the BIG BULGE and could be doing a targeting run like a D version.

"The thing is", he went on, "*Yarra* with only her short range PDMS won't be able to do anything if the Bear keeps out of range but the aircraft will still be able to spot for a submarine if the Indians have one out there. I'd tell *Yarra* to start looking for a sub. We still can't locate all the Indian Navy submarines."

HMAS *Yarra*, Indian Ocean

DTG 260827Z MAY
IMMEDIATE
SECRET
FROM: MHQ SYDNEY
TO: *YARRA*
             PERTH
             11 SQN
             DEFENCE CANBERRA
YOUR260805Z BANDIT ASSESSED AS INDIAN BEAR-F
POSSIBLY ON TARGETING FLIGHT YOU SHOULD ASSUME
SUB IN VICINITY STOP FOR 11 SQN P-3 REQUIRED FOR
ASW TASK VICINITY OF MERCHANT GROUP *YARRA* AS
SCENE OF ACTION COMMANDER STOP FOR DEFENCE
REQUEST ROE BE SIGNALLED ASAP

Bellano read the signal and checked the plot. The merchant ships were now 36 miles away bearing 041° while the Bear continued to orbit at 33 miles bearing 344° from his ship. The BIG BULGE transmissions had commenced again and all three groups were closing.

He was closing the others at high speed but this prevented him from listening for submarines on his passive sonar. It would also reveal his presence to any submarine in the vicinity.

At the same time, high speed was an advantage if he faced a threat from the Bear. Fortunately, his gas turbines gave the ability to accelerate rapidly.

"PWO, let's go to action stations. Bring speed back to 10 knots and alter towards the Bear. We'll see what the bludger does. Tell the bridge to stand-by for some high speed manoeuvring in case he decides to throw something unpleasant at us. Also let's stream the tail and carry out a very careful passive sonar search."

Bellano was glad MHQ had asked for a Rules of Engagement update. Under the current rules, he could not use his weapons except in self-defence. Even an attack on the merchant ships might not give him sufficient excuse particularly since they were all foreign-flag vessels. It would be some time before he had any answer though. The query would go to the politicians who would not want to make a quick decision.

Perth was still more than 100 miles away and would not join before dark. By that time, the Bear would probably have left anyway. Having the P-3 around would be useful but it would be at least 24 hours before the merchants were tucked up safely in Hedland. By that time, there could be another group to convoy either to or from Lombok.

The Ops Room was crowded at Action Stations but there was a hush over the group, broken only by the quiet reports of the air search radar plotter updating the picture. The Bear was maintaining his distance at about 30 miles from the ship, edging away as *Yarra* approached.

An hour later, the BIG BULGE transmissions abruptly ceased. Radar reported that the Bear had altered course to the west and was opening the range. It looked like she was going home.

With no sonar contact, Bellano secured from action stations. With additional units, he disposed his small force. *Yarra* with her longer range passive sonar and less capable weapons would take station 50 miles to the west while the P-3 ranged still further to the west and south-west. *Perth* would stay within 10 miles of the merchant ships where her more powerful long-range weapons would provide better protection.

16°42' South, 110°55' East

Dawn was three hours off as Shepherd 52 arrived in her patrol area and took over from Shepherd 54. Vidulic reported in to *Yarra* now 160 miles almost due east.

"Bravo Sierra Delta Four, this is Tango Seven One Foxtrot", he called.

A brief pause. "Tango Seven One Foxtrot, this is Bravo Sierra Delta Four! Authenticate."

Vidulic smiled to himself. Either *Yarra* was twitchy or her captain was going to play the operation by the book. He checked his authentication tables for the day's code group.

"Bravo Sierra, this is Tango Seven. I authenticate Whisky Five."

"Tango Seven, this is Bravo Sierra. Kilo."

The pilot rechecked his tables. The reply from the ship was the correct one. Now he would recognise the operator's voice but they would repeat the challenge from time to time to guard against spoof calls.

"Bravo Sierra, roger. Good morning. We are on task as briefed for another eight hours, give or take."

"Tango Seven, roger." *Yarra*'s operator was a man of few words.

The crew settled down to work. Shepherd 54 still had some live sonobuoys in the water and the acoustic operators quickly picked them up as they listened for submarine noise. A bathy probe established the layer at 90 feet so that sonobuoys would have to be dropped to search above and below that level.

Vidulic cut his no. 3 engine and settled the airspeed at 240 knots. Height would be held at 3000 feet as they listened to the buoys, flying a wide orbit to maximise radar coverage.

It was still dark when the report came.

"Tacco, Sensor 3! Riser bearing 192, range 30."

"Pilot—Tacco! Come to course 192. Sensor 4, initiate infra-red search. Navcom, inform Bravo Sierra we have a riser at approximate position 16°42' South, 110°25' East and we are prosecuting."

"Tacco—Sensor 3! Sinker. Lost contact."

"Tacco—Sensor 4! No contact on IRDS."

"Sensor 3—Tacco! Stand by for MAD. Six minutes to estimated datum."

The minutes passed. The aircraft lost height to level out at 600 feet. As it reached the datum, Vidulic began to circle. The magnetic anomaly detector remained quiet.

The tactical officer's display showed the datum which had been computed from the initial radar contact, as well as the aircraft's position. As time passed, he updated the furthest-on circle which showed how far the submarine, if there had been one, could have travelled in the elapsed time.

He called the pilot back to the datum, selecting sonobuoys as they approached. Labelled buttons lit up on his console. As they passed over the spot, he punched a button. "DIFAR ONE away—now!"

Giving Vidulic another heading, he dropped another DIFAR buoy, and yet another. The three buoys bracketed the furthest-on circle. The acoustic operators checked in. They were in contact with the buoys.

The DIFAR buoys were a passive sonobuoy which would listen for submarine noise. Tacco had dropped them for a search below the layer, assuming the submarine commander would go deep if, as was likely, his ESM had picked up the aircraft's radar transmission.

Vidulic called up *Yarra*. "Bravo Sierra, this is Tango Seven. We are prosecuting a sinker at the datum. No contact with Jezebel at this time. Request check for friendlies."

"Tango Seven, this is Bravo Sierra. Roger. No friendlies in the area."

"Tacco—Sensor One! Faint contact on DIFAR TWO. Not good enough for blade count." The acoustic operator punched in the data which showed up as a symbol on the Tacco's console. No other buoy indicated a contact suggesting the submarine was heading away from the datum and had passed DIFAR TWO.

"Pilot, Tacco! This bugger's pretty quick. Head for the new fly-to point on your screen and I'll try to bracket him again."

Vidulic hauled the big aircraft around in a tight turn. More sonobuoys were dropped, above and below the layer but without result.

Time passed. The faint contact on DIFAR TWO faded out and no other buoy picked up any sound. BARRA buoys, the advanced directional sonobuoys, were dropped without result.

"Pilot—Tacco! I think we've lost this one, boss. Suggest we hunt back towards *Yarra*."

"Roger, Tacco." Vidulic switched to his radio. "Bravo Sierra, this is Tango Seven. Lost contact. Classified POSSUB LOW ONE. The original contact was consistent with a snorting diesel-electric. We got one faint Jezebel contact but unable to classify. Intend sweeping back in your direction. Over."

HMAS *Yarra*, Indian Ocean

"Tango Seven, roger. Bad luck but at least you've put him down and, if he was charging his battery, he may have to come up again. Bravo Sierra, out."

Bellano put his microphone down and grimaced at his PWO. The tactical picture was not too bad. The Bear had gone home but he surely would have reported the merchant group to the submarine—assuming there was one—and it was sensible to make that assumption.

On the other hand, the submarine had been put down possibly with a low battery almost 300 miles from his charges. They would be safe in harbour before the submarine could make up the distance.

The broader picture was not so good. There was at least one unfriendly submarine out there, a very quiet diesel-electric type, getting targeting information from an aircraft. He would be slower than a nuke but would compensate by being very quiet and difficult to detect. The iron ore ships had to keep moving and time was on the submarine's side. If the sub got in too close, it might well be able to fire torpedoes on sonar information without having to pop up and have a look for targets. Looming also in his consciousness was the fact that he and *Perth* would have to follow the merchants in to Hedland for fuel before covering the next group.

As well, if those bloody politicians could not make up their minds soon on Rules of Engagement, they would lose merchant ships before he could retaliate. He hoped the air force could keep their P-3s going flat out to keep the sub down.

CHAPTER 10

Cocos Islands

Jeffreys woke with a start. The sergeant was a dark mass in the black night. The moon had set and there was a heavy overcast. For two days and nights, they had holed up in the coconut plantation as the Indian paras had swept through looking for them. Carefully burying their food containers and scraps to conceal all traces of their presence, the five remaining SAS troopers had evaded the search with comparative ease, flitting between the trees, silent as shadows, and infiltrating back behind the searchers.

Tonight, there had been only routine patrols, in vehicles and making no attempt at concealment. Perhaps the Indians had decided it was a waste of time, that the Australians had been withdrawn on that first night after the firefight. They had taken the opportunity to snatch some well-earned sleep.

Silently, the patrol moved off through the night, navigating by the luminous dial of Jeffreys' compass. Moving towards the sound of the surf, they came to the beach, changing direction then to the left and keeping just inside the treeline. The low surf glimmered in the darkness as the slight swell broke over the reef, narrow here on the lee side of the island.

Reaching the big sand dune which marked the most easterly point of the island group, Jeffreys posted a sentry on the landward side of the dune and assembled the rest of the men on the beach. Using a starscope to collect and intensify the tiny quantity of available light, he scanned to seaward, looking for the submarine.

Then he saw the boil of foam as the sub surfaced, not more than 400 metres off the beach. The submarine stood out clear in the starscope as a long shadow on the sea, the sail appearing as a solid black block against the horizon. He nudged his sergeant and pointed. The man nodded and aimed his infra-red torch at the sail, flashing the code that would confirm their presence. There was no reaction from the sub.

Every two minutes, the signal was repeated. It seemed like an hour but was in fact only a few minutes before Jeffreys saw the phosphorescent wake of the small Zodiac powering in towards the beach, its silenced engine barely audible above the mutter of the surf.

He sent a man back to recall the sentry and the group moved down the beach to the spot where the inflatable had grounded on the sand.

"G'day, fellers. Which one of youse ordered a taxi?" The coxswain was on his own. "Get aboard and one of you shove off."

It took little more than three minutes to get back to the submarine, its casing almost flooded down so that they could easily climb aboard. Seamen helped them up and sent them down the forward hatch before recovering and collapsing the inflatable. This with the dinghy's motor then went down the hatch which closed with a thud.

A petty officer called the bridge. "All secure, sir. Party on board."

Jeffreys went aft to the control room as the submarine got under way. As he arrived, the sub's captain shot down the conning tower hatch and nodded a welcome to him before giving the order to dive. There was a rumble as water flooded into the buoyancy tanks. The bow dipped gently as the submarine slid beneath the surface. They were on their way home.

The Cabinet Room, Parliament House—two weeks later

Chapman took his seat and called the meeting to order. There was a full attendance, he noted. The ministers sat around a hollow square table in the big room. Only a few advisers were present but they included all the members of the National Security Council. The only item on the agenda was the crisis with India.

Grayling opened the discussion with a summary of developments. The Indians were on Cocos in some strength. The details were in the briefs available to ministers. Submarine surveillance indicated they were receiving supplies by sea.

Two bulk carriers, both Australian flag ships, had been sunk and the port of Dampier was still closed as they struggled to clear the channel.

It could be presumed that the Indians were concentrating on Australian-flag ships but that could change.

One RF-111 had been shot down over or near Cocos and an SAS patrol sent in to collect intelligence had lost a man before being taken off by submarine.

A large proportion of the navy and RAAF were now deployed forward to the north and were working around the clock. Some reserves had been called up and operating costs were rising rapidly as fuel and spare parts were consumed. At the same time, government revenues were down because Dampier was still closed.

There was another problem. Peacetime rules of engagement prevented Australian units from taking offensive action against potentially hostile forces behaving in a threatening way. They could not respond until actually fired on. Even then it was legally doubtful whether they could shoot to defend neutral shipping. The CDF had asked for a relaxation of the current restrictions.

"In my view, gentlemen", he concluded, "we cannot afford to let things drift any longer. We're being attacked by the Indians, spied on by the Soviets and sniped at by the Opposition and the media. If we don't do something soon, things will get worse."

Wonders will never cease thought McDonald. Eric bloody Grayling is turning militant—about damn time too!

There were others in the Cabinet anxious to make a gesture of determination. Trade wanted the navy to provide blanket protection for all foreign ships as well as Australian. "If we don't", he argued, "they'll stop coming here. The iron ore and all the rest will cost them more elsewhere but at least they'll be able to get it."

The Attorney-General wanted to know what Grayling meant by threatening behaviour. At a nod from the Defence Minister, McCarthy answered. "If we detect an enemy or unidentified unit behaving in such a way as to suggest it is about to launch a weapon, we want to get in first."

"You mean shoot first, even if you're only guessing about his intentions?" The A-G was horrified. "How can you be so sure?"

McCarthy was angry but concealed it with an effort. "This is a life or death situation, Minister. If they shoot first, we get killed—or the people in our care get killed.

"We might need to promulgate the fact that any military vessel or aircraft operating in a designated area would be considered hostile. We could limit that perhaps to such things as submerged submarines, surface vessels or aircraft in what we regard as an attack profile. What I am suggesting is that we place the onus upon them to demonstrate their innocence."

There was a shocked silence. The Attorney-General broke it. "But you can't do that. It's tantamount to declaring war on everyone. What about the Indonesians?"

McDonald answered that. "I don't think the Indonesians would be too worried. If we specify the area concerned so that it excludes their territorial waters, I doubt if we'll have a problem. In any case, it's my job to work out a deal with them. Just remember, they want this problem solved too, even if they won't help."

Only McDonald and Grayling supported the proposal. Eventually Chapman put forward the compromise suggestion that a declaration be made that all merchant ships would be protected by Australian air and naval units as far as Indonesian territorial waters. What would not be publicly said was that the Australians would be restricted to a "no first shot" rule.

Grayling was opposed. So was McDonald. "It's just a bluff", he insisted. "If it's called, our people are going to get killed. I'd sooner it was the Indians."

McCarthy was not asked for his view. McDonald called for a vote. Only Grayling backed him in opposing the new rules and they were adopted.

Chapman moved on to the question of recovering Cocos. He reported on his conversation with President Forrest. McCarthy was asked for his views on the possibilities.

He walked over to the map which had been set up on an easel, picked up a pointer and sketched out the problem.

"Well, Prime Minister, we've had a look at the task. Ultimately, we must put troops on shore across the beach. Subject to two basic provisos, if we do that, I am confident we can defeat the Indian garrison.

"The two provisos are that we take out their air defence on the islands and make sure they can't resupply by sea. I doubt if we could prevent an airborne supply but they won't be able to reinforce much by air anyway."

"Why can't you stop them flying in reinforcements?" McDonald wanted to know.

"Well, sir, Cocos is more than 1200 nautical miles from our nearest mainland airfield here at Learmonth. Even with in-flight refuelling, we could not maintain fighter cover over the islands."

"Couldn't we use the airfield on Christmas Island?", one of the ministers asked.

"Yes, sir. Christmas would be better. The transit is down to about 550 miles from there. If we could use the island, we could fly a lot more sorties against Cocos but nothing like a standing patrol. We would need good intelligence, better than we currently have on the Indians, to be able to run interceptions.

"The complicating factor is that we would have to do a lot of work to build up stocks of fuel, ammunition and spares there. That would mean a pretty big movement task. And if we can fly from Christmas, the Indians could also strike there. My inclination would be to leave Christmas out of the equation."

McDonald interrupted briefly. "I think we could have real problems with Indonesia if we started running intensive air operations so close to their territory. Sorry for the interruption, General."

"No problem, sir. I think that's the killer so far as using Christmas goes. Better to think of it in terms of an emergency airfield for aircraft returning from Cocos.

"We are going to have to run air strikes out of Learmonth to try to take out their air defences. The planners are looking at the details now.

"One problem is that we can't use our F-111s except for the most limited ops."

"Why not?", Chapman demanded.

"Not enough range, sir, and we can't use our existing tankers. The F-111s use a different refuelling system, the boom type instead of the probe and drogue." He paused in his exposition to outline the difference between the two. "It does tie our hands more than somewhat unless..."

"Unless what", Chapman interrupted. "Well, sir, my air people have suggested leasing a KC-10 tanker with the boom system from the Yanks. If we could do that, it would solve our problems. They did approach the Americans informally but the answer was that the approval would have to come from the President."

"All right, leave that to me." Chapman was confident.

"OK. If we can fix that, I believe we can cut out their air capability."

"Can't they just fly in more aircraft?", the Treasurer asked.

"Certainly, sir, but we'd be looking to knock out the fuel supply and the runway as much as aircraft. Not much point in having planes there if they can't be flown.

"Then, simultaneously, we would be looking to a submarine interdiction of any supply ships. We ought to take a lead from what the Brits did in the Falklands, declare a maritime exclusion zone around Cocos. Tell the world that any ships moving through the zone may be sunk without warning.

"In a sense then, the actual landing operation would be basically mopping up. Let me emphasise though, it would not be easy. We don't have a lot of shipping and the Indians would resist pretty fiercely. They have crack troops there."

"What about your paratroops?", the Treasurer asked. "I seem to remember that we dropped a battalion on to Cocos some years ago as a demonstration of a capability. Can't we use them again?"

McCarthy chuckled. "That was a PR exercise, sir. I was a half-colonel then, 1985 I think it was, but I remember the whole army thought it was a big joke, except for the poor devils who did the jump.

"It is simply not a credible operational proposition. We'd be dropping men into a small and well-defended area. They'd be cut to pieces."

He explained. "Paratroops are of value to capture an undefended area and hold it against opposition for a short while until backup arrives. They are simply not an option unless you want to lose three or four hundred élite troops. No, I'm sorry, it would have to be a seaborne operation."

"All right, then, I accept that", the Treasurer replied. "Now, I know I've asked the question before but what about cost?"

"I don't have a figure, sir, but for the Cocos operation alone, it's going to cost a lot of money. How much will depend on our losses which will have to be replaced after the event but I certainly cannot see us doing it for less than the $500 million figure mentioned by Mr Grayling back in April. "

And we have to count the cost of the shipping protection operations as well. We're running those ships and aircraft pretty hard."

"So you're suggesting maybe a billion is not stretching it too far?"

McCarthy nodded agreement. Social Security made his first contribution. "A billion dollars to recover some small islands and no more than 400 people? It's a big price to pay."

There was a growl of agreement to that. After more discussion, Chapman proposed that the CDF prepare a detailed plan for the recovery of Cocos with a Cabinet decision to await the outcome of the planning process. Again McDonald demurred.

"We just can't go on like this", he began. "We're running into real political problems with all this dithering. We should agree to the principle that we will invade Cocos and tip the Indians off. We could announce that and earn some kudos in the electorate. It won't hurt in some of the key regional capitals either.

"That way too, the military can at least get their teeth into the plan and maybe start to carry out some of their raids without having to look over their shoulder and come to us every time they want to do something."

He knew before he finished speaking he was wasting his breath. His colleagues were not only undecided about the operation but they were also unwilling to let the military off a very short political leash.

And so it was decided, a compromise which, as usual, satisfied no one except the procrastinators.

16°00' South 117°25' East, Indian Ocean (three weeks later)

Vidulic roared over the group of bulk carriers at 300 feet. There were four of them, all Japanese or Korean, None of them, he guessed, less than 150,000 tonnes deadweight. All were obviously fully laden and heading for Lombok Strait at 13 knots. It was just after sunset now and he calculated they would hit the entrance to Lombok just after dawn the day after tomorrow. Sooner them than me, he mused. Better to get along at 300 knots than 13 with nothing but seawater for company.

Vidulic would stay with them for another eight hours when he would be relieved by another P-3. They were operating out of RAAF Curtin at Derby, having moved up from Learmonth. It was pretty primitive but there was some consolation in doing a real job.

Yarra and *Perth* were sweeping about 100 miles to the north-west covering any approaches to the convoy's track, either by a submarine or the Bear.

It was still an open question whether they were at war or not. No one seemed to know for sure and the new Rules of Engagement were not much help. Down south, it seemed to be business as usual with politicians preening, footballers on the front pages and popstars philosophising on the box. It was a different if all too familiar world. The French had a saying for it, he reflected, but he couldn't remember what it was.

As usual, it was the Tacco who broke into his reverie. "Pilot—Tacco! Putting another LOFAR pattern down, boss. Watch for your fly-to points. LOFAR SIX away—now!"

There was no response. Above the layer, the merchant ships could be heard on the buoys and their characteristic noise filtered out by the acoustic processor. Below the layer, there was only ambient noise, the normal sounds of the restless sea.

Darkness fell and the aircraft roared on. More buoys were dropped, the aircraft searching out to the east and west as well as ahead. Occasionally, Vidulic was sent back by the Tacco to interrogate the buoys left behind. As long as there was life in their batteries, they could warn of a submarine that might be trailing the small convoy.

Tedium ate away at enthusiasm and alertness. Men rubbed tired eyes, sucked at packs of fruit juice and strained to focus on the screens in front of them. Vidulic handed over to his co-pilot and walked through the aircraft, stopping at each crew position to exchange a joke, a comment or just a word of recognition.

The night wore on. Suddenly—"Tacco, Sensor 3! Contact, bearing 214. Very fast—shit! Sir, bearing is changing rapidly, moving astern, range initially 17 miles shortening— "

"Tacco, Port Aft! I have it visual. Flare at 8 o'clock low, moving very fast."

The aircraft banked steeply to port as the pilot wrenched the wheel over and trod on the rudder. Vidulic stumbled, banging his head painfully on an equipment rack. Grabbing at handholds, he hauled himself back to his seat and climbed in. Almost dead ahead now, he could see the pinpoint of light, white in the blackness, moving fast and low from right to left across his nose.

Then there was a flash. White-orange flame billowed in the distance. He ignored it.

"I've got her", he snapped at his co-pilot. He hauled the aircraft around to starboard, heading west towards the approximate source of the contact.

"Tacco—Pilot! That was a missile, probably sub-to- surface. Give me a course back to the initial contact point and stand-by for submarine prosecution."

"Tacco—Sensor Three! No contact except the convoy."

"Pilot—Tacco! Steer 224. Estimated time to datum six minutes."

The seconds ticked by. Vidulic strained to hold his course. This was almost the worst part of the job, running down a datum with nothing on the screen while the submarine headed away from its launch point.

Throughout the aircraft, adrenalin overcame tiredness. Eyes burned into screens and sweaty palms were surreptitiously wiped on overalls. Fingertips toyed with buttons as they willed the aircraft sensors to reach out and pinpoint the killer.

"All positions—Tacco! This target looks like a nuke, probably the Indian *Charlie*-class. She's fired something like an SS-N-7 at the convoy and probably has a hit. This thing can do 24 knots dived but she's very noisy.

"Navcomm, get out a contact report to Bravo Sierra. Tell them we've got a real one here."

"MAD Mark!" The radar operator almost shouted into his microphone as the spike shot up his MAD screen.

Vidulic dragged the aircraft into a steep climbing turn and punched the button which opened the bomb bay doors. The Tacco marked up the new datum as he armed a Mark 46 torpedo. Back in the aircraft, someone was vomiting as the big plane toppled into a dive back on to the datum.

"Torpedo away—now!" The long cylinder dropped away from its grabs. Almost immediately, a parachute deployed to slow its entry into the water.

"BARRA ONE away—now!"

"Tacco—Sensor One! Torpedo running."

The Tacco watched his screen. The torpedo was circling, seeking a target. As he watched, the sonobuoy symbol acquired a vector. There was another sound source there.

"Pilot— Tacco! Steer 330,"

"BARRA TWO away—now! Pilot, steer 220. Let's box this bastard in."

Almost immediately, the second buoy acquired a target.

"Tacco—Sensor One! Torpedo is pinging."

The Tacco watched as the torpedo closed with the intersecting vectors. He held his breath. Nothing!

"BARRA THREE away—now! I think the torpedo homed on a noisemaker. On your toes, everybody. He's still out there."

Yokosuka Maru

The missile hit the ship on the port side below the bridge. With its rocket motor still running, it slammed its way through the thin plating and into a sleeping cabin before the warhead exploded.

There was an orange-white flash as the missile body dissolved into white hot fragments. The pressure wave blew out the bulkheads an instant before the unexpended rocket fuel vaporised and flashed into an expanding ball of white hot energy.

The two men asleep in the cabin died instantly. The deck was punched out into the engine room immediately below and the fireball reached down into the large space, hungrily sucking up the oxygen in the air. The three men on duty suffocated, their lungs collapsing as they gasped for breath. Then the fireball swept over their dying bodies, singeing hair and blistering flesh.

Three decks above, Captain Ito was flung out of his bunk by the blast. Stunned, he tugged at the cabin door. It was jammed. He kicked out the escape panel, struggled through and clambered up to the bridge.

The Chief Officer had cut the throttles and the ship was slowing although it would be three miles before it could come to a full stop. Below, automatic fire sprinklers had cut in and were pouring huge volumes of water on the fire.

Ito looked around. Broken glass crunched under his feet. One man was down on the deck, bleeding from a gash in the neck. Another was bent over him, vainly trying to staunch the flow of blood that was forming into a dark pool on the tiled deck. The wheel, he noted, had been lashed. There was not an intact pane of glass in the bridge windows. The cool night air which washed over him brought the smell of smouldering paint and woodwork.

At his nod, the Chief Officer left the bridge to take charge of the mopping up. Other crewmen came to the bridge, then to be sent below to help. There were not many of them.

16°00' South 116°55' East - Indian Ocean

"DIFAR TWELVE away—now!" The Tacco looked over his shoulder at Vidulic who had come aft to look at the screen. He switched on the small scale range display.

"My guess is he continued roughly east after firing to stay in touch with the convoy. Getting the MAD detection was a fluke for us but when he heard the torpedo drop, he fired off a noisemaker and went deep, very deep—and quiet.

"The furthest-on circle is not getting too big." His finger ranged across the screen, tapping to make his points.

"If it is their Charlie, he can make 24 knots dived but he is not doing anything like that or we would have heard him. I've given him a maximum of five knots so he'll be inside this circle, probably to the north or west, either heading to stay in touch with the convoy or going home."

Vidulic pondered before he agreed. He glanced at his watch. "Two more hours and we'll have to go home. Curtin have another bird in the air but it'll be another hour before he gets here." he said, returning to his position.

"Tacco, this is Sensor Two! Contact on DIFAR 12."

"Sensor One! Weak contact DIFAR TEN."

"OK. Good cross bearing on these two. Let's have another Barra down. Pilot, steer 195." He punched buttons on his console.

"BARRA FOUR away—now!"

"Tacco—Sensor Two! Contact BARRA FOUR, bearing 152."

"Pilot—Tacco! Steer 090." A pause. "BARRA FIVE away—now!"

"Tacco, Sensor One. Contact BARRA FIVE, bearing 018."

He watched his screen. Good! He had a course and speed on the target. He punched up another fly-to point for Vidulic and armed another Mark 46. He would come up behind the sub, drop on a predicted position and let the torpedo chase him. The target appeared to be on a course between the two BARRAS which were giving a good cross bearing.

"Pilot—Tacco! Come left 270. Bomb doors open."

"Tacco—Sensor One! Contact BARRA FIVE bearing 015."

"Sensor Two! BARRA FOUR bearing 156."

He updated his target position and track as the aircraft headed in. "Torpedo away—now! Bomb doors closed."

"MAD Mark!" Right over the top of the bludger! A perfect drop but which way will he go when he hears the torpedo? A guess. "Pilot, steer 330."

He watched the screen, barely hearing the reports. There he goes. Bugger! He's fluked it. Turned hard—right or left? And kicked on speed too. The Barras are in the wrong place. He's on a course in a straight line between them. Fired off another noisemaker and the torpedo is chasing it.

"Tacco—Sensor One! Signature evaluated as *Charlie*-One nuke." It was something but only confirmed his earlier guess.

"Pilot—Tacco! Target upgraded to PROBSUB. Let's try another attack. Steer 220."

Another hour passed. Two more attacks failed. On the first, the torpedo's engine failed to start and a lot of taxpayers' money sank to the bottom. On the second, the sub went quiet, dead quiet, and the torpedo's passive sensor lost him. The active pinging head just never found the target. It was a brave gambit by the sub captain but it worked.

Shepherd 57 joined and restarted the hunt. Vidulic, with fuel running low and torpedos expended, headed east for home.

RAAF Base, Tindal

This time, the squadron commander briefed the two pilots.

"You're detached to RAAF Curtin down at Derby. The task is to pick up the Indian Bear-F that keeps trailing the convoys." He pointed to the general area on the map. "You'll be directed by *Yarra*, call sign Bravo Sierra. Your call sign will be Dragon, as before. *Yarra*'s been picking up the radar from the Bear but can't get close enough.

"You'll be on stand-by at Curtin on the ground until the ship hears the aircraft. On previous experience, she'll be about 500 miles out so take as much fuel as you can plus AIM-9s and a full gun load. Leave your Sparrows behind so you can take more fuel.

"We'll fly a ground crew and basic spares down to Curtin but you'll have to rely on the base staff down there for everything else.

"*Yarra* will direct you as far as possible but she won't be able to give you a height read-out. Maintain complete EMCON until you are well within presumed radar range and then go for it."

"What do we do when we intercept?" Norris wanted to know.

"That's up to you. The rules say he has to be allowed to shoot first. Yeah, I know it's bloody stupid but the politicians don't want us to kill anyone just yet.

"Just don't get yourselves killed first. But don't take any shit from him either. Use your judgement, whatever that's worth. I'll cover you as best I can. Any more questions I can't answer? OK, be on your way."

Two days later, Norris and his wingman roared off the ground and headed west-north-west, climbing to 40,000 feet. Forty minutes later, *Yarra* came on the air. "Dragon, this is Bravo Sierra. Bandit bearing three zero seven range one three four."

Norris swung on to the new course putting his nose down to lose height. He punched the data into his computer. Intercept would be in about 17 minutes. Twelve minutes before he would be in radar range. Make that ten before he broke EMCON. He glanced over his shoulder. His wingman was there.

"Dragon, Bravo Sierra. Bandit has altered course. New bearing two niner six, range eight three."

Norris cursed into his oxygen mask. The bastard's running. Now I'll be chasing him up the tail, not even closing at this speed. But if I go faster, I'll be burning more fuel than I can spare.

He pushed his throttles forward and the aircraft leaped ahead, pushing him back into the seat. The HUD showed his speed at Mach 1.2.

"Dragon—Bravo Sierra. Lost contact. Bandit out of my radar range."

Furious, Norris triggered his own radar. Contact. The computer produced the intercept solution—course, relative height, time to intercept.

Then his fuel warning sounded. He had programmed the computer to tell him when it was time to go home. Now that seductive female voice in his headset was telling him to fly home or he'd have to swim. Bitch, he thought. Why can't we get a frigging tanker up here?

Sadly, he throttled back, flashed his wings to his partner and commenced a long turn on to a course for Derby. He broke radio silence.

"Bravo Sierra, this is Dragon One. Bandit has evaded. Gained contact but have to go home for fuel. Sorry, mate."

"Dragon One, this is Bravo Sierra. Bad luck. Still, he can't do any damage if he's running for home. Thanks for that."

Eighty minutes later he landed back at Derby. His wingman who had the job of keeping up had about enough fuel left to boil a kettle. By that time, though, Norris had cooled down as he walked away to make his report.

Defence Operations Centre, Canberra

Forbes was briefing the CDF. "The Bear ran, sir. *Yarra* had a good intercept set up but he just took off for no apparent reason. Maybe he was at the end of his time on task. Maybe he just guessed we might have Hornets on the way. It doesn't really matter. The Hornets gained contact but they were operating at absolute maximum range for fuel and had to turn back.

"Without a tanker up there, it's a no-win situation. The pilots are watching their fuel state all the time. They have to leave their Sparrows behind to carry enough fuel. Not that that's a real problem anyway with these Rules of Engagement. We can't touch the bugger unless he shoots first and he can't do that at Sparrow range."

"So, what's the answer?", McCarthy asked.

"The only real answer is to run a tanker in support. We'll have to do it out of Darwin, I think, otherwise we'll be putting too much pressure on the fuel stocks at Derby and Learmonth, if we operated from either place.

"As it is, I've had to ask the supply people to get a lot more fuel up to all the northern bases. We're going through it very fast."

McCarthy pondered the problem. "All right, do it. Now, tell me, is *Yarra* doing enough?

"Not really. She's not much more than a radar or sonar picket in this situation. She gave the Hornets a good intercept although with that tinpot radar she's got, she can't give a height. And, if the Bear keeps out of gun range, she's pretty useless. She just doesn't have the weapons.

"To be fair, she can't shoot at the Bear even within range under these bloody rules. I'd be more worried about her ASW difficulty if a sub gets in close. She hasn't got much to hit him with.

"We'll have to get the navy to send out the DDGs or the FFGs. At least, they've got an area SAM system that can knock an aircraft down at long range. They're better ASW ships too."

"OK. Talk to Cartwright and get him to pull *Yarra* back. If she can't do anti-air or ASW, she might be useful as an escort for the invasion—if that ever gets off the bloody ground. What a friggin' mess!"

CHAPTER 11

16°22' South 110°40' East, Indian Ocean

Yarra was sweeping west with *Perth* in company three miles to starboard. Shepherd 52 was 50 miles to the north conducting a radar search. Almost a month had passed since the attack which damaged the *Yokosuka Maru* and there had been no trace of any submarine in that time.

Shipping was moving again but Bellano was sure some of the shipowners were getting nervous. If there were any more attacks, it might not be long before some of the ships, particularly the foreign ones, began to drop out of the trade.

He lounged in his bridge chair, flicking through the signal log, the collection of mostly administrative traffic about stores, defects, personnel matters and the rest. Most of it would be looked after by his department heads; he checked through to make sure there was nothing important that should be referred to him.

It was a good day to be at sea. A long swell rolled in from the south-west making the ship pitch gently as it lifted over and down each wave. Spray flew, glistening in the sun, as the sharp bow cut through the water with a loud swish. A brisk breeze from the west blew the tops off the larger waves and rattled the signal halliards outside the open bridge doors. Far away on the horizon, heaped-up thunder clouds dropped grey sheets of rain in locally violent squalls.

Almost subconsciously, Bellano heard the afternoon watch piped to dinner. He was more interested in watching *Perth* away to the south. Despite her age, she still looked what she was, a lean powerful destroyer, heavily armed, fast and dangerous.

The Ops Room 'phone buzzed. The Officer-of-the-Watch snatched it up. He listened briefly, then turned to his Captain.

"Ops reports racket bearing 183, sir, classified as SNOOP TRAY. Looks like a riser."

"OK, I'm on my way down. Come left to 183 but maintain this speed." Bellano heaved himself out of his chair and disappeared down the after ladder to the Ops Room.

In the Ops Room, Bellano leaned over the plot. "What have we got?" he asked the PWO.

"Only the racket, sir. We are in Patrol State Quiet with *Perth* coming up on our port beam at 10 miles. Speed is six knots. We have TASS and Nixie streamed, radar and Mulloka shut down. Shepherd 52 is about 10 minutes away.

"The sub is still transmitting. EW has no range but believes we would be within detection range. I recommend we ..."

"Ops—EW! Transmission has ceased."

"Roger. Sir, we should go active on radar and sonar."

"Yes." Bellano agreed. "And call in the P-3."

The bulkhead speaker crackled again. "Bravo Sierra, this is Tango Seven. I have a sinker bearing approximately 180 and three, repeat three, miles from you."

"Jeez, he's a bit close, sir." The PWO was startled.

"Yes. Clear the TDA and have the helo stand by. And let's go to action stations."

"Bravo Sierra, this is Oscar Romeo." It was *Perth* on the secure voice channel. "Sonar contact bearing 352, range 14,800 yards and moving left. Request approval for Ikara attack."

Bellano shook his head. "Tell him to stand by but hold the contact." He swore to himself but the Rules of Engagement stopped him from launching an unprovoked attack.

"Let's open it up a bit. Come left to 110 and tell *Perth* to keep to the west of the datum. Hasn't sonar got anything yet? Wake them ..."

"Torpedo in the water, bearing 202 and constant." The PWO snapped on his microphone.

"Bridge, Ops! Come hard left 022, speed 24."

Men hung on as the ship heeled hard to starboard away from the turn. Loose gear rolled off tables and the gas turbine note rose up the scale as the ship accelerated away from the torpedo.

"What's today's call-sign for all units?" Bellano snapped.

The PWO looked up from the screen. "Mike Alpha Three Zulu, sir."

"Mike Alpha, this is Bravo Sierra. Target has fired a torpedo at me and we are attempting to evade. Command approved for attack."

The speaker crackled back immediately. "Bravo Sierra, this is Oscar Romeo. Attacking Ikara. Tango Seven, scram west."

Despite the tension, Bellano grinned at the last. Perth was telling the aircraft to clear out of the firing line. P-3 crews were notoriously unhappy if they had to share airspace with the Ikara missile, although the chances of collision were pretty slim.

"Mike Alpha, BASSETT away bearing 147. Dogbox 1152."

Perth's Ikara was in the air and no more attacks would be made until its torpedo ran out at 1152.

The seconds ticked by, each seeming like minutes. "SCR—Ops! How's that torpedo running?"

"Still closing, sir. Constant bearing."

The submarine's torpedo was chasing him up the stern. There was little he could do except try to outrun it and hope the Nixie would seduce it.

"Ops—SCR! Torpedo is pinging. It's acquired something."

The explosion jolted the ship. A column of water shot up in the ship's boiling wake. White water thundered down on the quarterdeck. Throughout the ship, men were knocked off their feet and lights went out. A few seconds later, they came back on.

Bellano looked at his PWO and grinned. "Scratch one Nixie. Get me a damage report, please.

"Bridge—Ops! Come right 130, speed 21. SCR, you'll be coming out of the baffles now."

"Ops—SCR! Torpedo in water bearing 206. Sounds like a Mark 46."

"That'll be *Perth*'s Ikara", the PWO offered.

"Ops—SCR! Target has evaded. He fired a decoy and kicked away. We seem to have a diesel-electric boat but sonar conditions are not too good at this speed." Was there a note of reproach in the sonar chief's voice?

Bellano studied the plot. The standard evasive tactic was for the submarine to put on speed, fire a decoy and make a large course alteration to put a knuckle in the water. Then he would dive under the knuckle and go quiet.

His own best option was to keep clear. He had no weapon which would outrange the submarine but *Perth*'s Ikara was ideal. His passive sonar was largely useless at this speed while his own sonar did not have the range of *Perth*'s SQS-23. Best to use the P-3 and *Perth* with himself standing off as a sonar picket. He would drop back to eight knots and listen on passive sonar, occasionally going active. He could set up a data link with *Perth* and the aircraft to give him a full picture on his own plot and thus control the action from his Ops Room.

With any luck, the sonar barrier would drive the sub away from him although he suspected the enemy captain would be aware of his vulnerability. Now, too, he could get his helicopter in the air to box the sub in.

He looked up to give the order but the PWO forestalled him. "Helo's U/S, sir. Pilot was thrown off the aircraft when the torpedo exploded and broke a leg."

"Tango Seven, this is Bravo Sierra. Can you give me a active sonobuoy barrier east-west three miles south of the last datum? Oscar Romeo, continue active prosecution."

Tactically, the submarine was now positioned inside a box of sound waves. To the south was the barrier of sonobuoys, low-powered but effectively deterring the target from attempting to escape that way. *Perth* was now ten miles away to the west of the datum while his own ship was a similar distance to the east. Both ships would cover their sides of the box at 16 knots. The aircraft would close the gap to the north.

On the other hand, the submarine was quiet, too quiet for detection by passive sonar as long as he kept his speed low. The sub could use the layer to confuse the active sonar and, of course, low speed would help to conserve his battery. He was on the defensive, though. Firing another torpedo at one of the surface ships would disclose his position very quickly.

133

The loss of the helicopter was a blow. Its dipping sonar and mobility would have overcome the disadvantage of the layer and would have allowed *Yarra* to stand off further.

Time passed. It was almost six hours later when the P-3 gained what he thought was a contact from the southern barrier. *Perth* got a cross bearing on her sonar and the aircraft was guided in on a VECTAC, dropping another torpedo. Again, the submarine evaded by putting on speed and going deep. But he left behind an updated datum. The ring was closing and time was on the side of the hunters. Every sprint by the submarine not only disclosed his position more precisely but drained his battery further. Bellano decided to bait him; he opened his mouth to order the active sonar to shut down—

"Ops, SCR! Contact bearing 248 range 16000 yards."

"OK. We've got him. Too far away for us though. Oscar Romeo, this is Bravo Sierra. Attack Ikara on my contact. Tango Seven, stay clear and stand by for VECTAC."

The bulkhead speaker crackled. "BASSET away bearing 092. Dogbox 1743."

Sonar held contact on the target, constantly updating its position. The ship-to-ship datalink fed the new information directly to *Perth*'s Ikara control system which automatically updated the missile guidance. The submarine was held under the layer but was kicking on speed to try to evade. *Perth*'s sonar was scanning above the layer in case *Yarra* lost contact.

"Ops, SCR! Torpedo in the water bearing 261. Mark 46." A pause. "Torpedo pinging. Torpedo has acquired the target. Detonation. Lost contact."

All round the Ops Room, heads lifted from their consoles. Men looked at each other and grinned, relaxing from the tension of the past hours. There was no cheering, only a few words exchanged between neighbours. Later, the stories would start and be embellished, building up to the mock heroics with which they would impress civilians when they were next ashore.

The PWO grinned at his captain. "Nice one, sir. We got him that time." All that training, he thought, and when the real test came, we were good enough.

Bellano looked at them. They were a good team. And they had done their job well. But they had just killed 55 men, men like themselves with families who would never see them again, with homes which would never feel their presence. And for what?

Sure, the submarine had killed unprotected merchant ships. They had tried to kill him and his men. Why? Because they were told to by those in authority, those other men who would go home to their families, ambitious men who directed men and machines for political ends but who were detached from the reality and immune from the consequences.

He nearly said so but stopped himself in time. The reality would come home to them later. Instead, he picked up the microphone. "Mike Alpha, this is Bravo Sierra. Well done! Oscar Romeo, join me at the datum to search for survivors. Tango Seven, thank you for your assistance. "PWO, secure from action stations. I'm going up to the bridge."

Parliament House, Canberra

The media conference was packed as the Prime Minister entered the room accompanied by Grayling and McCarthy. As they took their places behind the table with its mass of microphones and tape recorders, the buzz of conversation faded.

Chapman waited for complete silence, building up suspense. He picked up the paper with the brief statement, looked around the room quickly and commenced.

"Thank you for coming, ladies and gentlemen." Of course they would come, he thought. Not only had they been told to but they would be spoiling for trouble. He continued. "Two days ago in the Indian Ocean, units of the Australian Defence Force detected an unidentified submarine which attacked HMAS *Yarra*, our latest frigate. The submarine was subsequently sunk by an Ikara missile fired by HMAS *Perth*. Only superficial damage was done to *Yarra* which is remaining on patrol with *Perth* and Orion long range maritime patrol aircraft of the RAAF.

"Only minor casualties were suffered, the worst being a broken leg. "I want to pay particular tribute to the professionalism shown by our sailors and airmen who responded so promptly and effectively to this unprovoked act of piracy.

"That ends the statement. My staff have copies for you. I presume you want to ask some questions."

"Prime Minister!" Predictably it was Reg Baker with the first question. "Whose submarine was it?"

"That's something we don't know, Reg. It was sunk with all hands as I believe the saying goes."

"Do we then make a habit of sinking unidentified submarines?" Baker sneered. McCarthy flushed but said nothing.

"Our forces are entitled to retaliate against any hostile act. A torpedo was fired at *Yarra*. Under current regulations, the ship was entitled to retaliate. She did so. What would you want our men to do, call a policeman?"

There was laughter at that. Baker subsided.

"Prime Minister, Mary Petrelli, ABC. Is there any evidence that this was an Indian submarine?"

Chapman paused. "As I said, we don't know whose submarine it was or even if it was acting with the authority of its government. I want to make it absolutely clear that we have no evidence linking this attack with India."

The experienced journalists brightened at that. Baker thought to himself that as soon as a politician insisted on making something clear, he almost certainly had something to hide. It was an almost Pavlovian response—by the journos as well as the pollies, he admitted.

Petrelli kept the floor. "Sir, is there any link between this attack and the Indian invasion of Cocos?"

Again, Chapman hedged. "We have no evidence to suggest that."

Norton from AAP interrupted. "Prime Minister, my sources tell me that a Japanese freighter was attacked and badly damaged by a submarine in the Indian Ocean a month ago. Could this have been the same submarine?"

Chapman conferred briefly with Grayling who, at one point in the muttered exchange, visibly shook his head.

"A Japanese flag bulk carrier was attacked with a cruise missile launched from a submarine", Chapman replied. "The submarine was counter-attacked by an Orion aircraft but without result."

There was a buzz of excitement. This was real news. Why had the government concealed that incident, they wondered?

Norton went on. "I also believe that the submarine was almost certainly a Soviet-built nuclear submarine of the Indian navy. Can you confirm that for us?"

"That's a very speculative view, Richard. We have no hard evidence."

Norton persisted. "But you agree that the ship was attacked by a cruise missile." Chapman nodded. "Who else has cruise missile firing submarines in this part of the world?"

McCarthy leaned over and whispered to the PM. Chapman nodded, then looked up to the room. "It is certainly a possibility that the submarine was Indian. There is some negative evidence to support such a conclusion but, as I said, we have no hard evidence to confirm that assessment. I can't be any more precise than that."

Baker returned to the fray. "Prime Minister, we have an Indian invasion force on Cocos, submarines, one of them in your own terms probably Indian, attacking ships trading with Australia. There's another submarine attacking our own warships. You say it's unidentified but you don't have to be a genius to guess whose it was. Are we at war with India and, if so, why? And what the hell are we doing about it?"

Before Chapman could answer, another reporter interrupted."Prime Minister, Sally Newell, *Finance Daily*. Is there any link between these events and the sinking of two of BHP's bulk carriers since last December?"

Chapman cringed inwardly. The government—he—was clearly losing control of the situation. He had not expected the surge of public outrage that was reflected by the questions. He decided to call a halt.

"Ladies and gentlemen, I understand your interest and concern. What you must understand is that the government is facing a very tricky situation in its relations with a fellow Commonwealth country. The Indian government has indicated that the military force on Cocos is made up of volunteers who do not have the backing of the Indian government—"

A voice from the back shouted. "Why don't you kick the bastards off then?" There was a rumble of agreement.

Chapman held up his hand. "It's not quite as simple as that. The other thing I want to say is that ships trading with Australia are being protected. We have almost all our shipping protection capability deployed to the north west and, I want to emphasise, we have sunk a hostile submarine. That will give whoever they are something to think about. Now, I'm sorry, but I have work to do."

Chapman ignored the chorus of questions. Getting quickly to his feet, he walked out of the room, followed by Grayling and McCarthy.

Later in his office, he watched the television news, appalled at the hostility. The editing of the press conference added to the reporter's commentary were as vicious as anything he had experienced. On Channel 6, Baker had called him the Australian Neville Chamberlain. According to his staff, the radio news commentaries were little better. With luck, he thought, the morning papers would cool the heat a bit after the hours of reflection they enjoyed over the electronic media.

Grayling and McDonald came in as the Opposition Leader was being interviewed on the current affairs programme that followed the news.

Newman was insisting that the country faced a serious problem and the government had to deal with it. "I don't want to make party political capital out of this", he declaimed, "but the government does not seem able to make up its mind what to do. It is drifting and the community won't stand for it.

"We have seen the public opinion polls which show conclusively that more than 70 per cent of the population wants strong and vigorous action from their government.

"I am absolutely certain that the great Australian people will support any government that resists this aggression. And any government which does that will have the unequivocal support of the Opposition."

Chapman grunted. "Bill's got his statesman's face on again. I'll bet he's been practising." He held up his hand as the interviewer went on.

"So, would you support an Australian invasion to retake the Cocos Islands?"

"Certainly." For a change, Newman made no attempt to qualify the commitment.

"Even if it means an all-out confrontation with the Indian military machine?" Newman pondered his answer. "I just don't think it would come to that. The Indians would lose enormous prestige. They know that, and that is why they are distancing themselves from their forces on Cocos with this myth that they are volunteers. It gives them the option of backing off if we go in hard."

Chapman flicked off the set. McDonald broke the brief silence. "He's right, you know. We are isolated and starting to look pretty silly. I had Andy Firebrace on the 'phone a few minutes ago. He won't be pulling any punches in his editorial tomorrow."

"We need time." Chapman sounded tired. "You know the feeling in Cabinet. Even if I wanted to go ahead with an invasion, I doubt if I could carry them. Eric, what are those planners of yours doing? We've got to have a proposition on the table before we can go any further. I'm not even sure any more."

"I'll hurry them up. In the meantime, is it any good, d'you think, putting out a 'D' Notice on the whole thing?" The 'D' Notice was a request to the media not to report or discuss specified matters of national security. It had no force of law and depended upon co-operation by editors.

McDonald was annoyed. "Don't be bloody stupid. As if we're not in enough trouble. Even if you got the committee to agree to issue a notice—and that's pretty doubtful—someone in the media would break ranks on it and then the whole pack would be out for blood. The mere fact that we tried to suppress the story would give them another stick to beat us."

Chapman agreed, somewhat mournfully. "I even thought of delaying the resumption of Parliament next week. But it is the Budget session and we've got to get that through. And, as you say, we don't want to make things worse than they already are.

"Tell me, are any of the media on our side?" Grayling thought not. McDonald agreed. "The big Sydney and Melbourne dailies are inclined to sympathise with the dilemma. On the other hand, they are always keen to bag us. The rest, I guess, will be pretty militant."

CHAPTER 12

Cocos Islands

Sharma was sitting at the wheel of his Landrover with a civilian as Squadron Leader Jaswal climbed down the ladder from the MiG-29. After three hours strapped to his seat, Jaswal was tired, hot and sweaty. He waved a casual salute as he walked over to the vehicle.

Sharma flicked a hand in acknowledgement. "Allow me to introduce Vivek Nadkarni who has just arrived. Vivek is from the Foreign Ministry and doubles as my political adviser and", he grinned, "ambassador to the Republic of Cocos." The two men shook hands without much warmth, the pilot wondering why the colonel needed a political adviser.

"Get in. Let's go for a drive." Sharma was impatient. As they parked on the beach, he turned to the pilot. "You wanted to talk to me, Devan. What's the problem? Anything that Vivek can't hear?"

"It's these dammed CAPs, sir. They're a waste of bloody time. We're just burning up fuel and aircraft hours. I doubt if the Australians are going to hit us. What does New Delhi say?"

Sharma paused before answering, looking out over the beach to where the surf broke on the reef. It was a glorious day. The sun shone, the breeze took the edge off the heat and there was little enough work to distract men from the hedonistic pleasures of a tropical holiday resort, however primitive and militarised it might be.

Jaswal's problem was yet another minor irritant. Sharma's own men were getting a bit restless. They were ,lite troops, uncomfortable with garrison duty on the remote outpost. There had been minor acts of indiscipline, nothing serious but the normal reaction of bored troops spoiling for a fight.

They had expected a stronger reaction from the Australians but, since the F-111s came over nearly two months before, there had been no air activity other than his own. Jaswal was right; they were burning up aircraft for no particular purpose.

The Australians had sent in a small party, presumably to gather intelligence on the ground. They had killed one of them at a cost of two of his own men but the others—he assumed there had been others—had got away.

According to Nadkarni, New Delhi did not expect the Australians to react. His latest briefing had told him of the indecision in the Australian government. Satellite intelligence provided by their Soviet friends indicated a build-up of naval and air units in the north-west of Australia but assessed these as a response to the submarine campaign. There was no sign of any ground force build-upin Australia, at least according to the Russians.

He explained this to his companions. Jaswal was morose. "Bloody Russians. I suppose we can believe them?"

Sharma shared his colleague's reserve. As an Indian, he resented the dependence on the Soviets that his country had encouraged. Nevertheless, the intelligence was good.

Nadkarni explained that the Soviet intelligence was confirmed by their own diplomats in Canberra. "I can't understand why they have not thrown our high commissioner out of the country. Our people think the Australians are content to let us have the place.

"We will know soon. Their parliament is due to resume shortly. The government is split and the opposition is usually a pacifist party so we expect they will formally accept the new situation.

"Also, I should tell you", he went on, "that the government is now looking to reducing the garrison here, perhaps increasing the air strength and relieving your unit, colonel. The tentative time for relief is late October or early November when you will have been here six months."

The pilot wanted to go on the offensive."We should get some more aircraft in here, use some tankers and hit them, maybe at Learmonth, certainly on Christmas Island. For sure, if we ever see any tankers at either place, we should strike at them to cripple their air force."

Not for the first time, the soldier envied his colleague's ability to project his power over long distances. He himself could only sit and wait for the enemy to come to him. He looked at the pilot quizzically.

"Well, you aggressive young man, it depends on how far you want to push them. We have what we want and look like being allowed to keep it. There's no point in further aggravation just for the sake of it, is there?"

"But what about the shipping campaign? Aren't the Australians enraged about that?"

Sharma shrugged. "Apparently not. They have mounted defensive measures and they did sink one of our submarines. If they have any sense in New Delhi, they'll call it off now that they've made their point. Still", he shrugged with the usual soldier's contempt for the high command, "who can know what those silly beggars will do, eh?"

"So, we just sit it out here, do we?" Jaswal allowed a touch of bitterness to show.

"That's it, my friend, until October anyway. Look, why don't you cut out the patrols. Run a few exercises and keep the radar going but don't push yourselves. And don't worry about attacking the Australian bases. Not yet, anyway."

The pilot shrugged. "OK. Can we go back now? I could do with a shower."

Parliament House, Canberra

McDonald sat at his desk, chin in his hands, staring unseeing at the wall opposite. He was facing the biggest dilemma of his long political life. Every politician at some time or another faced some crisis of conscience, he knew. Politics was about choices. Some choices were easy to make. Some were bloody hard. Usually, though, pangs of conscience could be assuaged by going with the party line, the decision of the majority. It was easier for a junior backbencher but became progressively harder as the years went by.

In his years as Foreign Minister, he had rarely faced an issue where he was so clearly out of sympathy with his colleagues. In the past, though, he had gone with the tide of opinion, reluctant to fight over questions he had rationalised as being of marginal importance.

The Indians had shaken him out of that complacency. The Cocos question was different, dammit! It was about Australia's standing as a sovereign nation. It was about taking a stand against international lawlessness. As he pondered, he wondered at his conviction. He had never felt so certain about anything. He almost laughed at himself. Brian McDonald a patriot, he thought. No one will believe it!

Tomorrow afternoon when Parliament assembled for the Budget session, Newman would jump the gun and move no confidence in the government. Was this a challenge to his principles? He had never considered not supporting his party in a parliamentary vote before. Now he was torn between the two loyalties, to the party and to the community. Was he imagining a conflict, he wondered? There had never been one before. The old security blanket of party loyalty had deserted him. No matter how he struggled with himself in his mind, he was forced to recognise the speciousness of his attempts to justify loyalty to the party as some infallible expression of the popular majority. Was this intellectual arrogance, he wondered? But there was conflict in his mind. Which was the greater loyalty? Every argument went around in circles, facing him again and again with the same fundamental problem.

It was almost a relief when the 'phone rang. It was John Markham, a West Australian backbencher from his own party.

"Brian, can you spare me a few minutes with Ian Hicks if we come round?" Hicks was another backbencher, from the backblocks of Queensland. Both were members of the backbench Foreign Affairs and Defence Committee. Equally, both were regarded as moderately conservative.

Markham wasted no time. Ensconced in an armchair, he launched into his case even as McDonald poured drinks for the three of them. Hicks merely nodded agreement with his colleague.

"It's this no-confidence motion of Newman's, Brian. We know that Cabinet has gone to water over Cocos and we know you are opposed to the appeasement line. Now Ian and I are not prepared to support the government. Are you going to toe the party line or will you cross the floor?"

McDonald was startled. "Are you bloody mad? A minister vote against the government? It's unheard of."

"Unheard of or not, Brian, we intend to cross the floor. I'm not sure about anybody else. We've done no canvassing."

"Have you told anybody except me?", McDonald demanded.

"No. But we intend to at tomorrow morning's party meeting."
"D'you realise that if I go with you, it will bring down the government? We've only got that majority of four, you know?"

"That's right. We've thought of that. But we also believe that this is a basic issue. If this country knuckles under to this aggression, we'll never have any moral right to resist anything else.

"Look, Brian, everyone knows you have been holding out for a strong military response. If you resigned as Foreign Minister and lined up with us at the party meeting, we might force them to do something, even at this late stage. Neither of us want to do this but we're committed unless the government finds some backbone. You could give it to them."

It was politician's hyperbole, McDonald thought, but he does have a point. And it adds weight to what I was thinking about earlier. Is it the only way, he wondered?

Yet, even now, he was careful not to commit himself. He temporised, promising that they would have an answer before the House sat.

"Have you talked to Newman?", he asked.

"I told you. We haven't talked to anybody except you. We're not going to run to Bill Newman behind our colleagues' back. He can make what he can of it but he won't get my support without a commitment to do something. I'll resign from Parliament first."

As they talked, McDonald found his attitude hardening. They were right, he thought. We could do this in the party room tomorrow. But I'll hold off until I sniff the wind then.

Defence Headquarters, Canberra

The briefing room was crowded. Even the limited presentation by the Cocos planning staff required the presence of most of the operations, intelligence and logistics staff of the Defence Force Headquarters. The room was regularly debugged and a security team had swept it for listening devices only an hour earlier.

The Director, Joint Plans was a navy commodore. Dressed informally in navy blue jumper and slacks, the broad gold ring of his rank on each shoulder gleamed in the harsh fluorescent lighting. He stood behind a lectern facing the room. Behind him, most of the back wall was covered by a map showing the whole of the Australian continent and the eastern half of the Indian Ocean.

The door was suddenly opened by the military police guard who saluted smartly as McCarthy strode in, followed by Noble and Forbes. Everybody jumped to their feet, standing to attention as the three senior officers walked through to the front of the room.

"Thank you, ladies and gentlemen. Be seated, please." As he sat down, McCarthy nodded for the briefing to commence.

Commodore Davies picked up a pointer, checked his notes and began.

"Thank you, sir. Firstly, this briefing on what we are calling Operation Imperious is classified top secret. No notes are to be made and nothing that is said here is to be passed on to any other person without the direct authorisation of CDF.

"The planning staff have been tasked with producing a plan for the expulsion of Indian military and air forces from Cocos Islands. The plan is subject to revision and is not yet authorised by the government."

Davies opened by describing the political situation, the Indian strength on Cocos and mentioned what appeared to be a low key but lethal campaign against shipping, designed, he argued, to dissuade foreign shippers from using Australian ports.

"The basic plan requires air strikes against Cocos to neutralise the Indian air defence system. It is small but quite dangerous and our ability to mount an amphibious landing does require that we effectively prevent any Indian aerial intervention.

"The second element is to ensure that any attempt by the Indian navy to intervene or resupply their force on Cocos will be neutralised by submarine and surface interdiction.

"Finally, it will be necessary to put a brigade on shore with some armour to round up the Indian ground force."

He went on to outline the preparatory measures required.

"We expect to operate a squadron of Hornets out of Learmonth with tanker support. At least two tankers will be required; four would be better.

"We have no tanker support for the F-111 force. Unless we can acquire a KC-10 tanker from the Americans, it will be necessary to operate F-111s from Christmas Island. This will require some upgrading of the airfield there. Quantities of fuel, ammunition and spares would have to be stockpiled.

"In general, we expect current stocks of air-to-air and air-to-ground weapons to be adequate but recommend some further acquisitions from the United States in case the operation does not go according to plan.

"A maximum effort will be required from the navy. We will deploy two to four submarines against the Indian fleet. The FFGs will bear the burden of air defence against Indian carrier aircraft in the maritime exclusion zone around Cocos which we would expect to be proclaimed. They will also be required to handle any surface threat to the landing operation.

"The DDGs will be needed for local air defence of the landing force and naval gunfire support. Unfortunately they are the only ships with a sufficiently heavy gun armament for NGS unless we bring *Swan* and *Torrens* back from reserve.

"Naval ammunition stocks are already inadequate and additional supplies of missiles, both surface-to-air and surface-to- surface, as well as torpedoes and gun ammunition will be required.

"*Tobruk* will be the main element of the landing force. She is the only ship capable of putting armour and vehicles across the beach. There are no significant berthing facilities on Cocos so all troops will have to be landed across the beach or by helicopter.

"It will be necessary to requisition and modify civilian ships to carry personnel and stores. They will have to be fitted with helicopter decks and davits to handle landing craft. We are proposing to use Fremantle as the concentration point for the landing force.

"The army task is assigned to 3rd Brigade, the Operational Deployment Force. Fortunately, the logistics are not too complicated. Cocos is so small that only a minimal number of vehicles will be required. Four only tanks from 1st Armoured Regiment are proposed primarily to deal with a number of strong points which, we judge, would be largely immune to naval bombardment.

"The ODF must be brought up to full strength and be trained for amphibious operations, especially against opposition. Ammunition stocks will require augmentation.

"As well, it will be necessary to bring 1st Brigade up to full strength in the event that reinforcements are required. Once 3rd Brigade has landed, the ships will return immediately to load 1st Brigade should that be necessary.

"We assess, however, that subject to the interdiction of the Indian supply system and the destruction of their ability to operate aircraft from Cocos, the rest of the operation should be reasonably straightforward.

"Command will be exercised by Commander, Joint Forces Australia who will establish himself at HMAS *Stirling* near Fremantle and take command of all assigned forces as soon as the government approves the plan.

"There will be some considerable delay in implementing the plan. Collecting stores, taking up ships from the trade and refitting them, bringing ground force units up to strength and upgrading the airfield on Christmas mean it will be impossible to complete the operation before the beginning of the cyclone season in December. Therefore, we would not expect to actually commence military operations before April next year.

"Finally, there are some political considerations. We assume that a KC-10 will be made available by the United States. If that does not happen, the availability of the F-111 force is highly problematic.

"Second, the use of Christmas Island will require the tacit approval of the Indonesian government. If that is not forthcoming, our options are even more severely restricted.

"Lastly, there is an assumption based upon current intelligence estimates that the Indian government will not wish seriously to escalate the conflict. If that assumption is incorrect—and any assumption about political intentions must be tentative—then we do not have the resources on our own to resist effectively.

"Are there any questions?"

Discussion was brief and there were no significant alternatives offered. Quickly, McCarthy brought proceedings to a halt. Back in his office, the CDF conferred with his senior staff and Davies.

"What are the implications of this if we don't knock them over quickly?", he asked Noble.

The VCDF thought there would be serious manpower problems if conflict was sustained. As well, he suggested that attrition of equipment would quickly wear down their small force.

"Are there any alternatives? Couldn't we just keep up sustained air strikes to persuade them to go home. Or have the navy off-shore bombarding them?", McCarthy asked.

Forbes shook his head. "Certainly we could run air strikes for a while. It would wear down our force and be costly in ammunition but there is no guarantee that the enemy would call it quits. That sort of air offensive tends to make people more stubborn than otherwise. As for the navy, what do you think, Davies?" He turned to the planner.

"I couldn't recommend that, sir. We just don't have the ability to cover the ships from the air. It would be a gilt-edged invitation to the Indian Fleet to intervene with their carriers and submarines. We would have to put all our assets into defending our own ships with the odds stacked against us in my view."

"All right." McCarthy was resigned. "I'd better go over to Parliament House and tell our masters. They wanted to know the score before their party meeting in the morning. You'd better come with me, Davies, and answer questions if necessary."

Parliament House, Canberra—the next morning

The government party room was packed. There was a loud buzz of conversation as members discussed the latest rumours. Although it was

Budget day, almost the sole topic of conversation was the conflict with India and the growing tensions in the government. The *Canberra Advocate* that morning had speculated that some government members would defect unless a strong line was taken. Its editorial had actually urged party dissidents to cross the floor on the Opposition's foreshadowed no-confidence motion.

No one had named any dissidents and journalists were swarming in the corridors trying to identify the possibilities. Names were being bandied around usually on the basis of pure speculation. McDonald had managed to avoid making any statement, waving his tormentors away with a quiet refusal to comment. Some noted an unusually grim face for the normally genial Foreign Minister. He looked as though he had slept badly, if at all.

The buzz faded as Chapman entered and took his place as chairman. The doors were locked from the inside as the Prime Minister called for order.

With a wry smile, he announced that the first order of business would be the Indian invasion of Cocos. He asked Grayling to outline the essence of the military plan. The Defence Minister was brief. Without going into the specifics of the plan, he highlighted the cost and the inevitable delay. Cabinet had met during the night, he told them, and had decided the military option was not viable. The government would use its best efforts diplomatically to have the Indians withdraw.

There was immediate uproar. Markham was first on his feet and got Chapman's nod. "Mr Chairman, I move that Cabinet's decision be rejected and that the government give orders that the Australian Defence Force retake Cocos as soon as possible." Hicks put up his hand to second the motion.

Markham's speech was cold and cutting. The government was making not only the party but the whole country look pusillanimous. A small force of troops had walked in and taken over Australian territory and the Australian government was not prepared to do anything except issue a condemnatory press statement. Where would they draw the line, he wanted to know? Their craven behaviour was an exhortation to aggression.

McDonald watched his colleagues' faces as Markham spoke. Some of them squirmed. Many were puzzled. Most, he realised, saw the whole thing as just another aspect of the game of politics. Some were clearly angry, not so much at the Indians as at Markham's ferocity.

As the debate wore on, Chapman realised that he had the numbers. There were members who criticised the government, who backed Markham and Hicks, but who would not rock the boat. He wondered if the two ringleaders would indeed defect, if they had inspired the *Advocate*'s story that morning.

The debate raged for almost an hour. Eventually, Chapman called a halt. Time was getting on, he said. The Treasurer still had to brief members on the Budget. On the vote, Markham's resolution was lost 70-42.

McDonald watched as first Markham, then Hicks, got to their feet and announced their resignation from the government party. There was a shocked silence as they left the room.

McDonald, too, got to his feet—wearily. He asked Chapman's indulgence to make a brief statement.

"Prime Minister, colleagues. As you know, I have always supported the notion that our long-term national interest demanded that we use what force we could muster to expel the Indians from Cocos and show that we would not submit tamely to naked aggression.

"I have listened to interminable debates in Cabinet and to you, my colleagues, this morning. I understand the reluctance of those who fear to engage in what could be a bloody and expensive war. I understand those who say we cannot afford it. I understand those who say that we have to live with a populous and well-armed India.

"But in understanding, I cannot agree and I say to you that we cannot not afford it, nor can we be seen to submit weakly to naked aggression.

"I say with very great regret to my colleagues in Cabinet entrusted with the government of our country that you must not back away from the hard option of war. If you do not know how to make war, if you do not know when to make war and when not to make war, then you are not fit to govern.

"I cannot support this decision you have taken. It is wrong and it threatens the peace and long-term security of our people. You cannot put a price upon that as you might put a price on some new government programme. With the deepest regret, I must tender my resignation as Minister for Foreign Affairs and as a member of this parliamentary party."

Ignoring the expostulations of the others, he shook off those who tried to stop him and walked out of the room.

The Prime Minister's Office

Barney Gills walked into Chapman's office. The Prime Minister was sitting at his desk, munching a sandwich taken from a plate on his desk. Opposite sat Mark Woolmer, his deputy and Treasurer. He was in no mood for food but gulped nervously at a cup of coffee.

Gills' expression carried his message. "Brian won't deal." He explained. "I talked to him. He had Markham and Hicks with him and a million journos beating on the door. The three of them insist on our endorsing the military option as a price for their vote on the no-confidence motion."

"I can't do that", Chapman protested. "You saw the vote; it wasn't even close. Have they done any deal with Newman?"

"They say they haven't and I believe them. Brian says they'll sit on the cross benches. They'll vote with Labor but only if Newman makes a commitment to the military option."

"Will he?" Woolmer clutched at that straw. "Can he carry his pacifists when it comes to the crunch?"

"Yeah, I think so. He hasn't had any problem with them so far." Chapman nodded agreement.

"What about the Senate? He'd have to cope with the angries there?" Gill's contempt for the small group of alienated single-issue independents which held the balance of power in the upper house was well known.

Chapman shook his head. "He doesn't need Senate approval to invade Cocos. It's an Executive decision. Even if he had to come back to parliament to get extra money, could we oppose him?"

He answered his own question. "I can't see it. He'd simply go to the people with a double dissolution and we'd be done like a dinner on the Cocos issue."

He paused, looking from one to the other. "Can either of you see a way out of this mess? I'm damned if I can."

Woolmer agreed. Gills picked up a sandwich and took a bite. "That's about it, boss. We go in there and go through the motions. It's really a question of whether you want a slow or a quick death."

House of Representatives

And so it turned out. Chapman barely had time to announce his intention to act as Foreign Minister following McDonald's resignation when Newman jumped to his feet to move his no-confidence motion.

The galleries were packed but the members, sensing the historic nature of the occasion, were unusually quiet. The small group of rowdies on both sides traded noisy insults but without their usual enthusiasm.

McDonald sat quietly and without noticeable expression with Markham and Hicks. Occasionally, it was observed that they exchanged a few words.

For his part, Newman was reserved. He was well known for extravagant language and occasionally cruel attacks on his opponents. Today, he was statesmanlike, his oratory filling the chamber with a powerful denunciation of what he termed "this government's ineptitude and cowardice".

In turn, Chapman was wholly defensive. He stumbled over his speech as he justified the acceptance of the invasion of Cocos to avoid unnecessary bloodshed. In contrast to Newman's moralising, he presented the government's decision as the result of a proper balancing of profit and loss, on human as well as financial grounds. His argument was for pragmatism over principle, the tradition of recent governments. But his heart was not in it. He knew the numbers were against him, that the debate was no more than theatre.

McDonald did not speak. Nor did his fellow rebels. They were conscious that Gills would use any opportunity offered to force an uproar. The suspension from the Parliament of just one of them would save the government, however temporarily.

Eventually, tiring of the charade, Newman demanded a vote. The government was beaten by two votes.

Immediately, Chapman got to his feet and announced that he would see the governor-general and resign his commission. He suggested the House adjourn. There was no dissent.

In Newman's office, chaos reigned as aides struggled with shadow ministers to gain the leader's attention. All expected that Newman would shortly be summoned by the governor-general and commissioned to form a government.

Newman listened with only half an ear. They seemed to have forgotten about the three defectors, counting them as uncritical allies. He did not see them in that light and had to make a deal which would put him into government with some stability so as to avoid having to ask for an election. Eventually, he got rid of them and picked up the 'phone to call McDonald.

The amenities were dispensed with quickly. He knew better than to flatter McDonald. He could guess at the emotional turmoil the man was suffering. Instead, he was blunt.

"Can I count on you three to support me if the G-G gives me the nod?", he wanted to know.

McDonald was equally forthright. Outlining the military plan, he spelled out his conditions.

"If you undertake to retake Cocos and do so quickly, a bloody sight quicker than the soldiers say, we'll back you. Any other programmes, we'll look at on their merits. That I promise." He looked at the two men sitting on the other side of his desk. They nodded. "I have Markham and Hicks with me here and they have confirmed their agreement."

Newman indicated that he understood. "You'll have no argument on Cocos. As far as the rest goes, I'm prepared to take over Chapman's Budget just so long as we get the money through. We can fine-tune it as we go along."

He paused. "You know I won't be able to offer you a job. The party rules won't allow it. But I hope we can consult a lot and use some of your diplomatic contacts."

He hung up as an aide put his head in the door. "The G-G would like to see you in half-an-hour, boss. I've told his office you'll be there.

CHAPTER 13

Parliament House, Canberra

It was later the same night. As staffers struggled to pack up files to move Newman's office into the Prime Minister's suite, the new PM conferred with two of his senior colleagues.

"I can't wait while we go through the process of electing a new ministry", he told his deputy and trusted political adviser, Len Darby, and shadow defence minister, Clem Taylor. "Most of the jobs can wait but you two are certain to be elected so we'll get things running on the Cocos scene straight away. Now, I'm going to be my own defence minister until the business is resolved. Clem, I want you to be my backup and look after the detail for the time being."

As Taylor nodded, he went on. "Len, I want you to be Foreign Minister. We need to get started right away on building up some support for what we need to do. Get McLeod in and work out a plot for us as the interim Cabinet to look at."

He bellowed to the outer office. "Is that directive ready yet?"

His chief of staff came in with a paper, closely followed by the CDF. Newman greeted McCarthy briefly before snatching the paper and reading it through. Satisfied, he scrawled his signature on the bottom, then looked up with a smile.

"Sorry, general," he apologised. "Please sit down. I think you know my colleagues." They exchanged brief pleasantries and Newman outlined his new ministerial arrangements.

"All right, let's get to business. General, I've heard about your plan to recover Cocos. I don't particularly want to know the details. That's your job. What I have got for you is a directive from me as Minister for Defence."

McCarthy took the proffered document. It was brief, only three paragraphs, and to the point.

MINISTERIAL DIRECTIVE FROM PRIME MINISTER AND
MINISTER FOR DEFENCE TO CHIEF OF DEFENCE FORCE

You are forthwith to organise and conduct such military operations as are necessary to expel Indian forces from the Australian territory of Cocos Islands. These operations are to be concluded by the beginning of the cyclone season this year.

Concurrently, you will assure the security of all merchant ships trading with Australian ports for such distances as are deemed operationally necessary.

You are to consult with me on any matters affecting foreign relations or additional resources required to implement this directive.

G.W. Newman
Prime Minister
20th August, 19..

McCarthy finished reading and looked up.

"Can you do it?", Newman demanded.

McCarthy smiled, ruefully. "You don't want much, do you, sir? I can't give you a guarantee. I think we can do the job but it will cost a lot."

"Yeah, well you leave the money and the politics to me. You just do the soldiering."

He turned to Darby. "Do we need a National Security Act to give us the necessary powers? And, if we do, can we get it through parliament?"

Darby thought it wasn't necessary. "I don't see a problem at this stage. If we need to, I think we can get it through pretty quickly. Chapman's people might want to put some conditions on it but I can't see them fighting too hard."

"OK. Let's talk about some political strategies."

Cocos Islands

Sharma mopped his face with a towel as the PT session ended and his men dispersed to their breakfasts. The early morning workout coupled with a run along the length of the airfield kept them all in peak condition. He saw Nadkarni walking towards him and waited on the edge of the parking apron.

"Good morning, Vivek. You should join us for the exercise."

"Thank you, colonel, but I doubt if my poor body would stand the exertion. A brisk walk before breakfast is enough to put an edge on my appetite. However, I have an invitation for you. I am to lunch with the president over on Home Island and he has asked that you come with me."

Later that morning as the boat took them across the harbour to Home Island, Nadkarni passed on the latest news that had come in that morning.

"Perhaps your headquarters have informed you as well?", he enquired. As Sharma shook his head, he went on, "There has been a change of government in Australia. The Prime Minister was defeated in a no confidence vote. Three of his hardliners defected and there is now a new government committed to retaking these islands. I think you may have a fight on your hands."

Sharma shrugged. "That's what we get paid for. It won't be too easy for them provided we are backed up here. What about Rahmani?"

"The president is enjoying life. He has moved into the old Clunies-Ross house which he calls his palace. He has grandiose plans for a new mosque and wants us to give him the money in advance of the Australian indemnity.

"Apart from that, his advent has not had much effect. The people generally ignore him although there are rumblings of discontent because their income from the Australian government has dried up. It's not very serious and so long as you have some soldiers over there, nothing much will happen, at least for a time."

Sharma grunted acknowledgement. He was not happy having his men used as policemen but there was little he could do about it.

He was not particularly concerned about the new Australian government. He would ask his headquarters for an intelligence update but there was no cause to panic yet.

Parliament House - Canberra

Darbywelcomed McLeod into what had been Brian McDonald's office. The two men knew each other well and got right down to business. McLeod handed over two documents which had been prepared late the previous night after a 'phone call from the new minister. Darby read them through carefully before signing them with his neat, almost pedantic signature.

"Who have we got first?", he asked.

"Natarajan's first cab off the rank. Thought I'd get the easy one out of the way. He was very curious when I called this morning but I left him in the dark. He's due now."

The Indian High Commissioner was wary as he was ushered into the office. He was introduced formally to Darby but his over-effusive greeting was received with studied coldness. Darby was cool and unemotional. "Please be seated, Mr Natarajan. I have here a note from my government for your government. Would you please read it."

Natarajan took the proffered paper and read it quickly. The half-smile was replaced by a shocked expression. It read:

The Government of the Commonwealth of Australia presents its compliments to the Government of the Republic of India.

The Australian government requires that the Indian government end its illegal occupation of the Australian territory of Cocos (Keeling) Islands in the Indian Ocean forthwith.

The Australian government further notes that Indian war vessels have carried out attacks upon Australian war vessels and merchant ships engaged in innocent trade contrary to the International Conventions on the Law of the Sea.

The Australian government considers the Indian invasion of Cocos (Keeling) Islands and military attacks upon innocent merchant vessels and national vessels of Australia to be acts of war incompatible with the maintenance of proper relations between sovereign states.

The Australian government reserves the right to protect its interests against this unprovoked aggression in accordance with Article 51 of the Charter of the United Nations.

In the existing circumstances, the Australian government is not prepared to welcome the High Commissioner for India in Australia.

The High Commissioner and his staff have been informed that they are to leave Australia within 72 hours from delivery of this Note.

Upon withdrawal of Indian forces from the Cocos (Keeling) Islands and the cessation of attacks upon merchant ships trading with Australia, the Australian government would be prepared to discuss the restoration of normal relations between our two countries.

The document concluded in formal diplomatic language by expressing Australia's high esteem for India. Diplomatic throat-cutting is an extraordinarily polite business, Darby ruminated.

He held up his hand as Natarajan opened his mouth.

"This is not a matter for discussion, Mr Natarajan. Any matters relating to your departure may be discussed with Mr McLeod who will also return your passports and credentials.

"In the meantime, I have to inform you that a guard will be placed upon your offices and residences. Neither you nor members of your staff or their families are permitted to leave them for any reason without Mr McLeod's permission and an escort will be provided in every instance."

He rose to indicate that the one-sided interview was concluded. Natarajan wanted to protest but was cut off, bluntly.

"Mr. Natarajan", Darby said, "there is nothing to discuss. I hope we may be able to welcome you back soon. But that is a matter for your government. Good morning."

As McLeod returned after seeing the Indian out, he grinned at his minister. "That'll burn up the wires to New Delhi", he commented. "Now, Ivan next? He's in the waiting room."

160

"Yeah, wheel him in."

Dmitri Sulkov was Chargé d'Affaires at the Soviet Embassy in the absence of his ambassador on leave. McLeod knew he was in fact the KGB Resident and had quickly briefed the new minister about the head of Soviet intelligence in Australia. Sulkov was a throwback to the old-fashioned Soviet operative, ill-dressed, ill-mannered and aggressive.

Back in the 1980s when the Soviets had been wooing Australia, they had staffed their embassy with a much more cosmopolitan team. Even the spies had been gentlemen in those days, McLeod recalled.

When the wooing had failed to detach Australia from the Western alliance, the Soviets had reverted to type. Sulkov was a good example.

"He's just an old-fashioned Soviet cop", McLeod had said. "He's more interested in spotting and terrorising dissidents in the emigré communities than anything else."

"Mr Sulkov", Darby opened after greeting his visitor, "my government has received disturbing reports of Soviet aircraft and ships conducting intelligence missions against Australian forces. Please", he held up his hand as the diplomat began his ritual protest, "you and I both know that these are facts. I merely wish to inform you that because of impending military operations by Australian forces and because of the special relationship enjoyed by the Soviet Union with India, there may be a danger that your units could become confused with Indian units.

"As you are no doubt aware, it would be possible for Indian forces to disguise themselves as Soviet units to gain an advantage over our forces. We are not prepared to put our people at such a disadvantage.

"It is therefore my earnest advice that you recommend to your government that any Soviet units operating close to Australia be withdrawn to ensure that no unfortunate mistakes are made."

Sulkov protested vigorously. Of course, that was to be expected, McLeod thought. It was all part of diplomatic ritual. What was really surprising was the toughness being shown by the new government although, he admitted to himself, all new governments start out aggressively, implementing the ideas they have had time to develop in opposition. It was later when they bogged down in day-to- day detail that they ran out of steam.

After the Russian had left, he asked Darby if he really meant his warning.

"We'll have to see", was the answer. "Of course, we can't do anything about their satellite snooping but I don't see why we have to put up with the Bear flights or that bloody trawler."

"You mean 'Snoopy'?"

Darby nodded. "We could arrest him for illegal fishing in the Exclusive Economic Zone. Set him free after the event and blame it on a junior officer's zeal." He grinned. "Highly illegal but it would make the point, don't you think?

"All right then, what's next on the agenda?"

United Nations, New York

Barbara McKinnon smiled to herself. It was going well, she thought. Sudjono, the Indonesian, had been nagging at her for weeks, asking what Australia was going to do about Cocos. Now at least, she had something positive to say. She looked at the slight, youngish looking Indonesian as he sipped his coffee. "As you are no doubt aware, Mr Sudjono, the new government in Australia has decided to expel Indian forces from Cocos. Our people in Canberra have undoubtedly discussed this with your government but I have not heard what the response is yet."

"Oh, I can tell you that, Barbara. As you know, we have been very concerned about the Indian presence on Cocos and we are pleased that you have decided at last to do something about it.

"My government has indicated to Canberra that it is prepared to publicly condemn the Indian invasion of Cocos. We will provide some escorts for convoys between Indonesian territorial waters and Australian ports if that is considered to be necessary and we will support any declaration of a maritime exclusion zone around Cocos.

"I have discussed this with my colleagues from the other members of ASEAN and they agree with us."

McKinnon felt a wave of relief wash over her. She put her next question. "I have been instructed by my government to seek a condemnation of the Indian aggression by the Security Council. Indonesia is of course a member of the Council at this time. Will you be supporting us?"

Sudjono did not hedge. "Yes, of course. And I will encourage other members of the Council to support you. Let us get it done quickly."

The Prime Minister's Office, Canberra

Arnold Buckmaster had been United States Ambassador in Canberra for just over a year. Appointed by President Forrest, he was a political appointee but one who had proved popular and effective. Indeed, Fred Soulsby had been heard to complain only half in jest that Australia had two ambassadors to the United States and Buckmaster was one of them.

He had met Newman several times but not since the change of government. As he was ushered into the Prime Minister's office, he saw that Newman was accompanied by Darby and the CDF, McCarthy. A high-powered meeting, he reflected.

The atmosphere was relaxed and friendly. Buckmaster registered the thought that for once the Australians were taking the initiative instead of having to be pushed. He waited for Newman to spell out what he wanted.

"Arnie, as you might imagine, we've got a shopping list of equipment, mostly ammunition and spares. This has been signalled to Washington and we've put the list into your normal supply channels as well."

Buckmaster glanced at the list McCarthy handed him. It was not long but the quantities were substantial. "I don't see any problem with this, Prime Minister. It's all stuff that has been cleared before and which you use routinely."

"OK, thanks—and call me Bill. Now, we are going to declare a 200 nautical mile exclusion zone around Cocos. The Indonesians have told us they are quite relaxed about that and will step up surveillance in

163

their own waters and up to the zone. I think we can expect some leaks of intelligence they might gather.

"What we need to know is what your Indian Ocean force will be doing while we go in to take Cocos back."

Before the American could answer, McCarthy interposed with a smile. "What we'd really like, Arnie, is for your carrier battle group in the Indian Ocean to conduct some operations outside the zone but between Cocos and India at the critical time—just to dissuade the Indians from resupplying their force, and to help us out with some intelligence."

The American paused before answering. "Well, gentlemen, I hear what you say. It sounds like a great idea to me but the OK for that is going to have to come from the President. I'll send it on with my recommendation but I'd get your boys in Washington to start working on our people over there, especially Bill Rauchberger. He's on your side. How soon d'you need to know?"

At a nod from Newman, McCarthy answered. "We plan on going in early to mid-November. I can't give you a better date at this time because we don't know ourselves yet. But we do need to know by not later than mid-September if you will do it."

Buckmaster made a note. "OK, I'll see what I can do. Anything else?"

"Yeah. What we badly need is a KC-10 tanker. We can buy or lease but we want to be able to put it into Australian colours and we'd want it as early as possible so we can get the F-111 boys trained to use it."

"Fine. I'll put it in the list. I'd better get moving if we're to stir our bureaucrats along."

Newman wrapped up the meeting. "Len is going over to New York to front our UN Security Council complaint against India. He leaves later today. Is there any chance he can get to see the President to put our case?"

The American nodded. "Good idea. Leave it to me. I'll fix it, no problem."

The United Nations, New York

Barbara McKinnon sat behind Darby as he faced the Security Council seated around its horseshoe-shaped table. The delegates were stony-faced, giving nothing away.

Darby had asked for a condemnation of the Indian invasion of Cocos. He had presented evidence that Indian submarines had attacked merchant shipping as well as invading Cocos.

His principal argument had been that the General Assembly resolution had not given India authority to invade the islands. As well, he pointed out that the very small vote with a greater number of abstentions on the Assembly vote had effectively denied it any validity as an expression of world opinion.

He argued strongly that India had engaged in outright aggression. Its alleged justification in supporting the Cocos Liberation Front was specious. He insisted that the CLF was no more than a tool of expansionist politicians in New Delhi.

He concluded by warning the Council that if it failed to act, Australia would assert its right under Article 51 of the UN Charter to the defence of its own territory.

Gupta was now speaking for India. In its essentials, the speech relied upon the General Assembly resolution which had rejected Australia's legitimacy in the islands. He dodged the issue of shipping attacks by denying the admittedly tenuous evidence presented by Darby.

McKinnon looked up as one of her staff came in and passed her a note. She skimmed it quickly before leaning forward to whisper in Darby's ear.

"Sudjono says we have the numbers all sewn up. He and the Malaysians have been talking to the Moslem countries arguing that we will be better protectors of Moslem religious rights than the Indians. That ties up all the Afro-Asian bloc except China. The Americans have fixed it with the Danes and the Latin Americans. We have no problem with the Brits or the French. That only leaves the Chinese, Soviets and the Czechs."

"Any idea how they'll vote?", Darby asked. She shrugged. "The Chinese are unlikely to vote for India. At worst, I think they'll abstain.

My guess is the Soviets will use their veto against us. They just don't want to alienate New Delhi. The Czechs will go with the Soviets."

"So, we lose?, he commented.

"Only on a veto. It will be a moral victory for us. The UN won't do anything concrete but they never have in the face of a permanent member's veto. It does mean we'll have a free hand to do what we want. It's the best we could get."

And so it turned out. As she predicted, Arbutov added another *nyet* to the Soviet's abysmal record in the Security Council. The Chinese contributed nothing to the debate and abstained. The final vote was 9-2 in favour of Australia's complaint but the Soviet veto prevented the Council from taking any action.

Later that day, Gupta rang McKinnon while Darby was still with her. She put the call on the speaker so he could listen in.

"Barbara, where do we go now?" he asked, smooth as ever.

"I think we are effectively at war, S.K.," she said, looking over at the minister. He nodded. "We are reserving our rights to self-defence under Article51", she went on. "I'm not privy tomy government's strategy on this but there is certain to be a military dimension to it. What form that will take I simply don't know." Not that I'd tell you if I did, she thought.

"Can we do a deal?", he wanted to know. Again she glanced at Darby. He shook his head.

"You've got one option only, S.K. Get your people off Cocos and stop the attacks on shipping. Tell New Delhi the gamble has failed. You should get out and cut your losses. You've already lost a submarine and its crew and the price is going to rise."

ACTU Headquarters, Melbourne

Stan Reeves was ushered into the President's office. He knew both men in the room. Charlie Stein had been head of the national trade union organisation for three years and he had day to day dealings with him as Federal Secretary of his Seamen's Union. Charlie was a factional opponent within the Labour Party but they got on in a pragmatic sort of way.

By contrast, the other man, David Rubens, was another right winger but a hardliner. He worked for the Federal Transport Minister who was himself one of the right wing's number crunchers. Their greeting was cool.

Stein got down to business with little preamble. "Stan, the government is going to requisition a number of ships to support military operations against the Indians. We need to know if you are going to make waves."

Reeves looked from one to the other. His union had been ideologically aligned with the Soviets for more than half a century and the Soviet Union was India's ally. If he went along with the government, he would have real problems with his Committee of Management. He could even lose his job. On the other hand, he knew the government had both the electorate and the media on its side. He temporised.

"What's in it for my members?"

Rubens answered that one. "They'll be looked after. There'll be a generous war zone allowance, compensation for death or injury and they'll be eligible for all veteran's entitlements if they operate in a designated war zone."

"And if they won't?" he asked.

"It's a job for volunteers, same as for the military. But we won't cop the union pulling the men out. Let me spell it out for you. The government wants to do this job quick and clean but it will do it regardless. If your members man the ships, they'll be looked after. If the union pulls any funny stuff, we'll go into parliament for a National Security Act, disband the union and draft the men into the navy. Don't forget they'll get a lot less pay as naval ABs than as merchant service seamen. And if they refuse duty, they'll be treated as mutineers."

Reeves was appalled. "You wouldn't bloody dare! You call yourself a Labor man, you bastard."

Stein intervened. "He means it, Stan. And the ACTU will back the government."

After that, there was nothing more to be said. Reeves left, wondering how to tell his committee.

167

The White House, Washington

Darby was ushered into the Oval Office. Although he had seen it in photographs often enough, it nevertheless overawed him. Forrest came round from behind the desk to greet him warmly. He was a tall man, lean and fit looking. But his hair had turned white during his term in office. His face was puffy too, and his skin had an unnatural flush beneath the tan.

Soulsby made the introductions. Danowski was the only other person present and he poured drinks for them as they relaxed in easy chairs around a small table.

Forrest lifted his drink in a toast. "Well, Mr Darby, I hear you guys are going to kick the Indians off your islands?"

Darby grinned. "We'll give it our best shot, Mr President. We're taking on a pretty big military power but we think we have a good chance."

Forrest picked up a sheet of paper. "I guess you need some hardware too. This list is pretty impressive."

"It's mostly ammunition. We've been relying on being able to build up war stocks as we needed the stuff. I hope there's no problem."

The president was dismissive. "It's already on the way, Mr Darby, and by air too. I guess you need it in a hurry. We'll talk about the bill some other time. Just put it to good use. Now what else is there?"

"We were hoping that your Indian Ocean force might put on a demonstration between India and Cocos at the right time, just to discourage any heavy intervention or resupply."

"Yeah. Y'know, that caused a bit of argument around here. The Indians got a bit uptight back there in 1971 when we sent a carrier into the Bay of Bengal. They still moan about it."

Darby's heart sank. He could see the refusal coming. The request was crucial to their success. He opened his mouth to speak but Forrest beat him to it.

"Look, in my opinion, that's all crap. That's just the Indians trying to push us around. I don't like it and I won't permit it. I had a talk to Admiral Rose out there in Hawaii at CINCPAC and he reckons he can do it, by accident sort of. All you need to do is give him about two weeks warning of your critical dates. And talk to our people down there in Canberra about where you want them.

"Remember though", he went on, "it is only a bluff. If the Indians call it, there's not much we can do except get out of the way."

Darby's gratitude was brushed aside. "As far as I'm concerned", Forrest said, "you guys are sticking up for all of us. We're hamstrung a fair bit and I guess you understand that. But we're on your side and we'll help all we can.

"Now that's the good news. The bad news is we can't let you have that KC-10. You tell him, Pete."

Danowski leaned forward. "It's like this. We can let you have all the ammunition and spares because that's all tied up in formal agreements. We can tell CINCPAC to co-operate because he's got his own programme and we can make it look like an accident. But the KC-10 is a new thing. It's not on order and there's no formal agreement. If we let you have the 'plane now, it would look like direct intervention in your problem.

"That direct intervention is something we can't manage. Partly it's the Indians. They don't have much of a lobby here but it does exist. The main problem is Congress. The president is up for election in November and the campaign is well under way, as I guess you've noticed. Now the president's party does not control the House and those guys over on Capitol Hill are spoiling for a fight.

"We want to be able to fight them on our issues and win. And, of course, we want to win that election. But ever since Nixon and Watergate and Vietnam, Congress has been restricting the president's authority on foreign policy and on military intervention.

"In my view, and the president agrees, we just could not win. Sorry, but that's the way it is."

Forrest resumed. "The other bad news is that Fred here had a talk to the Indian ambassador, to see if we could broker some sort of deal to get them off the islands. But they won't play ball. Told us it was none of our business. I guess that made it a bit harder to let you have the plane as well."

Darby professed himself as satisfied. And, deep down, he was. McCarthy thought they could manage without the tanker. They had a guarantee of the supplies and the US naval exercises would be important. But Forrest had one more offer.

"What we did tell the Indians was that we would not tolerate their interference with merchant shipping. That is consistent with one of our traditional principles on freedom of the seas. They know that. Congress knows it too, and supports it. My people think they'll back off on that.

"Now you go home and tell your people that if they don't and if there are any more attacks on normal trade, all you have to do is whistle and we'll come running with escorts, P-3s and whatever you want."

Darwin

HMAS *Yarra* was tied up to Fort Hill Wharf. The self-maintenance period was complete and tomorrow morning, the ship would sail for Fremantle to join the units gathering for the attack on Cocos. Bellano had not seen the operational orders yet but he expected to be used for long-range surveillance against any approach by the Indian navy.

Today though was special with thoughts of war a long way away. Using an old ship's bell from the first HMAS *Yarra*, a World War I torpedo boat destroyer, an Army chaplain from Larrakeyah Barracks was baptising his new daughter.

A surprising number of his crew were present on the helicopter deck aft. The younger ones were off enjoying a perfect Darwin Sunday afternoon but there was a strong contingent of his older officers and the chiefs and petty officers.

Anne stood close beside him and he wrapped his arm around her waist. It had not been a comfortable pregnancy for her in Darwin's heat but the actual birth a week ago had been smooth and uncomplicated. Getting used to it, she claimed. She loved these occasions when the navy demonstrated its unity as a family as much as a force.

Now they watched, communing silently, proudly, with each other as their eldest daughter, Margaret, played godmother to her baby sister. She was having difficulty controlling her emotions. Awe was mixed with giggles as Father O'Connell, a fairly typical Army chaplain, inserted his own special brand of casual good humour into the solemn service.

And then to the climax as he trickled the water over the baby's head: "Catherine Anne, I baptise you in the name of the Father, and of the Son, and of the Holy Spirit."

Later there were the congratulations with the new daughter the centre of attraction, holding court with mother and godmother playing ladies-in-waiting. And his three senior chiefs making their own contribution, a polished steel christening mug made in the ship's workshop and engraved with its crest.

The coxswain was spokesman. "It's still got to have her name engraved, Mrs Bellano. We couldn't get the boss to tell us what her name was so we had to wait until today to find out. But we'll give it to him as soon as it's done and he can bring it back."

She was more serious than usual. Quietly she thanked them. "Just make sure you all come back."

Neutral Bay, Sydney

Old Mrs Drubny was a favourite of her neighbours in the small block of flats in Baden Road. A widow in her seventies, she was still spry enough to walk up the three flights of stairs to her flat with its view of the city across Sydney Harbour. Not that she went out much. She had two sons living in Sydney with their wives and her grandchildren. They called from time to time and took her out. Neighbours called in for a cup of coffee and a chat but she kept pretty much to herself otherwise.

Mrs Drubny had a problem though. She had lived in fear ever since that man from the Czech consulate had come to see her. He told her he was from the StB, the dreaded Czech secret police. Her daughter, he had told her, was well. Magda had married in Czechoslovakia. Her husband was no good. She had never liked him but Magda was her daughter and Magda's children were her grandchildren.

The man from the StB had made it clear that Magda's well-being depended upon her mother's co-operation. Nothing much, he had said. From your flat, you can see the naval base at Garden Island and the submarine base at Neutral Bay. All you have to do is call this number every morning and tell the man who answers how many ships are there. He even gave her a simple code to make it sound like an order to the butcher—so many chops, so many sausages and so on. It was easy. Do it and Magda and the children would be all right. What choice did an old lady have?

This morning, all the ships were gone, except for one she could see in the big dry dock. There were no submarines either at the wharf on the other side of Neutral Bay. Sadly, she called the number and told the man who answered she did not want any meat today. "No chops?" he asked. "No sausages?"

"No, nothing", she answered, and hung up. In a locked room at the Czech consulate, the man put down the 'phone and looked at his colleague. "They've all gone except the FFG in refit. They must have sailed last night. Better put it on the wire to Canberra straight away." His colleague was blasé. "The satellites will pick them up. I'll bet they've gone west. They are going to hit the Indians."

Not far from Mrs Drubny's flat in an underground room, the ASIO technician took off his headset and rewound the tape on his recorder. He looked across at the field officer at the other desk who had also been listening.

"What d'you think?", he asked.

"That's enough to get them expelled, for sure. It's a clear case of espionage. We can put it together with the tapes over, what, the past three months and the voice prints that identify that shit of a deputy consul-general. Even those wet bastards down in Canberra who don't want to upset anybody can't weasel their way out of this."

"What about the old girl? Will they charge her?"

"Nah, not a chance. We'll have a talk to her and find out what they had over her. If it's a relative—and it probably is—we might try to get them out. But once we stop that operation, they won't try to start it up again. They'll put it down to experience and look somewhere else."

Cocos Islands

Sharma stood on the edge of the apron as Jaswal joined him. They could hear the helicopter but could not see it beyond the trees.

"What on earth do we want a helicopter for, Devan?" Sharma wanted to know.

"No idea, colonel. It's a navy machine, a Sea King from the *Viraat*. She must have come in close enough to launch the helo and is now getting out to sea again." Jaswal was referring to the aircraft carrier purchased from the British some ten years earlier.

He pointed. "Here she comes."

The big grey painted helicopter with the orange, white and green roundels landed not far from where the two men stood. As the engines spooled down and the rotors slowed, a young navy lieutenant in green overalls climbed down from the cockpit and walked over to the two officers.

He saluted Sharma. "Good morning, sir. Reporting for duty. I am Lieutenant Mishra."

"Good morning, Mr Mishra." Sharma introduced Jaswal who promptly asked the question.

"What are you here for?"

"Ah well, sir, my aircraft has been modified as an airborne early warning helicopter. The idea is to get up to my operating ceiling and give you a better all-round radar coverage than you can get from the CRU.

"It's a scheme the British used in the Falklands and it is quite useful. I can give you maybe 200 miles all round compared with 100 that you would be getting now."

Jaswal laughed. "Well, sailor, we can certainly use you for that if you can stay up there long enough. But I hope you don't hang around when the Hornets are buzzing or you'll be badly stung. Let's go and get you and your crew settled in."

CHAPTER 14

Defence Headquarters - Canberra

Fennessy and Pender arrived together, having flown from Sydney in the same aircraft. Neither knew the reasons for the summons but speculated, from its urgency, that it had something to do with the planned Cocos operations.

As they got out of the car they had shared from RAAF Base, Fairbairn, they paused to look across Lake Burley Griffin to Parliament House, seemingly dug into Capitol Hill. Spring was just around the corner and already Canberra's famed blossom trees splashed their soft pastel colours across the Parliamentary triangle.

Frost still spangled the grass where the sun had yet to penetrate the shadows. Above Parliament House, the huge Australian flag drooped in the still air, its dark blue fabric a stark contrast to the pale blue sky.

"Too nice a day to go to war, Mike." Commodore George Fennessy gazed appreciatively at the peaceful scene.

Brigadier Mike Pender grunted. He did not like Canberra, preferring the harsh reds and deep blue skies of the northern deserts. Glancing at his watch, he turned towards the main entrance to the Russell Offices where a young ADC waited for them.

The young man saluted and handed each officer a VIP pass to clip to his uniform. Then, guiding them past the guards, they entered the lift which ground its way to the third floor.

Turning right after leaving the lift, they were taken to the CDF's suite and shown into his conference room.

McCarthy welcomed the two and introduced them to the others. Noble was there with Peter Forbes and Davies, the planner. A young sergeant, McCarthy's secretary, took coffee orders and disappeared.

The room was dominated by the long inlaid timber conference table. Padded chairs were set along each side while another was placed at the head. Maps of the eastern Indian Ocean and of Cocos Islands were mounted on mobile displays along one side wall while a small lectern was placed close by.

The morning sun blazed through the double-glazed windows whose venetian blind inserts were angled to reduce but not shut out the glare. The dark blue heavy drapes made a pleasing contrast with the soft grey carpet. The other side wall was panelled in light-coloured veneer broken by three small paintings, all of military scenes, loaned from the National War Museum.

At McCarthy's invitation, the men took their places at the table. He wasted no time getting down to business.

"George, you're relieved from your current job. As of today, you're appointed Commander Task Force 325. Your responsibility will be to Phil as Commander Joint Forces Australia to transport landing forces to Cocos, put them ashore and defend the beachhead against any attempt by the Indians to intervene.

"Mike, you will retain your appointment as 3 Bde Commander but your primary job is to retake Cocos. I want you to leave your deputy in charge up there in Townsville while you and George work down here with Phil to develop your plan.

"As soon as we have got something workable, I want you to pick your staff and move over to HMAS *Stirling* in the West and run your operation from there.

"Phil will handle the air side of things through a subordinate formation we'll create at Learmonth and he'll also move to the West with you.

"You'll have whatever force you need subject only to Ian Cartwright's requirements for shipping protection in the north-west.

"The only stipulation I have is that the job has to be done by the end of November. So you've got three months. In normal circumstances, it won't be enough time so you'll have to do the impossible.

"OK. Let's start reworking the original plan." He turned to the Joint Plans Director. "Davies!"

HMAS *Stirling*, Garden Island

The two men were sharing an office in the operations centre. It was better that way, they had decided. Problems could be solved or disputes within their planning staff could be settled much more quickly.

The planning staff worked together in the main operations room. There were six of them, drawn from all three services, and they had been working in shifts around the clock since their arrival four days before.

It was almost midnight when Fennessy yawned, stretched and relaxed suddenly. "Time to call it a day, Mike. Can we have a quick look at what we've got so far?"

Pender agreed. "All right. You've got to move my people and their gear so let me just spell out what we need.

"First, numbers. I'm going to use something less than two battalions, say 700 men. That's the infantry force. Add to that two Leopard tanks and four Scorpion MICVs plus six Landrovers mounting 106mm recoilless rifles. I want to use six APCs mainly to carry ammunition and other stores, as well as evacuate wounded.

"That makes 12 vehicles that must go in across the beach. The Landrovers, at a pinch, could be lifted in by helicopter.

"I'll be relying on you sailors plus the armoured vehicles for artillery. We'll leave the guns behind.

"I want to put the main body, a battalion, ashore across the beach here at Rumah Baru on West Island." He used a pencil to make his points on the map spread out on the desk between them.

"According to the map, there is a track from there that joins the main road along the length of West Island. SAS intelligence says they don't have any fixed positions there but it is patrolled. If we can get in there, I can split their two main bodies. They have about 200 men camped up around the fuel tanks and radio masts.

"The other group, about 300 in all, is concentrated down around the quarantine station and the airfield.

"Now, I want to stop them getting away into the plantations south of the airfield so I want to put the balance of my force ashore by helicopter in this open ground near the old quarry. It's a narrow neck and they'll be sitting astride the road.

"According to the SAS, they've got a blocking position there but it's not manned. We have to assume that they'll man it up as soon as we arrive. I want our people to go in between the block and the southern end of the airstrip, deal with the block first and then turn about to stop any escape into the plantations.

"My force will be two platoons, about 60 men, plus two of the 106 launchers. You say you won't be able to land them there through the surf so we'll have to do it by helicopter. That means about eight loads for the first lift if we give them some Milan ATGW as well.

"All that assumes that we've knocked out their aircraft and that you can give us whatever fire support we need when we need it. If it goes according to plan, I don't see that we have too big a job. They'll fight hard but, on these small islands, they've got nowhere to go.

"Against that, I've got to make sure we have enough backup of men and stores in case they are resupplied and it takes longer than I expect."

The commodore nodded. "Right! Our problem is to get you there, put you ashore, provide fire support, keep you supplied and take off your casualties.

"There is a good anchorage there but it is a bit close in. We'll need to suppress any shore fire very quickly.

"At a pinch, we could do all the transfers outside but there's nowhere to anchor. It's far too deep and we'd have to unload under way. In any sort of seaway, we could have losses and breakdowns we can't really afford.

"We'll use *Tobruk* as our main unit. She'll be headquarters ship and hospital ship as well. She's got four landing craft of her own and effectively two helicopter decks. We'll put your Landrovers for the blocking force in her and fly them ashore.

"For the same reason, we'll put the troops for the blocking force in her."

"What about the tanks? Won't you land them from *Tobruk* across the beach?"

"Bit tricky, Mike. There's not much water inside the lagoon and I just can't bring her in close enough.

"No. I think I'll put all your armour and the other Landrovers into a couple of our LCHs. They're slow and not too good in any sort of sea."

He paused. "I want to be sure you understand this. If you want your tanks, we must use the LCHs. We can put them on the beach inside the lagoon.

"What it means though is we'll have to provide a ship as escort and time it so they arrive simultaneously. It's a hell of a gamble and I'm banking on the season giving us reasonably fine weather. We may have losses and I suggest we take an extra one with an extra load to be on the safe side."

The soldier nodded. "Tricky business, isn't it? OK, what else?"

"For the actual landing, we should put them on the beach about an hour before high tide. That gives us time to unload and get off before they're stranded waiting for the next tide.

"I would prefer the approach to be in the dark but I guess you want to land in daylight." The question was in the tone of voice rather than the words.

Pender nodded. "If it's just after dawn, they'll have the glare in their eyes as well. What about covering fire?"

"You give us the targets and the times. We'll give you what you want. We'll need to train pretty hard for that and we'd better have some naval gunfire liaison officers on board the ships.

"We'll use *Jervis Bay* as the main personnel carrier. We can pack all your other soldiers into her. She's in dock in Sydney now being refitted.

"We'll have to take *Success* with us as a supply ship but that will mainly be for my force. For your stores, food, ammunition and so on, we've requisitioned a merchant ship. She's the *Golden Sovereign*, a Ro-Ro ship. She's got big holds and a vehicle deck. We're putting two helicopter pads on her foredeck, cutting hatches and installing cranes we've had in store from the old *Stalwart*. She's got a ramp at the stern which we might be able to use with landing craft if the weather's kind to us. Otherwise, we'll use helos off the deck.

"Helicopters! We'll be using your Blackhawks. We can put two on *Tobruk*, another two on the *Golden Sovereign* and one on *Success*. That's the best we can do. I don't want to take the combat helos off the frigates but we might be able to use them occasionally for communications runs."

"Sounds OK, George. There's not a lot of room for error but you know what they say about beggars and choosers. It'll mean some pretty intensive training for the aircrews. I guess we'll manage."

Fennessy continued. "That should cover the transport side. For defence of the operation, Ian Cartwright is putting three submarines out to cover the exclusion zone. They'll stay under his command.

"I've got two destroyers and four frigates. Two of the frigates, *Swan* and *Torrens* we've had to pull out of reserve. They're not worth a pinch of shit for anything except gunfire support and we're only restoring them to the extent of their twin 4.5 inch turrets. Apart from that, they can steam and the galleys work so the ship's company can eat.

"*Adelaide* and *Yarra* have only light guns and I'll use them for NGS only if I must. They'll be more value outside as radar and sonar pickets. *Perth* and *Hobart* will be general dogsbodies because they can do just about everything. Basically, they'll be force escort providing air and submarine defence but available for NGS as well. The other FFGs are tied up with shipping protection."

"That's about it then", Pender summed up. "The only other thing is the SAS. There will be a team going in to do something for the air people. I'm not quite sure what but they're being put in by submarine several days before our circus gets going."

RAAF Base, Learmonth

Learmonth was a hive of activity with more than 20 front line aircraft dispersed around the base. The new organisation, No. 6 Group, was settling down as its aircraft, ground crews and support equipment were flown in from their main bases around the country. To the north of the main runway, the radar antenna of 114 Mobile CRU was slowly circling, tracking all aircraft within 100 miles of the base.

Noble had flown up from Perth that morning. His PC-9 with the three stars painted under the cockpit was parked close by the control tower. He had walked from there to the Operations Centre, watching as he went the flurry of activity. The roar of aircraft engines provided a thunderous accompaniment to the scurrying of men and olive-drab vehicles around the base.

In the Operations Centre, he conferred with the Group commander and his operations staff. The five men gathered around a large table littered with aerial photos and a large scale map of Cocos. Noble opened proceedings by setting out the task.

"Our primary job is to knock out the Indian capacity for air defence against the landing force. Obviously, we also need to protect our own aircraft.

"We have to time this so that the Indians can't interfere with the invasion but we can't do it so early that they have time to reinforce or repair the damage we do.

"At this stage, I can't give you a date for the invasion but you'll have to think in terms of not later than mid-November. The navy and army people have a bracket of four days from 17th November when the tide conditions are right.

"We have to assume that the Indians will know when they sail. We do know they're getting satellite intelligence from their Soviet mates. The transit time for the force will be about six days although one group of slower ships will be leaving roughly three days earlier.

"There's one additional piece of information you won't like. In addition to the four MiG-29s and the mobile CRU, they've flown in a Sea King helicopter. The experts tell us it's operating like an AEW aircraft so they'll have about 200 miles detection of any raid. So, how are you going to do it?"

Air Commodore Heylen, the group commander, looked around his staff. They were all silent for a time. Eventually, the Operations Officer, a wing commander, spoke up.

"The first task is going to be to knock out their CRU radar and the SA-8. I suggest we use a two ship F-111 strike for that with HARM missiles."

Noble interrupted. "Will they have the legs? You're not going to get the KC-10 to refuel them."

"No, sir. We've talked about this. If we give them full external and internal fuel and one HARM each, they should be able to make Christmas comfortably after attacking, and refuel there for the trip home. Our briefing was that we could use Christmas in those circumstances."

Noble nodded. "Go on." "Next up, sir, and virtually simultaneously, I'd suggest four Hornets to deal with the Sea King and any MiGs they actually get off the ground." He looked around but there was no comment from the others.

"We still need to deal with those ZSUs as part of the air defence system unless we go for high level attacks, above 10,000 feet. They can't touch us that high."

Heylen demurred. "I think we need low level attacks to be sure of our targets. Why not a pair of Hornets with CRV-7 pods. As far as I can see, they aren't moving these ZSUs around. We should be able to find them easily enough."

"Fair enough, sir. That should take care of the air defence. The next task will be to put the airfield out of commission. Two targets, I think. One would be the fuel tanks here." He pointed to the small cluster of white towers on one of the photos. They were in a compound near the jetty at the northern tip of West Island.

"The other target would be the runway itself. If we can crater that thoroughly with some Mk 84s from high level, they'll be tied down even if we don't knock out their aircraft."

Noble didn't like that idea. "I'm not persuaded that strikes on runways are all that useful. They do have repair equipment there and, remember, we will want to use the place ourselves. The fuel tanks are our best bet."

The five men discussed the concept briefly. Eventually, they compromised. The runway would not be attacked unless the strike on the fuel tanks was less than completely successful.

The wing commander continued. "In that case, sir, I propose a low level strike on the tanks with Snakeyes. A good cluster of those should do all the damage we need. It's a pity we can't use the F-111s. Then we could use the GBU-12s with their PAVE TACK."

They all nodded at that. The PAVE TACK system used laser designation from the aircraft and laser guidance heads on the GBU-12 bombs. All the F-111 navigator had to do was use his joystick to hold the sight on the target. The bombs, released in a ballistic toss on a trajectory computed by the system, would hit the target.

Noble again interrupted quietly. "What if I can get you an SAS team with a laser designator to put the aiming point on the tanks?"

They all beamed. "Bloody good, sir! We'd use the Hornets then to hit them with GBU-12s. That would take all the guesswork out of it. Two aircraft should be enough for the job. Where will the soldiers be?"

"This is strictly within this room, you understand?" They nodded at Noble's warning. "The idea is to put them ashore here on Horsburgh Island from a submarine. The island's uninhabited but does have some permanent water. They could stay there for several days undetected and join up with the landing force when they arrive.

"Any other suggestions?"

Another officer spoke up. "Could we use another pair of Hornets with Snakeyes to attack any aircraft on the ground? I'm thinking of that Il-38 and any MiGs which might still be on the ground."

Noble agreed. "Good idea. They can be briefed for any targetsof opportunity as well, armoured vehicles, headquarters building, any ammo dumps we identify in the open, that sort of thing.

"Anything else?" They all shook their heads. "OK, I'll leave you to the detail. Get back to me with any problems. I'll be in Perth now except for the occasional visit up here."

9°38' South, 95°08' East

HMAS *Orion* was at 300 feet with her towed array passive sonar streamed. She was patrolling at low speed across the general line of advance of any shipping from India bound for Cocos. According to the plot, she was about 30 miles inside the maritime exclusion zone. Under the current Rules of Engagement, any ships inside the zone were legitimate targets.

More than one member of the crew pondered on the old submariner's joke—there are only submarines and targets. Well, it was no longer a joke. This was for real.

Lieutenant Commander Malcolm Harland was relaxing in his bunk. They had been on patrol for five weeks now. Another two days and it would be time to head for Fremantle. His place would be taken by *Otama*, already on her way. He was tired; they all were. They had not been working hard, there had been no contacts but the tension all the time was palpable. In the three weeks, they had not surfaced but had contented themselves with coming close enough to snort and charge the batteries, freshen the air in the boat, listen for signals and update their position. At this time, he was as well off as any submarine captain could be. His battery was topped up, he had a full weapons load and he was shortly to head for home and a well-earned break.

Then—"Captain to the Control Room!"

It was only a few steps. "Yeah, what have we got?"

"Sonar contact, sir, bearing 295. Two ships. We're on course 235, speed three."

Harland checked the plot. There was not enough information to make a judgement yet."OK, keep tracking. Maintain course and speed for the moment."

An hour passed. "Bearing is now 286 and range is closing, sir. One of the targets is a warship. He's doing a sprint and drift pattern, presumably listening on a passive sonar. The other target appears to be maintaining constant speed.

"Assuming the other is a merchant ship with a speed between eight and 16 knots, that would give the target a course somewhere between 135 and 175 but those figures are rubbery as yet. I think we'd be getting more noise with a higher speed, sir."

"Yes." He studied the plot again. "Come left to 220 and make speed five knots."

Half an hour passed. "Target bearing is moving left, sir, now 280. Range is still closing."

"Keep tracking—and give me a target assessment as soon as you can. Come to periscope depth and raise the EW mast."

"Aye, aye, sir."

"Control—EW. Two rackets. Airborne radar at 264, distant. Ship radar bearing 275, classified as HEAD NET, much closer."

That ship radar was the warship. The bearing matched well with the sonar tracking of the merchant ship, suggesting the two were reasonably close. The airborne radar could be a patrol plane or a helicopter from the warship.

"Secure EW. Take her down to 200 feet and hold her just above the layer. Any sign of the target zig-zagging?"

"Negative, sir. Bearing change is constant. This silly bugger doesn't seem to know there's a war on."

Another 30 minutes passed. "Target identification, sir. One warship, estimate a frigate, *Godavari* class. The other is a heavy merchant ship, single screw. Targets now bearing 272 and the range is still closing."

On the plot, the tracks were closing neatly. The targets were crossing his bows.

"Estimate speed of the merchant ship to be12 knots, course approximately 145."

"OK. Come left to 200 and make your speed eight knots. Confirm targets are within the exclusion zone?"

"Confirmed, sir. Estimated position is 163 miles from Cocos."

That gave him plenty of room for error although they had achieved a good position update only the previous night. Harland knew the current rules of engagement allowed him to fire at any target regardless of nationality but he now had a good identification on the frigate as an enemy.

Now *Orion* would be crossing the targets' bows and Harland was ready to set up a fire control solution for Mark 48 wire-guided torpedos, firing at the frigate first.

"Active sonar transmitting ,sir, bearing212. Helicopter sonar, sir, below the layer. Range from the transducer is 14,500 yards."

Good, Harland thought. He'll be dipping ahead of the targets. "What's the bearing to the targets now?"

"257, sir. And I have the frigate ahead of the merchant ship now."

"Sir, range plots at around 12,000 yards. We have enough discrimination to target both ships."

The data was fed into the fire control computer which automatically set target bearing and radar seeker ranges for the torpedos.

"Frigate now bearing 243, range 7000 yards. He's just come off a sprint. Merchant ship bearing 250, range approximately the same but about 1000 yards astern."

"Flood the tubes!"

The attack team went through its practised routine. Tubes were flooded, the outer doors opened, firing solution set and checked. The first torpedo would be fired at the frigate. Get him out of the way first, then the merchant ship would be a sitting duck.

The boat bounced as, one by one, the two Mark 48s were fired from the tubes by compressed air. Their motors started and they streaked away, trailing their control wires behind.

"Torpedos running, sir. Four minutes to target."

"The frigate's heard the torpedo, sir. He's put on power."

Back in the submarine, Harland reduced speed. The submarine was barely making way just above the layer. Unless the helicopter raised his transducer to search above the layer, they were practically undetectable. Even then, they could slip below the layer before he could get any contact.

"Both torpedos pinging, sir."

In the control room, men watched the bulkhead clock, counting down the seconds.

"Sir! Detonation. And another. Two hits, sir."

"Control, sonar. Both ships have stopped engines. Helicopter has stopped transmitting." Harland beamed. Two kicks, two goals, he thought, even if that frigate captain was careless.

That'll give them something to think about. He looked around. The command team was celebrating—quietly.

"Good work, everyone. That's a couple of hits. There's an aircraft around though. Take her down slowly to 600 feet and leave them to it. Come left to 090."

Cocos Islands

It was just over two hours later when the Sea King landed at Cocos, packed to danger point with survivors from the two ships. The pilot reported immediately to Sharma.

"Both ships were badly damaged and will sink if they haven't already done so. Both have been abandoned although there does not seem to be too many casualties. There are many rafts in the water. The May is orbiting the scene to maintain contact. Can we get some boats to rescue them?"

Sharma cursed. The supply ship had more fuel as well as ammunition and spares for his aircraft. They were all gone, as was the frigate, the INS *Gomati*.

He controlled his chagrin with an effort. "Yes, the other Sea King is on the way and I have requisitioned all available boats. There are a couple of large barges which should be able to pick up the rest of the men. They may need you to show them the way."

"Yes, sir. But now I'll refuel and make another trip. My crew are stripping the equipment out so that I can fit more survivors in."

RAAF Base Pearce, near Perth

The ten C-130s landed at intervals of two minutes and taxied to the open area near the control tower. Ground crews waved them to designated parking areas.

Even before they had stopped and shut down their engines, the big tail doors swung down but it was not until the loadmasters had given the all clear that the troops began to file down to the ground.

Chivvied into line by barking NCOs, they picked up their weapons and kit bags before marching off to the trucks that would take them to Karrakatta Camp.

HMAS *Stirling*, Garden Island

The huge tank transporters eased their way across the causeway. Military Police escorts on motor bikes led the procession and brought up the rear. The lead motor cyclist accelerated along the causeway to warn the guard at the main gate.

The 12 transporters, each with a single armoured vehicle tied down with heavy chains on to its trailer, headed up the main road before turning down to the wharf area. Sailors from the base watched silently as the trucks rumbled by.

Out in Cockburn Sound, ships of the task force swung at anchor. At the main wharf, workmen swarmed over the *Golden Sovereign*. Welding torches glared in the bright sunlight as the finishing touches were put to her conversion. Other men working from stages and pontoons rolled grey paint over her civilian colour scheme.

HMAS *Yarra*

Bellano sat at his desk, working through the operation order for what was now called Operation Matchless. Yarra had been given the job of escorting the three LCHs with their precious load of armoured vehicles. D-Day had been set for 18th November and he would sail with his group after nightfall on the 8th, only two weeks away.

There would be a briefing tomorrow morning for command teams, then he would take his ship to sea for a couple of days to tighten up some of their drills. Then a few days local leave before the ship's company was confined to the base area. During that period, they would strip the ship, landing all the inflammable furniture and other surplus fittings.

He sat back in his chair, going through the operation order in his mind. It was a mixture, he thought. Most of it would be all right, especially the air ops, he reckoned. The naval side should be no problem unless the Indians intervened. But if they could not get the soldiers ashore or if they had too many breakdowns, especially with the helicopters, the whole thing could collapse.

Ultimately, it all rested on the soldiers. They had to do the job quickly. If they get bogged down, or if the Indian navy reacts in strength, we will probably lose, he thought. We just won't be able to keep it going.

His eyes strayed over his bookshelves, lighting on the christening mug. I should post it home, he mused, before we sail. They've done a great job on it, something he and Anne would treasure until young Catherine grew up.

HMAS *Otama*

Jeffreys leaned against the bulkhead watching in the dim red light as the depth indicator gradually wound itself back to periscope depth. The submarine's captain, a young lieutenant commander, stood by the periscope standard.

"Raise EW mast."

"Racket, sir, bearing 196. That'll be the CRU."

The captain checked his plot. On his best estimate, he was just north of Port Refuge. The bearing on the radar transmission indicated that Horsburgh Island was still somewhere to the west.

"Can he pick us up?"

"Shouldn't think so, sir. We've only got the EW mast up. Too small and too low for an air search radar."

"OK. Quartermaster, come right to 300. EW, keep reporting that racket."

With the submarine behind Horsburgh, the radar would be blanketed and the submarine could safely raise its periscope to check its position before surfacing.

"Racket's faded, sir."

"Did it cut out suddenly?"

"Negative, sir, just faded out."

"OK, we're probably behind the island. Let's have a look. Up 'scope."

The periscope was fitted with an image intensifier which magnified the available starlight. The captain could plainly see the low outline of the island almost filling his southerly horizon. A faint white streak showed the low surf breaking on the shore. He swung around. A cluster of lights showed low on the water bearing - he checked—135°. That would be the settlement on Home Island. To their left, there was another low shadow—Direction Island. He called out the bearings and the navigator plotted them on the chart.

"Down 'scope. OK, Peter. Here's where we are." The small cross on the chart was 400 yards off the northern tip of the island.

Jeffreys called his sergeant over. Each of the two men would control a Zodiac inflatable for the landing. The sergeant made his calculations. "Piece of piss, boss. Head due south, turn left when we get close in and follow the beach around to the landing place here."

He pointed to the spot on the south eastern tip.

"Surfacing now. Casing party, stand by. OK, soldiers, you've got 15 minutes. The casing will be just out of the water and you'll be able to float off when I submerge. Make it snappy."

The soldiers wasted no time on deck. The dinghies were hauled up through the forrard hatch. Motors and other equipment followed. On top of the sail, the captain checked his watch, silently urging them on. The surface was no place for a submarine, especially so close to a hostile coast.

The call came up the voice pipe from the control room. "Captain, sir. EW has a racket bearing 058. Aircraft radar. Could be their Il-38. Too soon to classify."

"Has he got us yet?"

A pause. "Negative, sir."

A quick calculation, then he made a megaphone of his hands. "Aircraft approaching. I'm diving in five minutes regardless."

The answer came back. "Roger, sir. We're on our way. Thanks for the ride."

Men piled into the dinghies while others jumped down the forrard hatch. He heard the thump as it shut and was dogged down. He sent the rest of the men on the sail down the hatch, then followed.

In the control room, he gave the order to dive.

Slowly, the submarine sank below the surface, leaving almost no swirl. As the two heavily loaded Zodiacs floated off, the engines were started, their silencers reducing noise to a low mutter. Both turned towards the beach and disappeared into the darkness.

CHAPTER 15

Defence Headquarters, Canberra

Forbes checked his notes before going into the press conference. The media had been screaming ever since the Indians had announced the loss of the *Gomati* and the supply ship. The Australians had said nothing but the Prime Minister had finally decided that a conference should be held. Because the government wanted to play the affair down, it had been decided that neither the PM nor McCarthy should appear.

He took his place behind the table, his uniformed public relations officer beside him. His opening statement was curt.

"Thank you, ladies and gentlemen. This conference is being held at your request. At this time, I have nothing to announce beyond the fact that certain military operations are pending. They will be announced at the appropriate time to your representatives accredited to the units concerned. I am prepared, however, to answer questions where operational security permits."

"Air Marshal Forbes, Richard Norton, AAP. The Indian government has denounced what it calls an act of piracy involving the sinking of two Indian ships by one of our submarines with heavy loss of life. There has been no Australian confirmation and no comment. Could you confirm that this reported sinking was the result of Australian military action and, if so, could you comment on its necessity?"

There was dead silence as Forbes looked round the room. Everyone present was hanging on his answer.

"No, ladies and gentlemen, I cannot confirm the Indian claim." He held up his hand for silence as questions were shouted from around the room. "Please. Give me a chance to answer rationally.

"If an Australian submarine did sink these ships, it was because they had intruded into the maritime exclusion zone around the Australian Cocos Islands territory. Such an operation is a legitimate defensive measure as was set out by the Prime Minister eight weeks ago when the zone was declared.

"I might add that the warning we have given is in marked contrast to the sinking of unarmed merchant ships by what we assess were Indian submarines in recent months.

"We are not able to confirm the sinking because the submarines we have on operations are under instructions not to report until they conclude their operational patrols."

"Can't you ask the submarine to confirm the attack?" It was Norton again.

"Yes, we can but we will not do so. Any report back by the submarine threatens its own security."

"So, you let the Indians win the media war?" Reg Baker intervened.

Forbes nodded as his PR officer whispered in his ear. "Well, Mr Baker, we may have some difficulty with the media war but so long as we win the real one, that's all that matters. We are not prepared to risk the safety of our men to beat the Indians to a headline."

Baker was not dismayed. "When are we going to see some action, then?"

"All in good time, Mr Baker. You can't expect us to telegraph our punches. Your own people are reporting on the preparations being made in the West." He looked around. "Are there any other questions?"

Mary Petrelli put her hand up and got Forbes' nod. "Why are you releasing so much information about your preparations if security is supposed to be so important?"

"Thank you, Miss Petrelli. That's a fair question if you don't mind a lecture in reply." There was a chuckle at that before he went on.

"The reality is we are releasing information about what we cannot realistically conceal. We accept that the Australian people should know as much as we can tell them without threatening the security of our own troops.

"Now, the government has said we will retake Cocos. We are making preparations for that. Many of those preparations cannot be concealed. We expect that Indian intelligence will have a lot of information about these so there is little point in concealing them.

"Those are the obvious things. There are some things, such as specific operational plans, time factors and one or two tricks we might have up our sleeves, which we are not going to talk about and, I guess, most of you would not want us to, anyway."

Petrelli persisted. "You talk of Indian intelligence. Are you saying there are Indian spies in this country?"

Forbes hesitated briefly. His reply was cautious. "No, I am not saying that. But we do have evidence that Soviet bloc intelligence personnel in this country are taking an interest. We do know that Soviet intelligence-gathering satellites have extensive coverage of Australia and we assume that the information they collect will be passed on to their Indian friends."

HMAS *Stirling*, Friday 8th November

The darkness shrouded Cockburn Sound like a blanket. The broad stretch of water could be discerned only by the outline of the lights on shore. None of the ships in the Sound were showing lights and the approaches were patrolled by naval and civil police in small boats. They had strict orders to keep stray craft out of the naval area.

Bellano's visitors were dim in the red night lighting of his cabin. Noble, Fennessy and Pender were making their farewells before *Yarra* took the three LCHs to sea. Noble was speaking.

"Look after them, Tony. The weather forecasts look good so you should be all right, barring accidents. No queries?"

"No, sir. Just a bit curious about the security measures, that's all."

"Well, we don't want to give away more than we have to. If the Soviets are a bit slow passing satellite intelligence to the Indians, we delay their knowledge by just that bit more. Their bureaucracies are worse than ours so the odds are good that there'll be a stuff-up.

"And if they have any human assets on the ground here, the night time departure without lights will slow them down even more. They can't be sure where you've gone, although they could make a pretty good guess.

"Anyway, off you go. We'll get out of your way."

They made their farewells at the gangway as the three senior officers went over the side into their boat. Bellano went to the bridge and got the ship under way. By sunrise, they were well over the horizon heading for Cocos.

RAAF Base Learmonth, Tuesday 12th November

Heylen was in the operations centre when the signal came in. He scanned the slip quickly. It did nothing for his peace of mind.

```
DTG 120352Z NOV
IMMEDIATE SECRET
FROM          DEFENCE CANBERRA
TO            6 GP LEARMONTH
              17 ADR WOODSIDE
              36 SQN RICHMOND
INFO          COMMANDER JOINT FORCES AUSTRALIA
INTELLIGENCE ASSESSES INDIAN IL-76 DETECTED COCOS
AIRFIELD 07 NOV MAY BE TANKER AIRCRAFT CAPABLE
OF SUPPORTING RAIDS ON LEARMONTH 36 SQN TO UPLIFT
ONE RAPIER AND ONE RBS-70 BATTERY OF 17 ADR TO
LEARMONTH WITHIN 24 HRS
```

"Shit, that makes my bloody day. Make sure we've got a section of Hornets on immediate readiness for an intercept mission from now. And make sure the troops down at 114 CRU are on the ball. Is there any way we can bring our ops forward?"

The operations officer scratched his head doubtfully. "Maybe a day, sir. But we're pretty committed to the timetable now, especially with the pre-op training."

Heylen picked up his secure 'phone. "OK. See what you can do. I'd better talk to the boss."

HMAS *Stirling*, the same day

Noble had the same signal in his hand when the call came from Heylen. He listened briefly before making his decision.

"No, Gary. Leave things as they are. Jindalee plus your own CRU should be able to give enough warning of a raid. Tie the defence in with the SAMs when they get there. Just keep a section available for local interceptions and another to go after their tanker if they do show up. In the meantime, I've got another card to play."

He hung up and walked across to his operations centre where he conferred briefly with an army officer. Then, collecting his cap, he left the building to be driven down to *Tobruk* at the main wharf. It was time to farewell the main assault force.

Cocos Islands, the same day

Jaswal walked into Sharma's office, his face lit up with anticipation. "I've got it all worked out, colonel. According to the satellite reports, they've got two of their tankers on the ground at Learmonth. There's nowhere for them to hide and they've got no SAM defence there. I can take a strike of two aircraft in low and hard and go for the tankers. If we hit them about noon, they should be more relaxed and thinking about lunch."

Sharma looked at the younger man with some affection. A typical fighter pilot, he thought. He thinks he can do everything. Slowly, he shook his head.

"Sorry, Devan, but our masters don't want to stir up the Hornet's nest". They both chuckled at the pun before Sharma continued. "Basically, they don't want to carry the fight to the Australian mainland because that would encourage aggressive American intervention, especially since it is so close to the North-West Cape communications base. I'm afraid the defensive mentality rules back home, although, I must say, in this case I think they are right.

"What I do want you to do, though", he continued, "is plan to hit this group of landing craft and its escort when they come within range. It's slow and its escort is only one lightly armed ship—one of their new

ANZAC class. We can assume they will have air cover for part of the way but, by about the 14th, they should be comfortably within range for you and out of range of their fighters."

Jaswal was mollified as they examined the chart. "I'll get on to it right away, sir." He saluted and left.

That night

Jeffreys and his partner crouched in the lee of the old shed. Forty metres away near the edge of the parking apron, he could see the huge Ilyushin squatting massively in the starlight. The two men were dressed in black coveralls, their faces smeared with camouflage paint. Both had shed their boots and were barefoot. Even rubber boots made a noise, especially if they were wet. Unarmed, except for a killing knife, they carried satchels packed with plastic explosive.

Jeffreys nudged his companion and pointed. Following his arm, the other man saw the sentry leaning against one of the 'plane's main wheels. His rifle was slung and he was relaxed, looking towards the headquarters building further along the apron.

The commando nodded and slipped away, silently. Jeffreys checked his watch. The faint phosphorescent glimmer told him it was just after 0230. Time to get moving. The two helicopters were another 200 metres away, beyond the headquarters building but on the runway side of the apron.

Keeping low to the ground in the shallow drain which enclosed the apron area, he moved carefully, stopping frequently to check for patrols or sentries. The grass was short and offered no cover but there was little light and the drain was in deep shadow. He circled around the tracked ZSU carrier, hearing the mutter of voices as the crew chatted among themselves even before he saw it dark against the night sky.

The two helicopters were parked close together on the grass between the apron and the runway. A solitary bored sentry leaned against a wheel fairing, his rifle slung over his shoulder. He had his back to Jeffreys whose head peered over the lip of the drain less than ten metres away.

Again, he checked his watch—0250. Time to move. Drawing his knife, he slipped noiselessly across the short grass. His right arm went round the man's neck, hard, to cut off any sound. As the sentry's hands went up, instinctively clawing at his arm to break the hold, the knife in his left hand stabbed upwards through the ribs on the Indian's unprotected left side.

The keen-edged long blade sliced through flesh, cartilage and lung until it reached the heart, carving a huge gash so that, in its death spasms, it pumped the man's lifeblood uselessly into the chest cavity.

He lowered the body gently to the ground before dragging it into the shadow of the big helicopter. Quickly, he shinned up the wheel fairing brace to the roof. Carefully moulding three lumps of plastic explosive around the main rotor hub linkages, he carefully slipped a 20 minute time pencil detonator into each before triggering them and then sliding down to the ground.

Another five minutes saw him completing the same task on the other helicopter. He didn't know which was the AEW machine. It didn't much matter, he thought. Take them both out in the same spot and there'd be no worry about the Indians cannibalising one to repair the other.

Down on the ground again and in the shelter of the drain, he checked his surroundings for sentries or patrols before slithering across the runway itself. Against the black bitumen surface, no one could possibly see him.

Back at the rendezvous in the coconut groves, his partner was waiting. They compared notes. The other soldier had placed his charge, a big one, high up on the Ilyushin's nose wheel actuating mechanism. If it worked as planned, it would fracture the main nose wheel strut and the link pins. No chance of repairing those on Cocos, Jeffreys agreed.

They did not wait. It was time to get back to the Zodiac hidden in the trees with another soldier on guard. A quick trip across the lagoon and they would slip through the passage at the northern end of Pulu Atas before returning outside the islands to their hidden camp on Horsburgh Island.

They had just shoved off when they heard the thump of the first charge going off. They could see no sign of it through the screen of trees. Their tension mounted as they waited for the others to blow. They knew there would be a delay but, as time passed, that knowledge did not ease the anxiety gnawing at them. There was an audible sigh of relief from the three men as another, louder, bang announced the second detonation.

This time, there was a secondary explosion followed by a ball of fire roiling up above the trees. A fuel tank had exploded as well. Jeffreys was satisfied. That would have been one of the helicopters, he thought. Even if the third charge doesn't blow, the second helo will be a write-off.

The silly buggers had them parked too close together, he reckoned.

14th November, Thursday

The two F-111s streaked in from the west at 200 feet. In the lead aircraft, the navigator peered into the shroud over his radar screen, occasionally checking with the radar pictures made up from the photos taken all those weeks before by the RF-111s.

Ten miles out, he made out the shape of West Island. A minute to go. Both men could hear the chirping of the threat warning receiver in the headphones. The CRU had acquired them. It would be vectoring the MiGs on to them by now but the Indian fighters would stay outside the ZSU-23-4 envelope, waiting for the Pigs to come out—if they came out—so as to hit them without being shot down themselves.

Their course could be better. He wanted to turn to port after his attack to keep as much distance as he could from the deadly ZSUs.

"Come left five degrees", he muttered into his mike.

The aircraft slid sideways a trifle and the navigator was satisfied. He glanced quickly to his right. The stubby HARM missile hung from the inboard pylon under the right wing. Now it was locked onto the transmission from the Indian radar. As long as the CRU kept transmitting, the missile would home on to the antenna.

The pilot was visual now. He could see the target, the clearing, buildings and the rotating antenna through his windscreen. He toggled the "pickle" button on his joystick.

The missile dropped away from its grabs and immediately fired, then streaked away from the aircraft which broke violently to the left. He cut in his afterburner and shot away to the north east.

The Indian operator panicked. He triggered his electronic countermeasures system instead of simply switching off. Too late.

The missile homed on to the radar antenna and blasted it and its carrier vehicle into scrap. Immediately, the MiGs lost their vector and spent precious time trying to find the Pig with their airborne radar. By the time they had gained contact, he was too far away to chase. An hour later, his drooping main wheels spat smoke as they touched down at Christmas Island.

The second aircraft was 2000 yards behind his leader. His HARM was programmed for the SA-8 radar but the navigator could not get a lock. Time was passing as he searched. Two miles out, he gave up. The bloody thing was not transmitting. He saw the flash as the leader's missile hit home on the CRU.

"Let's get out of here. Break left."

Too late. As the pilot hauled the aircraft around, two streams of tracers came up, one from dead ahead, the other from the right. Frantically, he dumped chaff to confuse the radars but the ZSU had him.

There were eight guns firing, each with a rate of fire over 800 rounds per minute. At least 30 of the 23mm shells hit the aircraft and it just came apart. Fuel from shattered tanks sprayed into the air and ignited into a huge orange ball of flame from which pieces of the 'plane fell into the sea.

No one got out.

15th November, Friday

The four Hornets were flying at 30,000 feet in offset box formation. The leader had his deputy a mile to starboard while their wingmen were almost two miles behind. All aircraft were maintaining strict EMCON.

They had topped up with fuel from the tankers just 15 minutes before. The fighters had eased up to the drogues trailing behind each wing of the two Boeing 707 tankers, each plugging his probe into the basket and sucking the fuel into the wing tanks and the 1200 litre tanks under each wing. A little more than five minutes was enough to top up before they broke away, leaving the tankers to orbit under more fighter cover until the strikes returned.

The four Hornets between them had eight medium-range AIM-7M Sparrow radar-controlled missiles and eight short- range AIM-9M Sidewinder heat-seeking missiles. A 20mm six-barrel Gatling gun firing 6000 rounds per minute completed their powerful armament.

Thirty minutes behind them, a second strike would drop down to 300 feet after refuelling. In the lead aircraft, Norris' threat receiver warned him of the MiGs. They'd lost their AEW aircraft and the CRU radar. Obviously they had a CAP in the air looking for inbound strikes. That was OK. His job was to trail his coat for the Indian fighters. He maintained EMCON.

Jaswal had a contact bearing 073. He and his wingman were orbiting south-east of Cocos. He focussed his radar which gave him a range of 30 miles and 5000 feet below his own height. He flashed his wings at his number two and eased his aircraft into a shallow dive, turning to port.

Selecting one of his AA-10 medium-range radar missiles, he continued to close his contact which was now revealed as two aircraft. Ten miles out and he achieved missile lock and fired. Almost simultaneously, his wingman fired one of his own AA-10s at the second target, Norris' number two.

The missiles closed rapidly, flying at better than Mach 3, homing on to the radar signal in their seeker heads. The threat receiver screeched insistently. Norris shoved his throttles forward all the way, cutting in his afterburner, then punched the red button on the left side of his cockpit, releasing a programmed spray of flares and chaff bomblets.

Breaking hard left, he dived trying to get below the incoming missile and break the lock. It worked. The AA-10 homed on a cloud of chaff. When it broke through, it failed to find a target and flew on until it ran out of fuel.

Norris' number two was less agile. He was slow to respond and the missile's fuze blew the warhead ten feet away from the trailing edge of his port wing. Fragments tore into his port engine, wing and fin, gouging huge chunks out of the structure. Fan blades in the engine shattered but were contained by the shield.

The pilot cut his port engine as he battled to retain stability. As he struggled with his crippled aircraft, Jaswal's wingman flew closer. Now within visual range, he fired an Atoll infra-red missile which homed on the crippled Hornet's tail pipe and blew the aircraft apart.

Norris' number three broke EMCON and powered up his APG-65 radar, turning into the Indians. Immediately he gained contact on the two MiGs. He called his wingman.

"Dragon Four, Bandits 237 range three miles. Fox Two. Sorted."

With his thumb, he flicked the weapon select switch on his joystick, arming a Sidewinder. Almost immediately, the growl in his headset told of missile lock-on and his index finger pulled the trigger.

The missile streaked away as his wingman fired another Sidewinder at his allocated target. Both aircraft broke sharply to port, spewing flares and chaff.

Jaswal was caught unawares. His radar had not warned him of the other two aircraft in their dispersed formation. Both Sidewinders found their mark, crippling the two MiGs. A jagged fragment of metal tore into Jaswal's cockpit, slicing through his helmet and tearing into his brain. He died instantly as his aircraft tumbled to the sea far below.

His wingman ejected safely, his parachute snapping open automatically as his seat dropped away. Minutes later, he climbed into his dinghy where a boat from Cocos found him next day.

The three Hornets formed up and turned away, heading back to their tankers.

The same day, 30 minutes later

The two Hornets screeched in from the south, banking gently to line up with the runway. The crew of the ZSU at the southern end were not quick enough. The turret was traversing but the radar was pointing in the wrong direction as the aircraft popped up over its radar horizon. The leading Hornet fired a salvo of CRV-7 unguided rockets which tore into the thin-skinned vehicle. The four man crew died before they knew anything was wrong.

The two aircraft flew low along the length of the runway, jinking to throw off the Indian radars and jamming hard. It took seven seconds before they reached the apron. The two pilots selected weapons as they sought targets visually through the Head Up Display painted on the windscreen. Dead ahead, the leader saw the big Ilyushin tanker drooping tiredly on it chin where the nose wheel had been blown away. To his right in two circles of burnt grass were the wrecks of the two helicopters.

As the lead aircraft bomb sight came on to the target in his HUD, the pilot triggered his "pickle" on the joystick. Three Snakeye bombs, Mark 82 500 pounders with retarding tails, dropped away from the port wing. The tails deployed, slowing the forward movement of the weapons, and they dropped well behind the speeding aircraft. One fell under the Il-38 May ASW aircraft sitting at the edge of the apron under camouflage nets. When it blew, the big plane broke in two across the fuselage. The wreck dropped into a growing pool of spilt fuel which flashed into a boiling orange and black cloud of flame and smoke.

The second aircraft fired his rockets at the other ZSU which, by now, had acquired his target. The gunner triggered off enough rounds to tear off the Hornet's port wing before the rockets shattered the tracked vehicle. The wrecked aircraft toppled over to port, ploughing into the two remaining MiGs. Bombs, fuel and ammunition combined in a series of explosions which demolished buildings alongside the apron, including the Indian headquarters.

Sharma, visiting the northern end of the island, was unharmed. The surviving Hornet broke away to starboard, went to afterburner and set course for the tankers. A single SA-7 was fired at him but the aircraft accelerated away and lost it.

At the northern end of the island, Sharma was on the jetty when he heard the thunder of explosions and the roar of aircraft. He saw the pillar of flame and smoke boiling up above the trees and raced for his Landrover. As he did, two more Hornets appeared from behind Horsburgh Island, flying low and fast towards him. Sharma forgot his vehicle and dived behind a tree for shelter.

In the lead aircraft, the pilot selected and armed the single GBU-10 hanging from the pylon under his starboard wing. To his left, under the trees on Horsburgh Island, two SAS commandos carefully sighted their laser projector on to the centre fuel tank they could just see in the distance. The aircraft's FLIR looked for the laser spot transferring data to the sight on the HUD and the bomb's guidance head.

Lock on! The pilot pulled his stick back and the aircraft shot into a climb. His right thumb toggled the "pickle" and the bomb released, hurled into a ballistic toss. He broke right as the bomb reached the top of its trajectory, then arrowed down, steered by the winglets on its guidance head, into the centre fuel tank where the laser spot shimmered, invisible to everything but the seeker head on the bomb.

The blast of the 2000 pounder sent steel shards tearing into all the tanks. Fuel spilt to be vaporised by the heat of the explosion and the whole mass billowed into a cloud of black smoke, shot through with roaring orange-yellow flame.

Both Hornets broke away to starboard before turning left to a course along the seaward shore. Lining up an approach between the two orange and white checkered steel towers, the second aircraft, now in the lead, tossed his bomb into the quarantine station clearing. Breaking left, they then turned on to a course which would take them over the cluster of buildings around the Flight Services centre. There they dropped their loads of Snakeyes adding to the carnage from the earlier strike.

Trailing flares and chaff, the two aircraft cut in their afterburners and headed out to sea, gaining height as they went. The whole raid was over in two minutes, leaving a scene of devastation.

At the fuel depot, rivers of burning liquid flowed into the retaining dams where it continued to burn. Occasionally, small clouds of vapour flared, the flame reaching into the clouds of black smoke. The heat was too intense for men to approach and Sharma, looking on, told them to forget it. He was too shocked at the speed and intensity of the attack to be angry.

The shock soon gave way to resignation. Now, they had no aircraft and no fuel beyond what was available for immediate use at the airfield. That would have to be conserved for his armoured vehicles—if I have any left, he thought. All they could do now was wait for the inevitable invasion and do the best they could.

He climbed into his Landrover and, detouring through the trees to avoid the burning depot, drove back to what was left of his headquarters, to count the casualties, to take stock and to organise his force for the assault which would come in the next couple of days.

CHAPTER 16

Sunday November 17

The two task groups had rendezvoused for the final approach to Cocos. The whole fleet of 13 ships was in loose formation with *Yarra* and *Adelaide* sweeping ahead of the force. Further out, unseen, the three submarines patrolled the boundaries of the exclusion zone hunting for any surface or submarine intruders.

The force had slowed to the speed of the LCHs. They wallowed across the sea, small, flat-bottomed vessels which had no business in the great expanse of the ocean. All three had made the journey safely and, as Pender realised, the third vessel's cargo gave him a small but welcome increase in his force. Looking across at them, he silently commiserated with the men who had bounced around in them for the past ten days.

The escorts had fuelled early this morning from *Success* and had moved back to their stations. The two NGS ships, *Swan* and *Torrens* were inshore, out of the way of any attack that might develop from seaward. With only their twin 4.5 inch turrets operational, they would be a hindrance should any other threat develop.

For most of the day, the helicopters had clattered backwards and forwards between the ships. Mainly, they were carrying the three chaplains to their last services before the invasion. These were well attended with masses and communion services being celebrated in the larger ships. In their sermons, the chaplains urged the men to place their trust in God. Most of the men prayed simply that they would survive.

Separately, the commanders mingled with the men, chatting informally. All the briefings had been done, the training was as complete as it could be, given, as Pender frequently and forcefully expressed it, "the stuff-ups that are going to happen regardless." They passed on the intelligence of the successful air raids two days before, emphasising the good news that they did not have to worry about air attacks, as well as the challenge to do as well as the airmen.

Soldiers carried out last-minute checks of their equipment, cleaning and oiling weapons. Ammunition and ration packs were issued and water bottles topped up. Then, like soldiers anywhere, they curled up in any available spot to snatch as much sleep as possible

As night fell, the ships made their final approach to the islands.

On Cocos, the same day

Sharma knew they were coming. Intelligence had given him a detailed description of the naval force and he had a good idea of how much armour they had. There was no accurate assessment of their infantry strength but the Indian knew they would almost certainly enjoy superiority over his small force.

Also, he knew where they were and he could guess they would come ashore next morning just before high tide. But where?

He cursed his lack of knowledge of amphibious operations. There would be limits to where they could beach their craft but he was unsure what those limits were.

He faced the classic dilemma of the defender against the mobility of a seaborne force. Back in 1944, Rommel and von Rundstedt had argued bitterly over whether to try to defend every possible landing place against the Allied invasion that was eventually to come in Normandy or to lay back and wait for the enemy to commit himself before hitting him with concentrated power.

In Sharma's view, there was only one answer. Although the scale was infinitely smaller, the principle remained the same. He would concentrate his troops at two points but not so far from each other that they could not give mutual support. At least, he consoled himself, I won't have to face the scale of air attack that Rommel had to suffer. On the other hand, the use of helicopters to lift troops rapidly around the battlefield added another dimension to the problem, one the generals of old had not had to face. And, he ruminated, I don't have too much room to fight in.

He had moved into a battle headquarters hidden in the coconut groves just north of the Beacon Heights housing settlement. It was not much more than a couple of rude huts but it was heavily camouflaged and close to the main north-south road.

He would depend heavily on telephones for communications to limit the enemy capacity for radio interception and location for artillery targeting.

He explained his tactics to his subordinate commanders at a briefing that afternoon.

"I expect they will bring their landing ships into the lagoon so you gunners will need to deploy to cover the anchorage. Keep your guns under cover and wait until they actually drop anchor before opening fire. That way, they won't be able to get away so quickly.

"1st battalion will concentrate around the radio transmitter towers and cover both the main road and the lagoon beach. Keep your men in the trees. Man up the strong points you have built but be prepared to move out to hit the enemy hard.

"Get your guard platoon back from Home Island. We don't need them there any more and we must have every man.

"2nd battalion will concentrate around the quarantine station. Have a strong detachment, at least a platoon, to man the road block south of the airfield. Put a BMP with that block. Make sure you cover any possible approach from the eastern side of Telok Jambu. If I were you, I would concentrate your armour at the northern end of the airfield to cover the two possible approaches.

"I want all the SA-7 gunners concentrated on the lagoon beach with 1st battalion. Their principal targets will be the helicopters. All clear?"

There were no questions. These men were professionals and Sharma's plan had been exhaustively discussed over previous months. They all knew what they had to do.

Monday 18th November

Jeffreys' intelligence had given Bellano a good idea of where the Indian guns were. According to the map he was scanning, they were in the trees just south of the jetty at the northern tip of West Island, covering the main anchorage.

The fuel tanks ashore were still burning and the pall of smoke that reached up into the night sky as well as the radar return from the wreckage allowed his gunnery officers to develop a sound fire solution—provided the guns were where he thought they were!

Bellano had been given command of the gunfire support group that had detached from the main force an hour before. Only *Adelaide* remained with the main force. With her weak gun but powerful area air defence missile system, she was best suited to the task. *Perth* and *Hobart* had been detached and now cruised some three miles off Ujong Tanjong on the northern tip of West Island. He had the other three ships offshore to the west where they could hit the whole length of West Island. His job in *Yarra* was primarily to carry out surveillance to seaward as the other ships went about their business.

He checked his watch. The main force would enter Port Refuge between Horsburgh and Direction Islands at 0300. His group would commence harassing fire at 0245 trying to draw a reply from the Indian guns.

Rumah Baru was nothing more than a picnic spot. A number of tracks converged there and the beach shelved gently to the lagoon. A narrow concrete boat ramp ran into the water from the top of the beach. At low tide, there was very little depth of water for some 700 yards out into the lagoon.

Jeffreys and his team had come across from Horsburgh the night before after dumping their heavier equipment. The two Zodiacs had been deflated and concealed in the rank undergrowth. The six men had spent the day patiently in strict concealment, relaxed but alert and occasionally catching glimpses of Indian troops as they moved to their positions. Mostly they slept, taking it in turns to keep watch.

Their job in the morning would be to mark the beach for the landing craft as they motored in to disgorge their loads of men, vehicles and supplies. They would then act as guides for the troops.

Commodore Fennesy looked up as Pender stepped over the hatch coaming and came into the Task Force Operations Room in *Tobruk*. The navy would run their side of the operation from here. So would the soldiers for that matter, until Pender's troops were firmly established on land. Then, their headquarters would move ashore and the brigadier would take command. The soldier's green combat uniform showed up black in the red night lighting.

"How goes it?", the soldier asked.

"Fine. We're on time. We'll anchor here". His finger stabbed the chart at a point by No. 1 beacon.

"By that time, we should have suppressed any shore fire and the troops can disembark straight into the landing craft. The infantry will go in first to secure the beachhead, then the LCHs can come in and unload the armour. H-hour for the leading wave of landing craft is still 0600.

"The helicopter force will get off as soon as we anchor. They've been given flight paths to take them well away from the island until their final run in, just in case the Indians have still got some SA-7s there."

Pender studied the chart intently. It was all going as planned. They had practised it exhaustively. Now, it only had to be done. Finally, he looked up.

"Well, it's been a pleasure cruise so far. Now to work. I'll see the boys on their way, then come back here, but I want to get ashore as soon as possible, certainly by noon." He turned and went out on deck.

A thud shook the ship. He looked up, glancing at the bulkhead clock. The bombardment had commenced and he decided to go up to the bridge to watch.

Monday, 0600 hrs

The leading landing craft grounded gently on the coral sand and the ramps splashed down. Troops poured ashore, moving quickly into the trees, seeking both cover and the enemy.

They had had a straight run in. The guns on Ujong Tanjong had fired a few rounds just as the ships had anchored. The fire was light as they sought the range and had attracted a storm of retaliatory fire from the destroyers and frigates. The Indian gunners had not even been able to register their weapons before they were demolished.

Engines rumbled as the landing craft went full astern, pulling off the beach, before turning in a tight circle and returning to the ships for another load.

Jeffreys had acted as beachmaster, directing the troops into the trees until a navy commander had come ashore to handle that task. He had a tactical operator with him for ship/shore communications.

There was a full company, 120 men, ashore now. The company commander pushed sections out left and right as flank guards before the rest of the men deployed astride the track across the island and began their move to the western beach. At this point, the island was less than 250 metres wide. The leading company would drive a wedge across and cut the main road which ran along the western shore.

Across the lagoon, the big Blackhawk helicopters lifted off *Tobruk*. Both had Landrovers mounting the ugly 106mm recoilless rifles slung underneath. As they pulled away, two more dropped onto the decks and loaded soldiers. The four pulled away in loose formation, flying low and swinging away from West Island as they avoided the deadly SA-7s.

One of the troop carriers was first to land—on the neck of land at the end of the runway. It barely touched before the soldiers jumped down and deployed, looking for cover, facing south. The door gunner crouched over his weapon, also facing south, but saw nothing. The Blackhawk lifted off and flew out to sea, circling around to return to the ship for another load.

Next to land was one of the helos with an underslung Landrover. The vehicle bounced as it hit the ground but stayed on its wheels. The co-pilot unlocked the hook and the sling fell away. Again the helicopter touched down gently as the Landrover crew jumped out and set up their weapon. Quickly, the driver started up and drove hard for the tree line to get under cover.

A few seconds later, the third helicopter pulled away, pitching its nose down as it clawed its way into the air. The soldiers lost sight of it as it disappeared behind the trees. Then, moments later, it appeared again, clattering its way across the lagoon back to the ships. It looked bigger than the others. It was closer. Too close! A grey smoke trail shot out of the trees near the beach, closing rapidly with the big machine.

Then the soldiers saw a flash just before they heard the explosion. The SA-7 rocket exploded just by the engine exhaust, shattering the aircraft's main rotor. The blast toppled the helicopter straight into the water.

It didn't sink. The water was too shallow for that. But it settled on its side, rocking gently as the turbulent water subsided. There was no movement. No fire either. The fourth helicopter, the one with the second vehicle, pulled away out of possible range.

The soldiers looked in vain for the three-man crew to get out but were soon distracted by the rumble of a diesel engine and the clatter of tracks.

Just inside the trees, not quite on the road, was the Indian BMP.

Monday, 0700 hrs

The three LCHs rumbled in to the boat ramp. Above the noise of the vessels' engines could be heard the roar of diesels as the armoured vehicles on board started engines and ran them up.

The first vessel nosed into the beach and, at a signal from the shore, dropped its bow ramp. The big Leopard tank clanked down the slope, splashing through the shallows before rumbling up the beach. Guided by its commander standing in the open turret hatch, and scattering sand and broken palm fronds from under its tracks, it steered its way into the trees.

It was an hour before the three vessels completed unloading their cargoes. Meanwhile, other smaller landing craft came into the beach on either side of the ramp, disgorging more troops and stores into the rapidly expanding beachhead. Soldiers laboured to stockpile rations, ammunition and drums of fuel into hastily cleared dumps. Others loaded stores into the M113 armoured personnel carriers which would carry the supplies forward.

At the southern end of the runway, the gunner on the 106mm could not get a sight on the BMP. Standing beside the Landrover, he tapped the driver on the shoulder and motioned him forward, slowly beyond the tree line.

A bitch of a weapon, he thought. Sticks out like a bloody dogs balls, and as soon as you fire, every bastard is on to you.

There, he had the sight on. Ready to fire. But the burst of automatic fire from the trees cut him down.

The driver put his foot down and accelerated out into the open, to the shelter of the troops digging in. The BMP fired a shot from its 73mm gun but it went wide. The driver jinked around, putting the BMP gunner off his aim. He skidded off the track behind a mound of coral rubble and braked hard. Out of the line of fire. Now, to find a gunner and get a shot at that tin bastard.

The Australian platoon commander knew he was in trouble. He had few men while the 106, his only heavy weapon, was effectively out of action. He picked up his radio and called for help.

Monday, 0800 hrs

Bellano was on the port wing of the bridge. Peering through his binoculars, he could see the BMP just inside the trees quite clearly. His own ship was well within range and he pointed out the target to his gunnery officer. The trouble was, he was inside the BMP's gun range as well. They'd have to make it quick.

The 76mm banged out. They were firing visually. The first shell was high and exploded against a tree. Splinters tore through the foliage.

The Australians in their shallow holes hastily scraped in the sand cringed. I hope those bastards know where we are, the young lieutenant thought.

The BMP swivelled on its tracks. Its gun banged out at the ship but the shell went wide. The ship was picking up speed and the BMP's gunner, hampered by the narrow field of vision in his periscopic sight, could not train his weapon quickly enough.

A soldier jumped out of his hole and raced forward with a grenade in his hand. He was cut down by the Indian infantry firing through their armoured slits.

Again *Yarra* fired. There was a loud clang as the shell struck the BMP on the side of the cupola. It ricocheted away, exploding harmlessly in the trees.

The BMP's driver slammed the gears into reverse, to pull back under cover of the trees. Too late. The third shell hit squarely under the sloping bow of the amphibious vehicle, skidded off and buried itself in the sand before it exploded.

The blast lifted the vehicle into the air and toppled it on to its side. Splinters carved through the lightly protected floor of the troop compartment, killing and maiming. The survivors were shot down by the Australians as they tumbled out.

After that, it was a simple mopping up operation for the Australians. Most of the Indians quickly surrendered. More troops were flown in as the prisoners were removed. Another 106 came in and the small force reversed the roadblock, determined to prevent any Indian escape down the track into the plantations.

Monday, 1000 hrs

The Australian battalion commander had his headquarters near the main road junction with the cross-island track from the landing beach at Rumah Baru. He had deployed a company across the east coast track. With two of the Scorpion MICVs in support, they were pushing north, searching for the Indian positions.

Another company was guarding the approaches from the south, supported by the tanks. They probed cautiously down the main road, infantry in the lead in the long lanes between the coconut palms.

He had sent his support company down the peninsula on the eastern side of Telok Jambu with orders to secure the area and set up their heavy weapons to bombard the Indian positions at the head of the airfield.

The other rifle company was pushing north astride the main road with the other four Scorpions.

Further down the road, Jeffreys moved cautiously through the trees. They were not in touch with the enemy yet although he would not be far away. It was only another 600 metres to the quarantine station. The Indians would have to make a stand soon.

Sixty metres behind him and moving at walking pace along the edge of the road was one of the big Leopards, its commander standing up in the turret directing the driver. Another crewman manned a machine gun mounted at another hatch. The big turret gun pointed straight down the road, as if sniffing for a target.

He heard the clang first as the armour-piercing shell hit the Leopard. The crash of a gun came later and then the muffled explosion as the shell blew inside the tank. His mind registered a shell rather than a missile, probably one of their PT-76s. He couldn't see it. He looked back. Smoke mixed with flame was already pouring out of the hatches on the big tank.

Across the road, the two men in the turret hatches on the other tank had disappeared. He heard rather than saw the hatches bang down. Then the tank reared back as its 105mm gun fired down the road. And again. The Indian was shooting back. The noise was incredible, battering at the mind as well as the ears.

In the crippled tank, two bodies lay stunned, half in, half out of the turret. As he watched, one of the men dragged himself clear and jumped, almost fell to the ground. The other was struggling, jammed in the hatchway.

He raced across the long grass, dropping his rifle as he vaulted on to the Leopard. The man in the hatchway screamed as flame licked up his body, searing his unprotected face. Jeffreys climbed on to the turret behind the man. No time to be gentle. Reaching down, ignoring the flames and smoke, he grabbed him under the armpits and heaved with all his strength. Something ripped. He heard it despite the crash of gunfire and roar of explosions. The man screamed again but his body came free. Jeffreys rolled him off the tank before jumping down himself. The man's clothing was burning and blood poured from his ankle. His right foot had gone and the artery was pumping blood.

He rolled him in the grass to smother the burning clothing. He bellowed for medics as he gripped the severed artery between finger and thumb to cut off the blood flow.

Two soldiers came panting up with red cross armbands and medical satchels. They took over. "We've got him, sir. We'll take it from here." They dragged him none, too gently, into the trees as the flames roared up through the tank's hatches and ammunition began to explode.

212

Jeffreys rubbed his hands over his face. It was sore and singed. His eyebrows were nothing but stubble. The hair was gone from the back of his hands, he noticed. Suddenly, his knees wobbled and he began to shake all over. The sky was turning black. He decided to sit down. Or did his knees decide for him, he wondered.

"You OK, sir?" It was one of the medics. He shook his head to clear it and looked around. The man was standing over him, a look of concern on his face.

"Yeah, thanks." He took a pull at his water bottle and felt better. Picking up his rifle, he moved off into the trees after the leading infantry.

Monday, 1045 hrs

It was over, Sharma admitted to himself. They really never had a chance once they lost their aircraft and New Delhi decided not to support them.

He looked at the map. They had lost contact with the blocking force at the end of the airstrip. Dewan's 1st battalion was still fighting but the Australians were closing the ring.

Pandya's 2nd battalion was in fair shape and had dished out some heavy punishment. But they had lost practically all their armour. The attempt to concentrate fire from the head of the airfield on the ships and landing craft had attracted a storm of shelling from the warships.

What's my duty? he asked himself. To fight on? So the book would have it but at the cost of all these good men? Am I fighting for my country's safety? Or only for its pride? Or even for my own perverse honour as a soldier?

No one can advise me. I am in command here. My superiors have abandoned me. Or have they? Is there relief on the way? I don't know. My radio link with home is jammed.

He looked across the table at his intelligence officer who was pretending to examine the map. He's really looking at me, wondering what I am going to do. I can't ask his advice. I know the issues and the responsibility is mine.

The signaller interrupted his agony. "Lost contact with 1st battalion, sir. The 'phone went dead."

He nodded acknowledgement. Was it just the 'phone lines cut? Or had Dewan's headquarters been overrun? This was what they called the fog of war. He had seen it often enough on exercises. You made the decision and hoped for the best then. But men were not torn apart by bullets and shells in exercises. He shook his head angrily. It was not fog of war. They were beaten and he must surrender to avoid useless loss of life. He turned to the radio operator.

"See if you can raise the Australian commander on the international distress frequency."

The man turned to his set, punching up the numbers. The intelligence officer looked at his colonel sympathetically. It was hard but it was the right decision, he thought. But he kept the thought to himself.

Monday, 1050 hrs

Pender was at battalion HQ. He'd ridden up from the beach on the back of an APC bringing up ammunition. With the battalion commander, he looked at the map, marked up from the reports pouring in from all the units.

"Organised resistance has ceased up on the point, sir", the young colonel was explaining. They're still holding out down south. We've lost one of the Leopards and two Scorpions. Casualties are not too bad but they've still got at least one tank down there and some anti-tank stuff. Their mortars are still pretty busy and the ships' guns are having trouble getting fire on to their targets through this heavy overhead cover.

"It's only a matter of time, though", he concluded.

Pender agreed. "Yeah. I wonder if he wants to quit. Let's give him a chance. Tell your people to hold their positions for the moment and we'll see if we can raise him. Sharma's his name, isn't it?"

"Sir!" It was one of the signallers. "*Tobruk*'s calling you." He passed over a headset. "You're on secure voice, sir."

"That you, Mike? George here. We've just had a message on the distress frequency from the Indians. They want to call it quits."

Pender raised his eyebrows at his battalion commander. He felt the relief flood through him as his free hand clenched to a fist and punched the air. "George. Tell him I agree. Immediate cease fire and I'll meet him on the main road in 15 minutes."

"Roger! Well done, mate. I'll pass to all the ships to cease fire."

Monday, 1100 hrs

Trooper Anand cradled the SA-7 launcher in his arms as he squatted under the trees on the beach near the quarantine station. He had spent most of his time watching the ships. They were a good five kilometres off shore. Every now and then, their guns had banged away, adding to the roar of battle he could hear further up the road.

There were only two ships in sight. The other one, the one with the helicopter on the stern, had raced away to the south earlier. He had willed the captain to fly his helicopter and give him a shot but it hadn't happened.

Just then, his mate nudged him and pointed. The ship was coming around the point on his left. He was close in, too close. I can hit him, he thought. Just let him come within range. He rolled back further under the trees, watching the ship as it approached, measuring the range with an experienced eye.

He picked up the launch tube and switched on the power pack, sighting on the ship's stubby funnel, the hot spot. The red light in the sight flickered at him, mockingly. The ship was still out of range.

Then the light turned green—lock on. He waited, following the ship in the sight as it came closer in. Then he took a deep breath and squeezed the trigger.

Monday 1105 hrs

Bellano had just received the cease fire order. The ship was at action stations still and would remain so. He set course to join the rest of the group, starting to relax as the gunfire ashore slowly died away.

He stood on the starboard wing of the bridge, searching the shore through his binoculars. Columns of smoke showed where fires were burning. Too close in. He started to turn, to tell the officer-of-the-watch to take her further offshore. Then he saw it—a smoke trail, very faint.

215

He swung round urgently, bellowing, "Phalanx action starboard—missile inbound!"

Too late. The range was too short. The Phalanx was fast but not fast enough. It swivelled, its automatic radar seeking the missile. Before it got a lock, the SA-7 arrived. Aimed at the funnel, it passed close to the bridge structure which triggered the proximity fuze.

When it blew, the ship's structure absorbed most of the blast. Splinters clattered off the steel. There was only one casualty. One of the canard wings from the missile tore into Bellano's chest hurling him backwards against the bulkhead. He was dead before his body hit the deck. He was the last casualty of the war.

Monday, 1110 hrs

Pender stopped in the middle of the road. He was unarmed. His escort, cradling a rifle, took up a position on the treeline with a good field of fire in case anything went wrong.

The tall brigadier watched as the slightly built Indian in rumpled dark greens walked wearily towards him.

"Funny", Pender thought, "a beaten soldier always looks buggered. The poor coot's got the weight of the world on his shoulders."

Sharma drew himself erect as he came up to the Australian. They stood almost eye to eye although the Australian was heavier, bulkier, a bit overpowering. Sharma's salute was smart as he introduced himself.

Pender's salute was equally smart. But his tone was gentle. "Let's call it quits, shall we, colonel. You've done your bit. It's time to stop the killing."

EPILOGUE

The Prime Minister's Office, Parliament House

Newman was a happy man as he poured drinks for Clem Taylor and Len Darby. They had won Cocos back and humiliated India, one of the world's biggest countries. Now that the strain and tension was over, he was thinking like a politician again. What could they do with it?

He'd have to go for an election. It should be easy enough to force a situation where McDonald and his group would refuse their support for the government. He'd get his election and win in a landslide if he was quick about it.

As he turned back to his ministers with the drinks, the door opened and McCarthy was ushered in, together with Fennessy and Pender. The last one who followed them, a young soldier, must be that chap who distinguished himself in the invasion. Jeffreys, he recalled the name with an effort, was getting the Victoria Cross.

"Come in, gentlemen. We've got something to celebrate. What can I get you?"

As the introductions were made and drinks passed around, the two task force commanders recounted some of the less publicised highlights of the operation. Jeffreys listened quietly, only speaking when asked about his own part in the operation. It was all very cheerful.

Pender expressed his admiration for Sharma. "A real professional and a thorough gentleman. He's staying with me until the arrangements are made for his men's return to India."

Just then, there was a knock at the door. Newman's chief of staff put his head around the door, a startled look on his face. "Sir, I've just had a call from Defence. Another ship's been sunk!"

FINIS